MW01439849

Putting A Ghost To Rest

Ricky Ginsburg

Putting A Ghost To Rest

Ricky Ginsburg

©2023 by Ricky Ginsburg

All rights reserved. No part of this book may be reproduced, stored in a retrieval system or transmitted in any form or by any means without the prior written permission of the publishers, except by a reviewer who may quote brief passages in a review to be printed in a newspaper, magazine or journal.

The author grants the final approval for this literary material.

First printing

This is a work of fiction. Names, characters, businesses, places, events, and incidents are either the products of the author's imagination or used in a fictitious manner. Any resemblance to actual persons, living or dead, or actual events is purely coincidental.

ISBN: 9798332970382

Printed in the United States of America

Also by Ricky Ginsburg

K47

Boulong's Cheese

Sushi, Burgers, and Rocky Mountain Oysters

When Life Gives You Beef, Make Burgers

A Tasty Murder

The "Bird" Series featuring Detective Valarie Garibaldi:

The Blue Macaw

Shooting Limpkins

Clouds Full Of Ravens

I did not begin when I was born, nor when I was conceived. I have been growing, developing, through incalculable myriads of millenniums. All my previous selves have their voices, echoes, promptings in me. Oh, incalculable times again shall I be born. -
Jack London

Photo by the author

With Many Thanks To...

Carol Miller, proofreader extraordinaire, grammarian, and girlfriend, is without question my most valuable writing asset. All the tiny words my brain misses, she finds. Every plot-hole that needs to be filled is found by her careful assessment of the action as it unfolds. And when I wake at two-forty-five in the morning and need someone to discuss a scene, Carol rolls over and together, we solve the mystery. Every writer should have someone with her talents. No, sorry, I'm not sharing.

Jimmy da Bead Man, a Jamaican friend who works Seven Mile Beach in Negril, Jamaica for teaching me the Rastafarian way and always making me smile. That's him in the photo, pointing to a loose coconut over my head.

The many law enforcement officers and writers on the **Facebook page "Cops and Writers"** for answering the questions that help tie fiction and fact together.

The men and women of law enforcement. Hardworking people who stand up and say, "Not on my watch" and are willing to pay with their lives to make that happen.

Prologue - The Past

Bedford Jail, Bedfordshire, England, August 5, 1843

She shuddered with the memory of being hanged. She always remembered the moment of her death. Not so much the rope or the fall or the sudden stop, but the abrupt ending of her life–the darkness. It had been colder than today, but then she was barefoot. The walk from the prison cell to the gallows this morning had been through fresh-fallen snow. She had hoped to live until spring. It was too cold to die that day as well, but her chance at mercy was gone. What was left of her clothes did little to keep her warm in the last few hours of her life as she stared at the noose.

Throughout the march to her death, a man in a robe recited a catalog of her crimes in a singsong tone of voice. Even as she forced herself to recall his face now with her eyes closed, he might not have been clergy, but rather a government official assigned to the grim task. He did have a regal purple sash hanging from the robe that she kept watching as it swung back and forth, making slits in the snow.

Murder upon murder, the man's narration matched her footsteps as they covered the short walk across the prison castle's courtyard. He listed six deceased, crying out their names for the assemblage to hear. She knew there were twice as many, none of the bodies intact and all spread across the county where they would never be found. No one had seen her smile.

All the dead were lovers and husbands to another woman at the time she killed them. All had died at the moment of supreme joy as she slit their throats and leapt from the bed before their blood could splatter on her laughing face. She could still taste the metallic spit in the back of her throat. Men who had betrayed their oath, purchased pleasure, and then lied about it to the women who loved them. Lured to her bed with the simple temptations of flesh, tempered by drink and fooled by her promises, they were mindless prey.

She would find them in taverns. The men sitting at a table with their wives but staring at her as she loosened a few buttons on her blouse. They would talk to others at their table, but she could see their furtive glances as she flipped her shoulder-length red hair from side-to-side.

Later, they would seek her out. She would ask for a drink. Fate would have its way.

Had a chambermaid not discovered her as she left the room with her last victim still gurgling, she might have killed a hundred, just for the sport. She wasn't simply the serial killer she'd been in her past life. She was an animal, hungry for blood. Men were her quarry in this incarnation, more so than they had ever been in so many past ones.

Today was a warm, sunny day despite the early morning snow and she had let the wool shawl slip from her shoulders as they reached the gallows. Hanging wasn't the worst way to die. That much she remembered quite clearly.

Texas - Oklahoma Border, October 22, 1947

The bank robbery was a total failure. Police waiting outside the First National Bank of Oklahoma shot two of his accomplices on the steps of the building. No one knew about the silent alarm system that had been recently installed. One of the cops had been walking toward the bank, part of his usual beat, and had seen the three masked men run inside. The bank manager tapped the alarm switch and locked himself behind the bars of the teller's cage. He shot the manager twice while the man was cowering in a corner.

The younger teller passed out, collapsing under her counter. Handing him the entire cash drawer, the older bank teller pleaded for her life. He dumped the drawer on the marble floor and scooped up as much cash as he could with one hand.

His two friends, guys he'd gone to high school with, ran out of the bank empty-handed when he shot the senior teller. Had they dropped their guns inside the bank, they might have survived the day. Ten officers with machine guns and semi-automatics ended their short criminal careers before they reached the sidewalk.

Perhaps if there had been more money, fewer robbers, and no alarm system, he might have let the woman live. But his patience, thin that it was, had run out days before.

Their getaway driver had gotten out of the car and run around to an alley to empty his coffee-filled bladder. Heading back to the sedan, parked in front of the bank, the driver saw a line of police cars careen around the corner on two wheels and made tracks for the open desert, leaving the car behind.

Hearing the sound of gunfire from outside the bank, the red-haired killer went out the employees' entrance on the side of the building and stole one of the police cruisers. With tires throwing pebbles and dirt into the windshield of the black and white behind it, he headed east through Elk City, Oklahoma, toward the Texas border.

Rounding a corner in the stolen police car, he slammed into a delivery truck, forcing it off the road and into a nearby grocer's stand. The grocer, who never saw the truck coming, was pinned against a brick wall and died instantly. The impact flung the truck driver through the windshield where the glass shards ripped his body to shreds.

The Elk City sheriff, in pursuit of the robber and the stolen police car, radioed ahead to the Texas Rangers, who set up a roadblock just west of the state line. With Oklahoma State Police close behind him, the sheriff raced down the newly completed interstate at over one-hundred miles an hour.

The robber came over a rise on the four-lane highway, fifty yards away from the Rangers, firing his pistol out the window. He managed to squeeze off two rounds before they returned fire with high-powered rifles. A total of sixteen bullets struck his body. At least half of them would have been fatal on their own. Fifty-eight-years-old on his last birthday.

"Idiots. I should've gone alone," was his last thought, as this life faded away.

Good Faith Nursing Home, Liberty, NY
New Year's Eve 1987

Her goal, etched into her mind on her twenty-first birthday, was to kill one-hundred soldiers. She hated every person in a military uniform from Salvation Army bell-swingers to the young kids' home on leave who couldn't bring themselves to wear normal clothing around civilians. They seemed to be everywhere in their camouflaged uniforms, making that stupid "boo-rah" sound when they met on the street or in the checkout line at the supermarket. Bravado fueled their pace. Disdain for non-hackers and civilians beset their path.

She had a vivid memory of her husband leaving for Vietnam in late July 1967. They had celebrated his twentieth birthday a few days earlier. Hers followed three months later, the same day the soldiers came to her door and told her that her young husband wasn't coming home.

The Army dropped the assault charges. And even though she'd spent a night in jail, they buried the record of her arrest along with those of the other grieving widows who'd attacked the innocent messengers. The steak knife she'd used to stab one of them was returned to her along with a written apology for the way she'd been roughed up by the arresting officers.

It was a full year of heartache and disbelieving that led up to her twenty-first birthday wish. She whispered her plan in her mother's ear as her last living relative lay dying of a broken heart. She would avenge both her and her mother's loss. One hundred soldiers would pay for the needless death of her husband. She'd kill them one at a time and save the last bullet for herself.

Over eighteen years, she murdered eleven soldiers at military bases in the Northeast. She became known as the "Camo Widow" owing to her various outfits, all of them fashioned from used camouflage material she bought at surplus stores and the number of women she turned into widows by killing their husbands. The few witnesses to her killing spree were never able to give an accurate description of the killer. Several even insisted it was a man.

Some claimed the person was a blonde, but most who briefly saw the killer without a hat saw light reddish hair. It was cut too short to be a woman, or the hair was too long to be a man, depending on the witness and the accuracy of their eyesight. Only one living person saw the killer without sunglasses. She'd bumped into the Camo Widow as the killer was walking into a shoe store where a sailor on leave was about to die. The impact of the collision knocked the killer's sunglasses askew and the woman could clearly see deep blue eyes that she described to detectives as, "The color of ice on a frozen pond."

Her last and most violent episode was played out in public at a restaurant in South Brooklyn. Its location, just across the boulevard from Fort Hamilton, was a frequent dining destination for the commanders of the U.S. Army Garrison at the fort. Soldiers of every rank ate there. It was a target-rich environment. Same as her husband had described Vietnam before shipping out.

She'd stalked the Major for several months, watching him eat there every Thursday evening with his wife. Quite often, he'd dine with other officers and their wives. She'd considered taking out the whole lot of them in one mass execution. But the soldiers were always carrying a sidearm, and she didn't want to risk dealing with return fire, knowing that her aim was shaky at best.

She'd followed the Major to his suburban New Jersey home, planning to kill him in his driveway. One neighbor, to his right, was a detective that worked odd hours and both times she'd attempted to dispatch this evil soldier, the cop had been repairing a car in his driveway. Another neighbor, across the street, appeared to be housebound and spent all his daylight hours sitting on his porch, smoking cigars. Too many witnesses was her conclusion.

It was Labor Day, 1987. The restaurant was rarely busy on Mondays. She assumed that was why the Major favored it for dinner on that particular day. She got there shortly before he arrived with a woman she didn't recognize and another couple. The man was military as well. The Major had a regular table, even when he didn't come with his wife. She took a seat at a table facing away from him. Her camouflage clothes were concealed under a long raincoat.

Cocktails arrived, and the foursome toasted each other. Waiting until their appetizers were served, she stood from her chair and turned to face the Major. Letting the raincoat slip from her shoulders, she walked up to him and aimed the gun in his face. In the few seconds she stood in front of him, all she could focus on were his eyes. Too intense to be forest green, almost emerald, with a tinge of iridescent blue on the edges. They were the eyes of death. The eyes of a government killer. In that instant, she could see her husband's dead body in the Major's eyes.

Her first shot was less than three feet from his face. It blew him backward, away from the bowl of soup he'd never get the chance to taste. She spun and killed the second officer as he was reaching down to pull his sidearm from its holster. The Major's woman managed a single scream before she fired a bullet into the woman's open mouth, silencing her forever. The other officer's date fell sideways toward her dead companion, and she had to walk around the table to shoot her twice, despite the woman's cries for mercy.

Dropping the pistol on the floor, she walked out of the restaurant and hailed a passing cab. The four murders had taken less than thirty seconds. They would be the last people she'd kill in this lifetime.

Lung cancer from years of smoking unfiltered cigarettes stopped her long before fulfilling her dream of wiping out one-hundred members of the United States military. With the last of her husband's life insurance payout, she booked herself a one-way ticket to the grave in a comfortable nursing home in upstate New York. Her final journey would take four months, going from purgatory to hell.

On her last day of this life, she hadn't been able to get out of bed for the New Year's Eve ball drop at midnight. The nurse who checked on her at two in the morning wrote in her log that the woman had raspy, but regular breathing and her color was good. However, her pulse was dangerously slow and the young nurse, who had been hired three weeks earlier, considered calling the doctor, but it was New Year's and the woman didn't have long to live anyhow. The patient was only thirty-nine years old.

Her last conscious thought was regret for having failed to reach her goal, but she knew she would get another chance...if she remembered next time.

Chapter One
Politically Correct Cops

New York City, present day

David "Duke" Garvey put his left foot into the 84th Precinct detective squad and then pulled it back. He stood outside the open doorway, flipping the file folder from one sweaty hand to the other, working up the courage to walk in and meet his new squad. After eleven years as a beat cop, he'd finally received a promotion to detective and was awarded his gold badge. Even after his lieutenant had read him the letter from the Chief of Police, for the second time, Duke was having trouble believing it had finally happened.

The treasured promotion was not without a price. It had taken three months of physical therapy to repair the damage to his right shoulder where the bullet had punched through. But he'd saved the little boy's life and killed the hostage taker. It was front-page news for almost a week until the Yankees clinched the division and seemed to be destined for another World Series.

Duke looked at the door and sighed. It was Brooklyn and not one of the prestigious midtown precincts. But the way his mom glowed at the promotion ceremony was enough to convince him he made the right choice. He could have waited another six months. An older detective in Midtown South had taken a bullet in a shootout and was talking about early retirement. A friend in Central Robbery offered an entry-level position, but Duke wanted a job in Homicide. Even the opening at twice the pay in New Jersey wasn't enough to get him across the river. He'd spent too much time on the city streets to succumb to the boredom of suburbia.

When all was said and done, the Jamaican born cop's decision came down to stylish clothes versus what uniformed cops called "the bag." Getting out of the blue serge uniform had been goal number one. Of course, the bump in pay was a nice finishing touch, but Duke Garvey was a man known first for his wardrobe. Despite the washer and dryer in the basement of his building, all of Duke's clothing went to a professional laundry. T-shirts and jeans came back starched and ironed. Even his socks and undergarments were dry-cleaned. Every suit in his closet came from a bespoke tailor.

The wardrobe and his soft voice were the keys to his successful nightlife. Women spoke in hushed voices about his sexual prowess. His phone number was passed around more than the city's best restaurant. One recent girlfriend bought him a hoodie with the words "Satisfaction Guaranteed" stenciled on the front. It was rumored that he'd had intimate relations in the hospital with two different nightshift nurses while he was recovering the gunshot wound.

Rounding out his resume was Duke's skill in the kitchen. His friends and fellow cops raved over his culinary expertise and constantly sought him out for recipes and advice. Duke's name was first on every guest list for a summer barbecue, departmental dinner, or gathering of cops over a keg and grill party. Duke, the chef, always came dressed for the occasion. For a simple two-person barbecue, he had a choice of six clean aprons, matching toques, and oven mitts. It was a struggle for his girlfriends to outshine him on a date, and none of them cooked as well as the young Jamaican with red hair.

His thirty-third birthday, the previous weekend, had been celebrated with Juliana Tolkowski, his NYPD partner for the last nine years and current roommate. They'd been living together for just over two months, but had been shacking up for several years. Their affair was the worst kept secret in the precinct.

Joking that he'd probably make her move out now that he was plain clothes and a much higher pay grade, Juliana had pulled her suitcase from his storage closet and dusted it off when Duke left for his first shift that Monday morning. No one prior to her had lasted as long in his apartment.

Closing the top button on his sport jacket, Duke took a deep breath and strode into the squad, trying his best to hide his apprehension. He made it as far as the second footstep when a much shorter man leaned out of a glass-enclosed office and shouted at a senior citizen who appeared to be desperately in need of a meal, seated to Duke's left.

"Loviccio, we've got a DOA. 1070 Park Place on the second floor, apartment 2B. Uniformed officers are already on the scene." He walked over and handed the man a small, pink piece of paper.

The somewhat malnourished detective, who Duke surmised was Loviccio, rolled his chair back from the desk where he was sitting and nodded at the piece of paper. "Jankowsky's still at the hospital with the rape victim from 147 Midwood Street."

Gazing around the squad, the shorter man shook his head and folded his arms across his chest. He had a yarmulke with an embroidered Jewish star clipped to his hair that fluttered as he swung his head back and forth. "Where the hell is the squad?"

Loviccio brushed back his gray curls and shrugged. "Busy day. Everyone's still out on the street. I'll head over there and start working the case. Radio Jankowsky and let her know to meet me there when she's done at the hospital."

The short man shifted his attention toward Duke. "Can I help you?"

Duke smiled and held out his paperwork. "Perhaps I can help you. I'm your new detective."

Raising a single eyebrow, the short man walked over, took the folder, and dropped it on the nearest desk. "Lieutenant Bernard Moscowitz." He held out his hand. "And you are?"

"David Garvey, but everyone calls me Duke." Shaking the lieutenant's hand, Duke relaxed and looked around the squad.

"Well Duke, no one gets paid to stand around and admire the artwork here." He spun on one heel toward the skinny man who'd gotten up from his seat. "This is Detective Ronald Loviccio. He's four years from retirement, he's cranky, but he's the best detective to ever investigate a crime." Lieutenant Moscowitz smiled at the senior sleuth. "Ronnie, take Detective Garvey and see what you can teach him about dead bodies."

Detective Loviccio walked over to Duke and poked him in the stomach. "Too many carbs." He shook his head slowly. "Turns to fat that you'll never lose. And who did your hair? I've never seen a black man with red cornrows. You tie that shit yourself?"

Startled, Duke took a step back and pointed at the hollows of Loviccio's cheeks and freckled forehead. "You stand around too long and some mortician is going to pump your skinny face full of embalming fluid. And yes, I do my own hair. My girlfriend tried and couldn't get the knots tight enough." Folding his arms across his chest, Duke furrowed his brow. "Anything else you'd like to know?"

With a deep sigh, Lieutenant Moscowitz turned slowly and walked back into his office, slamming the door closed behind him.

Loviccio led the way downstairs and out to the chaotic array of marked and unmarked police vehicles parked on Tillary Street. Walking over to a brown Chrysler sedan with dents on both driver side doors and no hubcaps, he jingled the keys and looked over at Duke.

"You know your way around Brooklyn?"

"Not yet." Duke scratched an itch on the back of his neck. "I worked patrol in Midtown North and a short stint on Staten Island right out of the academy. Haven't spent much time in Brooklyn."

Loviccio nodded. "I'll drive, but you need to spend some time reading maps and driving around the borough. They don't like it when I drive." He pointed at the dents and shrugged. "Not all of them were my fault."

They got into the sedan with Duke in the passenger seat, buckling his seatbelt before he closed the door. Loviccio started the car and tapped the switch to turn on the emergency lights. Looking over at Duke, he laughed. "First time that seatbelt has ever been used."

"You said–"

"Relax, Duke. I'm actually one of the safest drivers in the squad." He started the engine and peeled out from the curb, a cloud of white and gray tire smoke behind them.

During the twenty-minute drive from Tillary Street to Park Place, they had three narrow misses, including a pedestrian who flipped them his middle finger as he jumped back onto the curb. Detective Loviccio, who drove with one hand, two feet, and minimal attention to the outside world, told Duke about his lifelong battle with his weight. From his childhood years as a fat baby and then an overweight toddler, to constant ridicule from his school friends, and finally a failed romance with a woman who crushed the scales at three-hundred pounds.

Loviccio had vowed to lose the weight before he entered the police academy. He joined the Peace Corps for a yearlong assignment in Guatemala, where he promptly got sick and lost over a hundred pounds before his bowels stabilized. Having reached a weight that he felt comfortable with, the detective went out of his way to maintain it.

However, his conversion from fat to thin brought with it a need to preach healthy living to anyone who would lend an ear. In the detective squad, that meant no one. On the streets, his words struck anyone overweight who came within the sound of his voice. Over the years, he'd been cursed at, had all sorts of small objects thrown at him, and twice a mildly obese person had attacked him– once with a baseball bat and the second time with a frozen leg of lamb.

"So what do you eat?" Duke reached into a pocket of his sport jacket and pulled out a pack of chewing gum, offering a stick to Loviccio who refused.

"Well, I'm a vegetarian, so no meat of any kind."

"In a city famous for its hot dogs?"

Loviccio slapped the steering wheel. "Poison on a bun. Do you have any idea what's inside those dirt-water dogs?"

"Hebrew National? Nothing but beef."

"Bullshit. You ever been to one of their factories?" Spinning the wheel hard, Loviccio brought the big Chrysler around a corner on two wheels, banging into the curb with the rear tire.

Duke tightened his seatbelt. "What about fish? Sushi comes straight from the sea."

"By way of a freezer, a defrost, maybe frozen again and then cut on a bacteria-infested countertop by chefs who sneeze on the fish, cough on the rice, and spit on the seaweed paper to get it to stick together." Loviccio rolled the window down and blew a chunk of phlegm across two lanes.

"So I'll ask again, what kind of food do you eat?"

He rolled the window up and switched hands on the wheel so he could point at Duke. "Fresh vegetables, none of that frozen, processed crap. I bake my own bread using only organic ingredients, and I drink tea instead of coffee."

"That's it?"

"Well, that and an occasional bottle of whiskey."

Duke closed one eye and stared at Loviccio. "A bottle?"

"Know anyone who can have just one drink?" Loviccio grinned. "Plus, there's no meat in whiskey. Just barley, malt, water, and time."

"How often?"

"As needed." He adjusted the rearview mirror. "Once or twice a week."

"And you think that's a part of healthy living?"

Detective Loviccio pulled up to the crime scene and threw the Chrysler in park. "No. That's just to keep me sane in this crazy city long enough to put in my papers."

They squeezed through the crowd of uniformed cops, nosy neighbors, and wailing family members to get into the bedroom at 1070 Park Place, apartment 2B. The body was male, approximately twenty-years-old, splayed out, face up on the bed in the master suite. The corpse was dressed in a white t-shirt with two bloody pools on opposite sides of the chest and nothing else. The look of surprise on the dead boy's face and the position of his arms out to the sides made Duke think the kid wasn't expecting to die today.

"He looks so peaceful." Duke shook his head. "Relaxed."

Loviccio sighed and reached into his back pocket, tugging out four disposable gloves. He handed a pair to Duke.

"Rule number one of detective work is to never add to the scene of the crime." He pulled the gloves onto his hands and stepped over close to the corpse. "Your body is filthy. You constantly shed skin, hair, and fluids. You must keep them from contaminating the crime scene."

"So, no sex with the victims?"

Loviccio looked at Duke with his eyebrows raised and put a hand on Duke's chest. "You're not one of 'them' are you?"

"Them?"

"Necros. Nut jobs who get off seeing a dead body. Maybe even having intimate relations with it." He dropped his hand and stepped back from the bed, looking hard at Duke. "We had a Medical Examiner who couldn't keep his hands off the corpses, especially the females."

"You're serious?"

He nodded. "As a hangnail."

"He screwed the dead bodies?" Duke's face curled in horror.

"Six of them before he was collared." Loviccio pointed at the dead kid on the bed. "Two of them were boys just like this one."

"Jesus."

"Yeah, that's what the judge said just before he sentenced him to seventeen and a half years in prison." Walking around to the other side of the bed, Detective Loviccio knelt and lifted one of the dead boy's arms. "Rigor has set in. Has to be dead at least five or six hours." He looked at his wristwatch. "Close to dawn. Probably four or five o'clock in the morning."

One of the uniformed cops came into the bedroom. "Parents said he came home from a party after midnight with a friend. Male. The parents expected to see their son at breakfast. When he didn't come out of his room, they knocked, went in, and found him like this."

"You speak directly to the doorman?"

"Yeah. He said a well-dressed man with a cane and Mets cap came out around quarter after five. He'd never seen the guy before tonight, but he was certain it was the same guy who walked in with the deceased just after midnight."

Duke grinned. "They're never Yankee fans."

"And of course, the well-dressed man didn't sign the guest register." Loviccio lowered the boy's arm. Lifting the t-shirt from the boy's waist up toward his neck, he moved some chest hair out of the way and examined the bullet wounds. "Large caliber. Close range. Look at the powder burns on the t-shirt."

"The parents didn't hear anything?" Nodding toward the door, Duke looked at the officer. "Was the door closed?"

The cop shook his head. "I don't know about the door. It was open when I arrived. And as far as the parents go, they both take medication to sleep. Could have shot the kid with a bazooka and they'd have slept through it. But they did say he's had several different friends spend the night recently."

Loviccio scanned the room. "Anybody find a cellphone?"

Another shake of the head. "Parents said he has one and tried to call it, but the call went straight to voicemail. No other cellphones in the house."

"What time did they find him?" Loviccio fixed the dead boy's shirt and turned to the cop. "Did they say?"

"Yeah. The eight o'clock morning news was just comin' on the television, according to the mother."

Duke picked up a magazine from the floor. "*Chains and Cheers?*"

"Whips and leathers." Loviccio pulled another issue of the same magazine from a pile on top of a nightstand. "The favorite journal of the rough trade crowd."

"Gays who beat each other?"

He nodded. "And worse, as evidenced by our dead body. You got a name for the deceased?"

"Vincent Marsden. Twenty-one on his last birthday." The cop tore a page out of the small notepad he'd been reading from and handed it to Duke. "Parents knew he had homosexual leanings, but they didn't know about the other shit."

"Anything missing other than the cellphone?" Looking around the room, Duke found a wallet on the floor and placed it on the bed.

The cop checked his notes. "Nothing, according to the parents, and the wallet has thirty-one dollars and a credit card, so it doesn't look like a robbery. I put it back on the floor where I found it. Looks like two faggots had an argument and one lost."

Loviccio glared at the cop, raising a hand of admonishment. "Yo, watch that shit before you get stuck in a re-adjustment class for a few nights of unpaid overtime."

"Sorry." The cop raised his eyes toward the ceiling. "Two *homosexuals* that had an apparent disagreement."

Duke looked down at his Italian leather shoes and smiled. He'd been through a couple of readjustment classes in his eleven years on the job. Words were far more powerful today than when he'd graduated the academy. No one called him 'black' or 'negro' anymore. The 'N' word was never uttered by a cop, even when talking about the most despicable skells. Political correctness was the new normal, and every cop was expected to preach it.

Even the term 'African-American' had taken on derogatory meanings. Duke was proud of his Jamaican heritage, even though his bloodline was tainted along the way with racial hatred of a different kind. His mother, who could trace her lineage directly back to Marcus Garvey, one of the earliest leaders of the black freedom movement, had raised him to ignore skin color and treat all people as equals.

He still bore faint scars on his lower back where she'd smacked him with a stalk of raw sugar cane when words he didn't fully understand popped from his mouth in anger. His mother had gone so far as to cut open the boy's thumb with a knife to show him his blood was the same color as a white boy whose nose Duke had crushed with a fist in anger.

When they left the island, a month after Duke's fifteenth birthday, his friends taunted him that he was going to live with the white man and follow the white man's laws. Duke's mother explained that there were only two sets of laws: God's and man's. Color had nothing to do with it. Break God's laws and he'd have to answer to God and his mother in order to be forgiven. Break man's laws and he could go to Hell for all she cared.

Duke saw that it came down to a choice between the clergy and the cops. He figured he'd have a better chance with criminals than with angels and signed up for the police academy on his eighteenth birthday at his mother's urging. The worst of it was having to trim his shoulder-length red dreadlocks that he'd started growing as a toddler. A barber across the street from the academy shaved his head half an hour before he reported on the first day. Duke had been weaving cornrows on his scalp ever since.

Rolling the body over, Detective Loviccio checked to see if the bullets had gone through the corpse and were underneath it, awaiting discovery.

"No luck. The Medical Examiner will have to find the slugs. They're still inside." He let the dead boy roll back. "Any of the neighbors hear the shots?"

The cop shook his head. "Nothing, but they all said there was loud music around three this morning. One of them called it in, but the officers who responded met the neighbor in the downstairs lobby. She told the cops that the music had stopped just before they arrived."

Loviccio let out a long breath. "And I'm guessing there are no security cameras in this building."

"Correct." The officer closed his notepad and shoved it into his back pocket. "Nobody other than the doorman saw them arrive. It's possible that the guy the doorman saw leave was the shooter, but according to him, the guy was too casual about the way left. Just kinda sauntered out of the building. Looks like another one of those cases where nobody saw nothin'." He walked over to the doorway and turned back toward the two detectives. "Good luck, gentlemen."

Duke took a long look around the bedroom. "You think there are many well-dressed men with canes wearing a Mets cap in Brooklyn?"

"Nah. Most of them would be wearing Yankee's hats." Loviccio lifted the crime scene tape and stepped out of the bedroom. "The Mets suck this year."

Chapter Two
Jamaican History Lesson

With the canvass of the building underway and little to go on, the detectives gave the apartment at 1070 Park Place over to the Crime Scene Unit and the Medical Examiner. Paperwork called, and they inched their way back through the late morning traffic to the squad to begin the tedious process of filing reports. They'd spoken briefly with the parents, offering their condolences for the loss of their son and to verify what was in the officer's notes.

    The doorman confirmed what the uniformed officer had reported. He said that he would probably recognize the man with the cane if he saw him again, but it had only been for a few moments each time. According to the doorman, Vincent Marsden had been bringing older men home for several months. Having been evicted from his apartment in Queens and jobless, Vincent returned to the nest. He'd moved back with his parents in apartment 2B into his old room just before the beginning of the baseball season. The doorman had carried the boy's luggage and helped move several pieces of furniture around in the room.

    A married couple who lived on the same floor, but wished to remain anonymous despite standing in their open doorway, told the detectives they'd seen three different men walking hand-in-hand with Vincent through the lobby since his return. The husband, who did all the food shopping, mentioned seeing Vincent in the bodega on Saint Marks with a man in a Mets cap, but he wasn't sure about the man needing a cane.

Duke made a note of the apartment number and added the anonymous couple's name from the mailboxes in the lobby.

The canvass of the neighborhood produced similar results. Vincent with a well-dressed gentleman at least twice his age, buying wine at the local bodega was reported by several witnesses. The boy with an Hispanic construction worker leaving a bar around the corner from the apartment was mentioned by two others. And one lucky break: young Mr. Marsden kissing the older man with the Mets cap, as the man got into a taxi in front of 1070 Park Place the previous Sunday morning.

"A mystery man in a Mets hat seems to be the most likely suspect. But the Hispanic has also been a frequent visitor. No video cameras and the lady who saw the man get into the taxi on Sunday didn't get a plate or medallion number." Duke shook his head. "Where do we start?"

"Breakfast." Loviccio pulled over to the curb and put the car in park.

The diner on the opposite side of the street reflected the late morning sunlight into Duke's eyes as he got out. He slid the sunglasses off the top of his head and shielded his eyes with one hand. "You're going to eat in a greasy spoon? You, Mr. Vegetarian?"

"Second rule of detective work: never judge a crime scene from the outside." Loviccio locked the doors with the key fob and dropped it into his pocket. "Come on, junior. Time for a healthy meal."

From an exterior of gleaming stainless steel and neon, suggesting bacon-wrapped, deep-fried everything, the interior became California foothills with soft music, servers in overalls and flowered shirts, and a menu that featured the same plants as the local garden center. Fortunately for Duke, they also served eggs, but alas, no bacon.

"I can see how you'd lose weight eating here." He laid the menu on the table and sat back in the booth. "How does an Italian not eat sausage?"

"Easy, once you've seen how it's made."

"And bacon?" Duke took a sip of water. "Bacon and eggs, right? How do you just eat eggs?"

Loviccio waved at the server. "I don't eat eggs, so bacon's not an issue."

"Does your partner dine this way, too?"

"Jankowsky? Nah, she's a good twenty-five pounds on the heavy side. But don't tell her I said so. I've been trying to convert her to a healthy diet for the last six and a half years. You'll like her. She eats those hot dogs, too. Hot onions, mustard, and ketchup. Two

Pepsis. None of that diet shit. And extra napkins because they drip all over the place."

Duke shoveled the last of his scrambled eggs into his mouth and wiped the plate clean with a slice of whole wheat bread...his least favorite. His mother, a devout Rastafarian, had done her best to raise a child who favored green vegetables over red meat. She'd failed to steer his diet but had instilled the values of truth and mostly healthy living to her sole offspring. Bread was one food group where Duke had refused to compromise. When he shopped, the white bread on the bottom shelf in the supermarket was the only loaf he bought.

While he had an addiction to street vendors of all types, Duke limited the amount of fried food he ate to French fries, only had a steak on his birthday or an important date, and drank a juice mixture for breakfast that resembled baby poop mixed with mud. According to his mother, the juice would enable her son to live a healthy, natural life despite his penchant for what she called "man's trash in de crepe wrapper." Only, she pronounced the word "crepe" as "crap."

Their server dropped the check between the two detectives and stood waiting to see who was going to pay. Loviccio pulled it closer to his side of the table, tugging his wallet from a back pocket at the same time.

"Breakfast's on me. Least I can do for having you suffer from a lack of bacon." He gave the server his credit card and shifted his attention toward Duke. "So, Garvey, what's your story? Slum kid turned cop? On your way to law school and this is just a stepping stone?"

Duke shook his head. "My mom's idea."

"To be a cop?"

"Yes." Wiping his mouth with the clean side of his napkin, Duke moved his plate off to one side and folded his hands on the table. "She was raped by a white American tourist on the beach in Negril, where she lived. I'm the child of that attack."

"Jesus, Garvey." The senior detective paused Duke's history lesson and jumped in with a question. "She wouldn't get an abortion?"

"Catholic women don't get abortions, especially in Jamaica. They have children, period."

"Italian families get cable television, Netflix, and a lifetime supply of condoms."

Duke laughed. "And yet you still have enormous families."

"Hey, not everyone watches TV or wears a raincoat to bed. Some of us get fixed." Nodding toward his lap, Loviccio smiled. "When you're firing blanks, you can shoot at as many targets as you like and not worry about hitting anything. So the rape, that's what got you interested in police work? Sounds like revenge to me."

Shaking his head, Duke took a drink of water before explaining. "From my earliest memories, all I watched on television were cop shows. When my mother took dinner to the police station on Christmas, I walked with her and waited while the officers on duty ate. She was the one who was enthralled with cops." He shrugged. "It rubbed off on me whether I wanted it to or not."

The server returned with the credit card and receipts. He placed them in the middle of the table along with two large, wrapped breath mints. Loviccio put both candies in his pocket. "For later when the kale makes me burp. You won't need them with eggs and toast, but the lieutenant has a thing about bad breath. Just a warning."

"Something I'll remember." Duke looked up at the server. "I'll take a couple of those, too."

"So, your moms wanted you to become a cop to take out her revenge on the white folk? Is that why she dragged you around to the police station all the time?"

Duke shook his head. "No. It was to keep me from turning to a life of crime in a country where young boys, 'rude boys' they call them, reach a point where they could go either way. She wanted me to fight crime, not make more of it." Loosening his tie, Duke leaned his elbows on the table and held his head in the palms of his hands. "She forgave the tourist a long time ago. It's the Rasta way."

"Rasta? Like pasta?" Loviccio cocked his head to the side. "Headhunters?"

Laughing, Duke picked up a crumb from the table and dropped it on his plate. "Rastafarian. It's a combination of religion and lifestyle practiced by the most devout Jamaicans. They're vegetarians, believe in a natural life, and worship Jah." He closed his eyes and shook his head. "And they will tell you that they've been here before and will be coming back again."

"Reincarnation." Loviccio snorted. "I'm coming back as a dog." Filing out the credit card slip, he scribbled an illegible signature and looked across the table at Duke. "So, you believe that Rasta stuff, too?"

"Some of it, not all the food, and I don't smoke ganja."

"Ganja?"

"Jamaican word for pot."

"Ah. I hear it grows wild all over the island." Loviccio chuckled as he shoved the credit card into his wallet. "Kinda like Colorado except with palm trees and a beach. A buddy of mine went there on a cruise ship and said people were getting stoned as they walked off the gangplank."

Duke shrugged. "I couldn't tell you. My mother and I left the island when I was fifteen-years-old without me ever trying it. She lives in Jersey where it's legal and gets her stash delivered. I'm never in the house when she smokes it and she never offers."

"You don't like to be called 'David'?" Taking a sip of tea, Loviccio leaned closer to Duke. "Tell me she didn't name you after the guy that raped her."

"Jesus, Ronnie." Duke shook his head. "That's some cold shit."

"Hey, I had to ask."

"David, as in David and Goliath. It's a name of strength, even to a Rastafarian."

"And what about Garvey. That a popular name in Jamaica?"

"Worshipped." Sliding closer to the window, Duke put his feet up on the benchseat and retied his laces. "Marcus Garvey preached that all blacks should return to Africa, to the motherland. He was a great reformer and outspoken about slavery to the point where it almost cost him his life several times. My mother is one of his great-great-grandchildren. One of many who kept his name alive."

"And Duke? Where does that come from?"

"Sixties hit. *The Duke of Earl*. My mother's favorite song to sing when she drives a car."

Bursting into laughter, Loviccio slapped his hands on the table. "Your moms thinks she's the Duke of Earl? No shit?"

"Not her, Ronnie." Duke shook his head several times. "Me. She calls me the Duke of Earl. It's what she sang me to sleep with when I was a baby. Even on my birthday, she won't sing *Happy Birthday*, just *The Duke of Earl*."

Loviccio shook his head. "Now that's some funny shit." He nodded at Duke's hands. "No jewelry? No wedding band?"

"No wife." With his tongue in his cheek, Duke shrugged. "Just a girlfriend for now. But she's moved in. That's a new development."

The portable radio on the seat next to Loviccio squawked, calling out to their unit. *"Dispatch to 84 squad detectives on the air?"*

Loviccio reached down and keyed the mic button. "84 squad portable three. Go ahead, dispatch."

"Marine Park Nature Center. 10-10, shots fired. Report of at least two civilians wounded. Highway Patrol is on the scene. EMS enroute. Meet Detective Jankowsky on tach four."

"No rest for the weary." Loviccio slid off the benchseat and pulled the key fob from his pocket. "Come on, Duke. The fresh air from Jamaica Bay will do you good. Make you feel right at home."

With Detective Loviccio driving, they raced across Brooklyn to the Marine Park Nature Center. Four cars from the NYPD Highway Patrol, stationed just a few miles away, sat in front of the white brick building. Avenue U was closed in both directions by sector cars, and the Emergency Services truck was parked on the grass between the driveway and the avenue.

Detective Rita Jankowsky, who Loviccio had spoken to from their car moments after leaving the diner, was already on the scene and told the two detectives by radio that there were two wounded and one DOA. Apparently, there had been an argument between two men over a woman that both initially claimed was their wife. The female was dead from a single shot to the chest, and both men had sustained multiple gunshot wounds in their arms and shoulders.

Getting out of their car at the scene, Duke and Loviccio walked across the grass toward the crowd of uniformed cops and bystanders. Rita Jankowsky met them and lifted the yellow crime scene tape to let them into the secured area.

What was left of her flaming red hair was limited to Rita's eyelashes. Duke wondered if they had been artificially colored, but decided that the woman probably would resent the inquiry. Her gray curls had some flecks of red at the tips and her arms were fuzzed with pale orange hairs.

A tiny scar on her chin spoiled what could have been a perfect movie star's face. The small 'v' dead center would have been covered by a goatee if she had been a man. The rest of her features belied her age. To the unknowing, she could have easily passed for a college girl on a basketball scholarship. Loviccio had told him that she was going to be fifty on her next birthday, twenty-five years on the job.

She towered over most of the people standing near her. Duke figured that she was at least six feet tall. Her gold badge shared a neck chain with a Star Trek pin and a cross. The balance of her outfit was denim, from the calf-high boots to the jacket with rolled-up sleeves. She was the Marlboro Man in drag.

"Who's the kid?"

Loviccio smiled at Rita. "Is everyone going to be a kid now that you're hitting five-oh?"

Duke held out his hand. "Duke Garvey, recently assigned to the 84th."

"Well, Detective Garvey, take a look at the scene and give me your first impression." Rita stepped off to the side and held out her arms. "One body over there and two wounded and weeping over there."

"The woman got between them. Her bad luck. She took a stray shot in the chest from one of the two gentlemen who were arguing over her." Taking off his sunglasses, Duke squinted at the men. "Hispanics fighting over the woman's honor."

Rita doubled over with laughter. "Jesus Christ, did you fall out of a monastery or are you just a hopeless romantic?" Turning to Loviccio, she staunched the laughter and returned to a serious expression. "Drug deal gone bad. The woman is Olivia Gomez, thirty-five and a resident of Queens. The man in the red plaid shirt is Victor Polmesio. He's the driver. His brother Tito, in green, lives six blocks from here and smuggles cocaine and heroin from small planes landing illegally at nearby Floyd Bennett Field. Narcotics has had this place under surveillance for months."

"I thought the runways were shutdown by the Air Force years ago." Loviccio put on a pair of gloves and handed a second pair to Duke.

"Yeah, but that doesn't mean shit to the drug trade." Rita turned and pointed at the dead woman. "She tried to rip them off. Got off four rounds from a Glock 17 before Tito put one center mass."

Loviccio nodded toward the parking lot where an unmarked Chevy Suburban with its red and blue grill lights still flashing had screeched to a stop. "Speaking of Narcotics."

"This is a homicide, even if it's a drug deal gone bad." Rita swiped an errant curl out of her eyes. "I'm not giving up another collar today."

"Special Victims took over the rape?" Loviccio furrowed his brow. "Again?"

"They were waiting in the hospital lobby and insisted on sitting in on the interview."

Duke managed to get a word in. "Where are the drugs?"

Rita shrugged. "Haven't found them yet. Probably in the trunk of the Polmesio brother's car. We're waiting for a search warrant to open it."

"So, for all we know, right now there are no drugs. This is just an attempted robbery that's morphed into a homicide." Duke smiled. "Not a narcotics case."

"Morphed?" Rita looked at Loviccio and shook her head. "Who the hell uses words like that?"

A brief discussion with the four Narcotics detectives landed the case in the hands of the 84th Detective Unit. Duke was certain he'd heard Rita mention testicles several times during the negotiations. That and Rita's handcuffs they'd used on both brothers seemed to sway the minds of the four men. They left as quickly as they'd arrived.

EMS did some field patching of the bleeding men and transported them under police guard to the hospital. While the detectives documented the scene with video and collected the shell casings, a team from the coroner's office stood by, ready to take the corpse off to the city morgue.

"Looks like a simple case." Duke stored the small video camera in the trunk of the Chrysler and tugged off the latex gloves he'd been wearing.

"No homicide is simple." Loviccio opened a bottle of water and drank half of it in one gulp. "Some get solved quickly, others..." Pausing, he stared at the ground for a few moments. "Others never get solved, and then the lead detective retires or dies. Or the case grows so old that any trail it left behind is covered with dust. Sometimes a detective will waste their entire career on one case and never solve it. Somewhere, a criminal will laugh because he or she got away with the perfect crime. But left behind will be the victim's family with a pain that will never end. Unanswered questions break more hearts than unfaithful lovers."

Rita twirled her keys around her index finger, shaking her head slowly. "And some detectives spend their careers chasing the ghosts of those criminals and trying to answer those impossible questions." She leaned over toward Duke and stage-whispered, "Don't get him started about the Good Father Nursing Home."

"Good *Faith* Nursing Home. Jesus, Jankowsky, get the details straight for a change." Loviccio tossed the key fob to Duke. "Come on, junior. Let's see if you can find your way back to the squad without hitting anything."

Chapter Three
Paperwork, Tea, and Puking

Loviccio and Jankowsky had desks facing each other in the squad. Both had computer monitors and keyboards, but Jankowsky's equipment was covered with Star Trek stickers and unicorns. At first glance, it appeared as though some prankster had dumped several trashcans full of paper on her desk pad and tossed an assortment of pens and pencils on top of it for garnish.

Her partner's work area was a stark contrast to the disarray. Even without a protractor, it was clear that every item on Loviccio's desk was either parallel or at a right angle to something else. The wood grain was clearly visible and any hint of actual work was missing. It was as though the cleaning crew had come and tidied up the place, knowing that no one was going to use the desk for a while.

Loviccio rolled out his chair and lowered himself gingerly onto the padded seat. "Hemorrhoids." He grinned at Duke. "Comes with the job."

"Only when you spend too much time on your ass." Rita pushed her chair away from her desk with a foot, kicking it off to one side. "I've been requesting a standing desk for months, ever since I saw one on TV. Eventually, the department is going to figure out why their detectives are so out of shape and get rid of the damn chairs."

Lieutenant Moscowitz came out of his office and walked over to the three detectives. "Tough break on the rape case, Rita. I know you wanted the collar, but Special Victims gets all related crimes."

"SVU is gonna start doing homicides and robberies next month." Rita sighed. "I'll be fifty and writing parking tickets if that shit happens."

He turned to Loviccio. "So, how's the kid?"

"Fresh and clean, like my laundry, but he'll get dirty fast."

Duke folded his arms across his chest. "Dirty?"

"Right now you're a nice, clean sponge. Fresh out of the package." Loviccio paused to realign a notepad and pencil that had shifted out of position. "A month in the 84th and you'll be covered with grit and grime, your fancy shoes will be all scuffed to hell, and that perfectly folded pocket square will be replaced by tissues and napkins you've used at least once."

Rita joined in. "Street cops stay clean. Detectives dumpster dive, dig through pockets filled with needles, and touch the pieces of a crime that we warn uniforms to keep away from. You might start out the day with a clean shirt, but by noon you'll be wishing you'd put a spare in your locker."

"Especially in the summer." Pulling the keyboard closer, Loviccio nodded at Duke. "Come over and grab a chair. Despite what Jankowsky says, typing is best done while you're sitting. I don't know how she files reports with all that crap on her desk and standing up, like she's waiting for a drink at the bar, but paperwork is the key to this job and it requires comfort to be correct."

Lieutenant Moscowitz smiled at Duke. "You'll make First Grade only when you can conquer the paperwork. When you were a beat cop, you signed in at the beginning of your shift and signed out at the end. You had nothing compared to the DD5."

"DD5?" Duke shrugged. "One form?"

"One form that leads to many others, but the DD5 is the backbone of our reporting system." The lieutenant leaned over Rita's desk and shuffled through the mess, finally yanking a long sheet of paper from the pile. "This is the New York Police detective's Document Number Five. DD5 for short. It's the single piece of paper that we use to store data in the department's case management system. Every time you walk out of this squad and interact with the public, you'll return to your desk and complete a DD5."

Loviccio joined in. "And every box on the form must be filled. Every line must have correct spelling. For short, we call them the fives, but you'll find more colorful terms as your fingers begin to cramp."

"The instant you sign it, you're putting your John Hancock on a legal document. Screw up a DD5 and the shit that falls from above will bury you." Moscowitz dropped the paper on top of the mountain on Rita's desk. "Your shift ends when the paperwork is complete. You can go home after eight hours, but the paperwork will be there waiting when you return. It has no soul and couldn't care less if you're tired, your wife burnt dinner, or you got a flat tire on your way to work."

"Every time you interview someone, whether or not they're a suspect, you will fill out a DD5." Grabbing the falling paper before it could hit the pile, Rita waved the form in Duke's face. "This is your biography as a detective. A hundred years from now, anyone who needs to, can dig up your DD5s from the archive and make you look like either a hero or a fool."

"Your life as a detective will be spent in front of a computer screen more often than pounding the pavement and looking for clues." Getting up from his seat, Loviccio grabbed a coffee cup from the back corner of his desk and wiggled a finger at Duke. "But long before you touch a keyboard, you must have a hot beverage to warm up your mind."

"Coffee?" Duke smiled. "Now we're getting somewhere."

Rita laughed so hard that she started coughing. "Garvey, you'd best get used to drinking tea. Mister Green Jeans has converted the entire squad from caffeine to tannin. Part of his 'make the world healthy' program."

"My mother forced me to drink tea when I was very little." Duke's face contorted with the memory. "It made me puke."

"Yo, don't start puking in the squad." Loviccio shook his head. "It's bad enough when a skell does it, but we don't need our detectives joining in."

Duke held his hands out. "Not to worry, I haven't thrown-up since I was ten. Just about the same time she gave up on the tea and let me drink sodas."

"Soda machine is downstairs in the lobby." Lieutenant Moscowitz walked toward the door. "Come on, I'll introduce you to the captain and the rest of the vending machines."

In the five minutes it took to meet and dislike Captain O'Malley, four additional detectives had returned to the squad and were working at their desks. Walking around the room with a cup of steaming Earl Grey in his hand, Loviccio introduced Duke to the team.

"Peter Cheng claims to be Chinese, but to watch him eat a pizza, you'd think he was at the wrong end of Mulberry Street." Loviccio gave the bald Asian a tap on the shoulder. "He gave my wife a recipe for vegetable lasagna that was better than the one her mother had taught her. And you, with the sausage cravings, should go with Peter to the butcher. He knows more about Italian food than all the cooks in Little Italy."

Duke shook hands with Detective Cheng. Bowing, he said, *"Zao shang hao."*

"You speak Mandarin?" Cheng stood and returned the bow.

"Just enough to get in and out of trouble." Duke winked. "I've had a few Asian girlfriends over the years."

Loviccio looked at Rita. "Yo, we've got someone else to order Chinese food. Maybe you'll get the right entrée for a change."

Kelly Tang, the female half of the 'eggroll twins,' as they had been affectionately nicknamed by Moscowitz, stood from her chair and walked over to Duke. "Don't speak any of that Chinese crap to me. I don't understand a word and don't want to learn. And if you're ordering Chinese food, all I eat are fortune cookies and fried rice."

"Trust me, it'll be a long, snowy day in August before I'll take on that responsibility." Duke shook her hand and noticed the tattoo that circled her wrist. "Is that some good luck saying in Chinese?"

Detective Tang shook her head. "No, it's my name, date of birth, and my mother's telephone number. She made me get it the day I graduated from the police academy. In the event I die suddenly, someone will know who I am and who to call if I'm found naked and without identification."

"Jesus, wouldn't a nice ID bracelet do the same thing?"

"Assuming whoever killed me left it on my wrist." Tang shrugged. "Before she fled China, my mom saw her parents and three brothers put to death by the army. My dad was murdered by robbers who broke into the warehouse where he and several of his friends were working nights. The dead were all found naked and their wallets had been taken. It was over a week before my mom located the right morgue with his body and paid for the cremation."

Duke took a step back, blowing out a long breath. "Mother of God. I hope no one ever has the necessity to read that tattoo." Rubbing his wrist, he pointed at her running shoes. "You jog?"

"Every morning before work."

"Perhaps we can go for a run together." Duke flexed his knees. "I ran the New York Half Marathon last year and I'm thinking about the full one for this year."

"Marathon runners are crazy people." She cocked her head to one side. "You a crazy person, Garvey?"

Smiling, Duke nodded slowly. "I've been told that I can get crazy if the situation requires it. Do you like crazy, Detective Tang?"

"Oh, Jesus, he's in the squad fifteen minutes and he's hitting on the only blonde." Rita threw a wadded piece of paper at Duke that bounced off his back. "You'd best keep those hormones in check, pretty boy. At this level, the department frowns on personal relationships within its ranks. You might have got away with that shit as a beat cop, but detectives are judged by a higher standard."

Tang tossed a ballpoint pen at Rita. It missed and bounced off the desk and into a trashcan. "Don't worry about Detective Jankowsky, she's got no interest in men, but she gets jealous when the females on the squad stop worshipping her."

Seeing that Loviccio wasn't going to introduce them, Detectives Albertini and Jackson got up from their desks and walked over to say hello to Duke. Albertini, the daughter of a Russian mom and Sicilian father, was an inch shorter than Rita and could easily bench press more weight than anyone else in the squad. She wore her black hair in a crewcut but fussed with it constantly as she spoke.

Moe Jackson had darker skin than Duke, but his features were Caucasian. He had joined the 84th Detective Squad last month on a transfer and promotion from the South Bronx. Both of his parents had been cops. His mother hailed from a wealthy California family, who'd been cast out when she married her black philosophy professor from Rutgers where she'd been pre-law.

Together, the couple decided that criminal justice was best handled at the street level and graduated from the police academy on the same day. They were shot and killed on the job a week apart, less than a month before reaching the twenty-year retirement plateau. Moe, who'd seen the wrong side of a jail cell only once in his life as a juvenile, lied about his age and joined the department six months later. He was only seventeen and was seeking vengeance.

That was over nineteen years in the past. The suicidal teen, who turned her gun on Moe's father instead of blowing her own brains all over her parents' bathroom, died from a drug overdose several weeks into her trial. His mother's killer lost his life at the hands of a rival gang member the following summer while in lockup. Not having any other plan for his future, Moe Jackson decided that being a cop wasn't the worst thing in the world.

Moe's long-term goal was to win the lottery and move to New Zealand before he reached forty. It took very little prompting to get him to speak with a fake New Zealand accent. Everyone who heard it swore he was trying to speak Irish. He'd never been down under but could describe tourist sights as though he'd been born in Auckland and raised sheep for a living.

The wall map of the dual-island nation hanging next to Moe's desk was so completely covered with newspaper clippings and postcards that only the southernmost tip of the South Island was still visible. He told Duke the name of the town where he wanted to live, but said it was buried under the memorabilia.

"Why New Zealand?"

Moe dropped into the proper accent. "Do you know how much a veterinarian gets paid, mate? Bloody hell, twice as much as a copper does here."

"You're a dog doctor on the side?" Duke shrugged. "I've heard of moonlighting, but that's a bit much."

Moe's accent returned to normal. "I like pets. They don't kill each other." He smiled. "Veterinary school is three years."

"What about college? Don't you need the undergraduate degree first?"

"Hey, screw you, Garvey." The kiwi-wannabe grabbed a sheet of paper off his desk. "I don't need anyone else in this squad pissing on my dreams."

Duke opened his mouth, but Rita hit him in the side of the head with another balled up sheet of paper. When he turned, she was wiggling a finger at him and mouthing the word, "No."

With the introductions complete, everyone returned to their desks and began hitting the keys. Loviccio walked over to an empty desk and tapped the power switch on the computer screen.

"This was Detective Gregory's desk. He retired two weeks ago. Now it's yours." He leaned over the desk and clicked the mouse on the NYPD logo. "This is the program where you'll enter your DD5s. You'll need a username and password. Sit down here and set yourself up. I need to drain the dragon. Be back in a minute."

Duke pulled the chair out from under the desk and sat down. All of his personal electronics were Apple-based. He had an iPad that was synced together with his iPhone, but other than that, no actual knowledge of the Microsoft world. He'd used a PC briefly in high school, but outside of the business community and the NYPD, everyone else had gone over to the fruity side.

Clicking the icon several times too many, Duke found the extra open windows and closed them. With the last one filling the screen, he entered a username of bobmarley and was surprised to see it was already in use. He tried petertosh, jimmycliff, and bobmarley1, 2, and 3 before finding marcusgarvey was available. "The old man's ghost is always watching," he muttered.

Loviccio returned as Duke was thinking about a password. "Keep it simple. You forget your password and you'll have to fill out forms and spend half the day getting it reset."

"What do you suggest?"

"Abc123cop. Same as everyone else." Loviccio looked around the squad and smiled. "If you can't trust a cop, who can you trust with your deepest secrets?"

Duke pulled the keyboard closer and typed the common password. But just to be different, he added a 4 in the middle when Loviccio wasn't looking. His mother had taught him to trust the police, but not with anything secret. It was one of her many lessons he'd taken to heart.

Chapter Four
The Ghost

One more desk sat unoccupied in the squad. It was an old institutional green metal relic with three original legs and a fourth made out of books. The pile of hardbacks was only the beginning of what appeared to be the squad's library. On both sides of the ancient desk, stacks of books had been made into walls nearly two feet high. The back edge had vertical tomes wedged from one paper wall to the other.

Newspapers filled the space not covered by paperbacks, hardcovers, and pamphlets. Duke walked over and lifted some of the yellowing sheets and read the dates, "1981, 1983, 1984. Looks like someone's researching an old case."

Loviccio rushed over and took the newspapers from Duke's hand. He laid them reverently back down on the desk and grabbed Duke by the shoulders. "The last person who touched this shit is still in the hospital."

Pushing him away, Duke dusted off his shoulders and nodded at the display "What is this?"

"The only case Detective Francis Nussbaum is still working." Lieutenant Moscowitz strode over to the pair and shook his head. "Sixty-four years old, one year short of mandatory retirement and this is his life's work." The lieutenant pushed the wooden chair under the desk and turned to Loviccio. "You want to tell him the story? You're the only one who's been here long enough to tell it right."

Loviccio nodded slowly. "Come on, junior. Let's go for a walk." He looked at the clock over the door. "We've still got time before the ghost of Frank Nussbaum makes his daily appearance."

The pair crossed Tillary Street and Flatbush Avenue, taking over a vacant bench in McLaughlin Park. Loviccio unscrewed the bottle of water he'd grabbed as they walked out the door and took a long drink.

"1987, Labor Day. Two couples sit down for dinner in the Narrows Diner on Battery Avenue. It's gone about five years. Burned to the ground. Arson, according to the reports." He took another swig and continued. "Anyhow, these two couples are the commanding officer of the Army garrison at Fort Hamilton and his aide along with their girlfriends."

"No wives?"

"Uh, uh. You know what a 'goomah' is?"

Duke smiled. "Yeah, I watched *The Sopranos*. Every guy had a wife at home and a goomah in some sleazy hotel room." Scratching an itch on the back of his neck, he frowned. "Never worked out so well for the goomah."

"There you go." Loviccio took another sip of water and burped. "So, the commanding officer, a Major, and his sidekick are at their usual spot having dinner with their goomahs, either before or after sex, and somebody shoots all four of them in their heads. This unknown somebody's first shot went to the Major's brain box from straight in front. Several witnesses stated that the killer stood there for a few seconds, staring at the Major before the first shot."

"Somebody?"

"Yeah, *somebody*. Not some guy. Not some woman. Somebody that a restaurant full of witnesses couldn't agree was either male or female. Somebody dressed in camouflage clothes who went so far as to leave behind a spotlessly clean .357 Smith and Wesson revolver." Placing the bottle of water on the grass, Loviccio stretched his arms out on top of the bench and took a deep breath before he let the mic drop. "The Major was the father of then patrolman, Francis Herman Nussbaum."

Duke's breath caught in his throat. "Holy shit."

Loviccio held up his hand. "But wait, there's more. Turns out, this was the last murder by a serial killer who mostly targeted military personnel. At least eleven of the twenty confirmed dead got government paychecks. All of them murdered by a killer dressed in homemade camouflage. Lots of different patterns sewn together. Navy, Army, desert, jungle, all sorts of shit, so they knew it was fake."

"No photos, video?"

"Nah, this was the seventies and eighties, that shit was at least a decade away."

"What about fingerprints?"

"The killer always wore gloves. Cheap ones like you'd use to clean the kitchen. Those were usually found not far from the scene."

Duke tried to switch his mind into detective mode. This was unfamiliar territory, not the regular routine of the sector car or the beat he'd walked. Street cops develop instincts early in their careers or they leave the job...often in a box. They learned the street, the city, and how it could kill you if you dropped your guard. However, the transition from the bag to street clothes, as Duke had done this morning, was no different from what happened on the day a cop graduated from the academy. This morning was the same as the first day after graduation. Duke was a rookie for the second time, and he was grasping at strands of dead grass. Detectives have to learn how to investigate. It was a brand new skillset for Duke Garvey.

"Hair, DNA, fiber samples? None of that?"

"Nothing, nada. The killer left behind a weapon only once, and it turned out to be the same gun that was used in all the other killings. Ballistics said it was a perfect match to every other bullet they'd been able to retrieve. The four dead in Brooklyn were the end of the killer's spree. A total of eleven military personnel from private to the Major and nine civilians lost their lives. An even twenty murders and not a single one of them ever solved."

"What about the Good Faith Nursing Home?"

Loviccio sighed. "The one lead that held promise. A patient there had been raving about killing soldiers. The Ghost got there too late to interview the woman. She died on New Year's Eve and he didn't find out about her until a month later. Frank was so pissed off that he left without interviewing anyone." Taking the last sip of water, Loviccio shook his head. "There was something about her that really freaked out The Ghost. Over the years, it was the one way to get him riled up." He smiled and let out a laugh. "One of my few pleasures on the job."

Duke chuckled along with Loviccio. "Damn."

Finished with the bottle of water, the senior detective stood, stretching his back to stare at a flock of pigeons. "Frank Nussbaum was promoted the day after his father was laid to rest. His moms blew her brains out with the Major's .45 while Frank was waiting in the car to take her to the funeral."

"Holy shit! Both parents, days apart?" Duke blew out a long breath.

"And that's where it all started." With a sigh, Loviccio continued. "For more than thirty years, Detective Nussbaum has been trying to solve his father's murder and the other nineteen killings. He's got less than a year left on the job before they force him out."

"Do you think he'll go? I mean, without closing the case?" Duke shrugged. "He could always turn it over to the Cold Case Squad or hire a P.I. or just keep researching it on his own. I'm sure the department would grant him limited access."

"The department would like to see him fade away. To many who eat from the trough before us, he's an embarrassment. They don't see any possible way to solve the case. The serial killer just stopped killing and disappeared. Did the killer die? Is the killer in prison for some other crime? The only clues are the gloves and one weapon. No footprints, fingerprints, or notes."

Duke got up from the bench and dusted off the seat of his pants. "My mother taught me that if you really want something, never give up. Never let an ill wind blow away your dreams."

Loviccio crushed the empty water bottle and dropped it into a recycle bin. "This ain't nobody's dream, junior. This is one old guy's worst friggin' nightmare." Sliding his cellphone out of his shirt pocket, Loviccio read the time, "Five minutes to noon. The Ghost will be parking in his reserved spot and Sergeant Williams will be clearing the lobby."

"This happens daily?"

"Like clockwork, junior. Come on. If we hurry, we can beat him upstairs to the squad."

The Ghost fit his name. Duke had never seen a living human with skin so pale. When the man moved from the doorway to his desk, it was as though his feet seemed to shuffle, but his body motion was smooth, flowing. He didn't float, but Duke was sure a gust of wind would have taken the old man off course.

Not a word was spoken and everyone in the squad stood until The Ghost had taken his seat and clicked on the small library lamp on top of the right-hand pile. And then life continued in the squad as though nothing had happened. No one acknowledged Nussbaum's presence. No one offered him a cup of tea or asked how his life was going. They all knew. Everyone in the squad could tell you exactly how many days were left until The Ghost would lose his parking spot, turn in his weapon and badge, and float off into NYPD history.

Duke watched the aged detective shuffle some papers and reach for a book at the top of the stack to his left. Nussbaum flipped through the pages, stopping occasionally to make notes on a yellow legal pad. Finished with the book, he returned it to the exact spot he'd taken it from, slowly sliding it in position with his thumb. He rotated in the chair so that the rest of the squad was at his back and folded his hands behind his head.

Leaning over toward to Duke, Loviccio whispered, "That's it. He'll stay like that until four o'clock and then leave."

"Four hours of thinking?"

"Sometimes he snores. Once in a while he'll fart. Not even lift his leg. Just rip one loose without moving a muscle."

Duke held back a snicker with his palm. "I'm glad we're on this side of the squad."

"Oh, it won't matter. You'll see an exodus starting with Albertini and Jackson. The lieutenant will slam his door and the rest of us will find some other part of the building to hang out in while the odor clears."

It was too much to hold back. Duke sputtered and let out a roaring laugh. The Ghost didn't move.

The man's lack of response along with Duke's laughter was enough to set Rita into spasms of knee-slapping chuckles. Cheng got up from his chair and stood in the doorway of the squad, facing out.

Lieutenant Moscowitz leaned out of his office. "Loviccio, Garvey, the M.E. has the slugs from your DOA on Park. Get over to Ballistics. Jankowsky, you and the eggroll twins, 42 Prospect Park West, apartment 4F. Home invasion. Two civilians on the scene beat up pretty bad. EMS is responding. Supervisor is on the scene. Apparently, she lives in the same building."

The flurry of activity ended as quickly as it began. Five detectives went out the door. The two who were left resumed their typing as though *War and Peace* was flowing from their fingers. And in his corner, The Ghost had hardened into a block of stone.

Chapter Five
Duke And The King, Royalty Abides

Tugging open the heavy door of the Ballistics Lab, Loviccio led Duke inside, handing him a pair of ear protectors as the door slammed closed. For a Monday afternoon, the lab was packed more than normal. Seven homicides by shooting in the last twenty-four hours meant at least seven bullets would be recovered. The most pristine would come from the corpses, the balance from walls, floors, and mattresses. All the slugs had to be matched to the weapon that fired them and catalogued before they went to the evidence locker.

One of the bodies had taken nine rounds from a trio of automatic weapons in a gang killing. Another from the same crime scene yielded six more. None of the technicians could assume that just because the bullets came from the same body, they were fired by the same gun. The weapons experts of the NYPD who worked in this unit were often the difference in the courtroom. Their knowledge of guns and bullets could be the deciding factor when it came to proving who was guilty and who was not. Today, however, the whirlwind of activity that greeted the two detectives was well beyond the norm for this early in the summer.

Even as a beat cop, Duke knew as it got warmer in New York City, the intensity of street violence went up with the heat. So far that summer, it had been much hotter than any of the weather prognosticators could remember. The humidity that afternoon had reached critical levels and storm clouds were gathering to the west. Fire hydrants had been cracked open and half-naked children were running through them. In the older neighborhoods, air conditioners dripped their excess sweat onto passersby.

The kidnapping that led to his promotion took place on the Fourth of July. Duke and his partner, Juliana, were just coming off dinner break when the radio call of a 10-34, an assault in progress, was broadcast. They were three blocks away from the scene and got there as the suspect was running out of the apartment building with a young boy under his arm. Spotting their blue and white approaching with its lights flashing, the suspect, a nineteen-year-old white male with a gun, dragged the boy back into the lobby of the building.

Out of the car first, Duke ran across the street and grabbed the door before it could close and lock. He cornered the assailant in the lobby, but Juliana was locked outside. The kidnapper was well over six feet tall and muscular. Able to lift the child and hold him as a shield, he fired twice at Duke. The first shot was wide, but the second one went through Duke's left shoulder.

Spinning from the impact, Duke managed to fire off one round that hit the kidnapper in his forehead. It was the only time in eleven years that he'd fired his weapon outside the range. The nineteen-year-old went down without firing another shot and was dead before his head hit the floor.

    A neighbor buzzed in Juliana and the rest of the Emergency Services Unit that had responded. The kidnapped child was unharmed except for scrapes and bruises. They promoted Duke to Detective Third Grade for his heroism, and he spent the better part of the winter and spring in rehab.

    While he was lying on a gurney in the emergency room, Duke's mother had rushed in and insisted on seeing her son. Juliana, who'd met her partner's mother several times, related the raw facts of the incident, including that her partner had gone in alone. She then led the woman into the examination room where Duke was waiting his turn for surgery. Mother Garvey, who was in her late fifties at the time, punched her son in the nose and told him a gentleman always waited until the lady got out of the car before running into a building. And, if nothing else, he should have gone around and opened the door for her.

    The slug that had gone through his shoulder was in a file somewhere in the massive Ballistics Lab. It had been dug out of the lobby wall. Duke had no desire to visit it and felt a chill, knowing it was nearby. Slipping on the hearing protector that Loviccio handed him, he followed the seasoned investigator over to a desk filled with computer screens and weapons.

Lifting one cup of the protective muffs from Duke's ear, he introduced the newest member of the 84th to King Percival, Detective First Grade and the only other cop on the job in the same age group as The Ghost.

"Duke? As in the *Duke of Earl*?" The King, as subordinates addressed him, hummed a few bars of the song.

"Yes. My mother's idea and it just stuck." Duke pursed his lips. "And so the Duke meets the King? Royalty abides."

"Shit, boy, you way too young to be royalty." The King stood with his fists jammed into his sides. "You graduate from the academy yesterday? Still got the starch in your uniform? Damn, Ronnie, I have shoes older than this kid."

Loviccio doubled over with laughter. "Percival, you have shoes older than just about everyone in the department. I've heard that your farts are so old most folks smell them six times before they dissipate."

"You best keep that boy around when you take a dump. I hear you ain't got the strength to wipe your ass no more. Goddamn nursing home reject." The King punched Loviccio in the shoulder. "What you doin' down here, white bread?"

"Boss says you got a pair of slugs from our DOA on Park Place."

"Yeah. Got 'em ten minutes ago." Turning, The King signaled with his finger. "Over here. One of the kids got 'em on a scope."

The trio walked to the end of a long bench filled with microscopes, Bunsen burners, and laboratory glass. A blonde with her hair tied back in pigtails was bent over a two-person microscope, fiddling with the spent rounds and the light.

"Thirty-eight caliber Beretta." She pointed at the slug. "See the extra wide groove? That's the key to identification with this brand."

"Any match to the database?" Leaning over to view the slug, The King adjusted the focus, switching eyes twice.

The technician pulled a keyboard closer to where she sat. "Nothing yet, but the system is running slower than usual this morning."

Duke nodded. "Another busy summer has begun."

"Bodies, bodies, everywhere and not a dime of overtime to be spent." Taking his turn at the eyepiece, Loviccio squinted. "I can't see shit."

"She clicked the light off, Ronnie." Chuckling, The King stepped back from the table. "You in a rush for this one?"

"Nah." Straightening his back with a bit of effort, Loviccio shook his head. "Two .38 caliber slugs from one of the most popular semi-automatics on the street. No video at the scene. Every middle-aged gay man in the city is a suspect. This case is going to require divine intervention for a solution."

"Or a lucky hit in the database." King Percival shrugged. "Isn't that how you usually solve these, Ronnie?"

"Kiss my ass, you old limp dick lab rat."

The King turned to Duke and winked. "White boy says a prayer every night that his dick will someday get as hard as mine."

Duke looked back and forth between the two senior citizens. "One thing's for certain. I'm not getting in the middle of you two and your dicks."

Driving back to the squad, Loviccio rolled the window down on his side and rested his arm on the door. In the few hours they'd known each other, Duke had yet to see the man use two hands on the wheel. Once, while his mother had been teaching him the fine art of four-wheeled navigation, Duke had taken his left hand off the wheel to wave at a group of girls. His mother had reached across with a flyswatter and smacked his arm so hard he had a welt that lasted for two weeks.

"You old guys like to talk about your sex life as though it's a sport."

Loviccio laughed. "Some of us are just happy to have a sex life at this age."

"You think The Ghost gets laid?"

"Yeah, he shares a goomah with the Pope." Switching hands, Loviccio pointed at a group of hookers standing in front of a liquor store. "You could line those girls up naked in front of The Ghost and unless one of them had a clue to solve his case, he wouldn't even notice them."

The radio came alive. *"Detectives 84 on the air?"*

Duke keyed the mic. "84 Detectives, unit three, go ahead."

"Saint Oda Catholic Church, 913 Sutter. See the priest there about a robbery."

"10-4."

Duke blew out a hard breath. "Robbing a church. Now, there's a shortcut to Hell."

The priest met the detectives outside the church and introduced himself as Father Xavier. Leading them around to a side entrance, he pointed out the damage. Fresh dents around the lock from a pry bar or large screwdriver and the deformed frame were clear evidence of forced entry. Duke bent down and pointed at a line of dried blood spots leading toward the street. They ended at the curb.

"Is there more blood inside?" He shot a few pictures of the blood trail and walked back over to the door.

Father Xavier nodded, tightening his sash. "Yes. There's a broken window where the thief got access to my office. Let's go around the front."

Following the priest around and into the church, Loviccio knelt and crossed himself. Duke took off his hat and held it in his hand, staring at the huge lifelike Christ hanging in front of the stained glass. It was a unique representation of the Son of God.

Jesus had Negro features and dark skin along with large crack in the wood of statue's left leg that ran from the knee to the nail in its foot.

Duke stared at the damage for a few moments and shook his head in confusion. Odd that it was, he thought he'd seen this particular black Jesus somewhere before. In fact, he was certain.

"I haven't been inside a church since I was five years old. But I'd swear on a stack of bibles that I've seen this statue. Was this damage in the news?"

"Not that I can recall." Father Xavier looked up at Jesus and shrugged. "I've been here for thirty-nine years and it's been cracked all that time. Why do you ask?"

Duke scratched the back of his neck. "Don't know. It just looks familiar." He started to cross himself, but couldn't remember the correct motions. He looked at the priest and shrugged. "As a Rastafarian, I worship wherever I feel the need. Jah is everywhere, not just a brick building with a cross on its roof."

Loviccio looked up at the dark wood and gold image and shrugged. "God is wherever you find him."

The priest spun around slowly and smiled. "Or her."

Father Xavier's office was down a short flight of stairs that ended in a dimly lit hallway. To the left, the blood trail led the way to the outside entrance. Turning right, the hallway widened and was more brightly illuminated. A long wooden bench sat outside the door to the priest's office. From the depth of the worn seat, it was obvious the bench was a common resting place before entering the priest's private sanctuary.

Loviccio shined his flashlight on the tile floor. The glass windowpane from the office door was in glittering pieces at the foot of the doorway.

Duke had filled his back pocket with gloves from a box on the floor of their unmarked car and handed a pair to Loviccio before the senior detective had a chance to get them from his pocket.

"You're learning. That's a good sign." Loviccio tugged the gloves onto his hands. "What's next?"

"Well, we have blood, so we're going to need a sample."

Loviccio shook his head. "Correct, but that's not our job. The Crime Scene Unit will process this area. They'll collect blood samples and fingerprints. So what's next?"

"Shoot photos of the crime scene?"

"Not yet." Turning to the priest, the senior detective pulled a notepad from his jacket pocket. "Tell us what's missing, Father."

Duke nodded his head. "Duh."

The thief, as it appeared to be a solo job based on the single set of shoe prints leading away from the doorway, had taken a cash box with over ten-thousand dollars inside. A good friend of the church had passed away several weeks ago, and the money was a cash gift from his widow. A solid gold crucifix that was on a bookcase behind the priest's desk was missing, and a credit card that arrived that day in the mail was also taken.

"Had you already activated the card, Father?" Duke shot a picture of the torn envelope and letter that lay on the priest's desk.

"No. The mail comes very early. I put this on my desk, thinking I'd open it after hearing confessions this morning. The thief must have broken in while I was upstairs."

Loviccio checked the time on his phone. "What time did you hear the first confession?"

"Ten o'clock sharp. I didn't come back to my office until after noon. That's when I noticed the broken window and the blood."

Loviccio looked at his phone again. "Father, it's almost four o'clock in the afternoon. Why'd you wait so long to call this in?"

Father Xavier's face folded in on itself. He wrung his hands and took several deep breaths. "I think I know who did this and I've been trying to get him to return the money and the cross. I don't want him to go to jail."

"Father, you're talking about thousands of dollars and a piece of art probably worth twice that. This is a felony, not some dime-store candy bar rip-off."

"You have to understand..." The priest's voice trailed off, and he looked toward the ceiling.

"No, Father." Loviccio leaned over with his hands flat on the priest's desk. "*You* have to understand. You can't save everyone.

God can't save everyone. Whoever did this should be in jail. What would have happened if you were seated here, behind your desk, and the robber came in with a weapon? Do you think prayer and forgiveness would have saved your life?"

The priest was adamant. "I know who did this. He didn't know there was that much money in the cash box." Pausing for a moment, he pointed to where the gold crucifix had stood. "No one else would have taken that cross."

Duke shook his head. "Anyone could melt that down in a kitchen oven and sell the gold for its value in ounces."

"No. He wouldn't do that." Father Xavier pounded a fist into his palm. "Emilio cleans this office twice a week. He could have stolen it a long time ago. No, you're wrong. You should see the reverence in his eyes when he polishes that cross."

"Emilio?" Duke wrote the name in his notepad. "What's his last name and where can we find him?"

The priest hesitated. "He's just a boy."

"A boy who could have cut your throat with a piece of that broken glass if you'd stood in his way." Loviccio pointed at the priest. "What do you think he's gonna do when he gets that cash box open and finds a lot more money than he's ever had? You think he'll spend it wisely? Maybe he'll call his stockbroker and ask for advice."

Ignoring the sarcastic remark, the priest looked at Duke. "I believe he'll return it."

"And if he doesn't?" Duke cocked his head to the side. "Then what?"

Crossing his arms over his chest, Father Xavier blew out a long breath. "He's a good boy. He must have needed a few dollars for food and was too ashamed to ask. I've given him money before."

Duke laid his notepad on the priest's desk. "The hardest thing for a man of the cloth to do is to see the bad side of anything. There's a flood, homes are washed away, lives are lost. I saw it happen in Jamaica. The Catholic priest stood on a dry hill and said, 'Yes, but the crops are getting watered.' A farmer who'd lost his house and livestock, told the priest that no one would live to eat the crops and the priest replied, 'That is God's will'."

"This is different."

"No, Father, this is exactly the same thing." Duke picked up the notepad and handed it to the priest. "If God is willing anything, he wants you to save this boy with our help and not His. A boy with thousands of dollars he's never had before is as dangerous as giving him a loaded gun. That big, gold cross makes him a target for thieves who do this for a living. If you really want to save this kid, give us his address and where he hangs out. We'll find him and bring back your stolen property before it puts him on an autopsy table."

Lifting a pen from his desk, Father Xavier wrote Emilio's name and address as requested. He held the notepad out to the detectives, but pulled it back before either one could take it.

"I don't want to hear that Emilio resisted, and you had to beat him to get him to confess."

Loviccio shook his head. "This isn't television, Father. They have video cameras everywhere now. Emilio will be taken with the least amount of force necessary. We'll reach out to you when he's in custody and you can talk to him before he goes to Central Booking."

Duke remembered how to cross himself. "Jah protect."

Chapter Six
Leaky Cash Boxes

The address was on Jerome, only a couple of blocks from the church. The detectives agreed it wasn't too hot or too late in the day for a walk and set off for the address on foot. Despite the lack of a photograph, Father Xavier's description of the boy's blue-tinted crewcut and lime-green overalls made it easy to spot the kid as he rounded the corner, strolling toward the two detectives.

Loviccio stopped and bent over as though he was tying a shoelace. Out of the corner of his eye, he saw Duke continue walking past the boy and smiled. The kid was carrying a brown paper bag, large enough for a crucifix...or a gun. Duke drew his Glock from his shoulder holster and held it by his side.

Several steps behind the boy, the former street cop spun on his heel and ordered the kid to freeze. Loviccio came up from his crouch with his gun aimed at the boy's chest and repeated the command.

"Don't shoot me," the boy pleaded. "I'm bringing it back to Father Xavier." He reached into the bag and pulled out the gold cross.

"Get on the ground!" Duke yelled at him, advancing forward a step with his Glock in the boy's face.

Loviccio ran up to the kid as the boy quickly knelt and then went spread-eagle with his hands slapping the pavement. "Is your name Emilio Cortez?"

"Yeah, but I was bringing the cross back. I didn't mean to take it."

"It just jumped into your hands?" Loviccio reached behind and pulled his handcuffs from their pouch. "Where's the cash box?"

Emilio shook his head. "I couldn't get it open so I threw it into the creek."

"Bullshit." Snapping a cuff on the boy's left hand, Loviccio dragged him to his feet. "Where's the box, Emilio, and no lies?"

"I'm serious, man. I couldn't get it open. I smashed the lock with a hammer and tried to pry it open with a screwdriver. It just wouldn't budge. So I tossed it into the creek at the end of Fountain Avenue."

Duke grabbed the boy's free arm and snapped the other handcuff in place. "You didn't know how much money was in the box?"

"No, man. There's usually a few hundred dollars from the collection plate." Emilio twisted his wrists around in the cuffs. "My wallet was stolen, and it had all my cash. I was just going to borrow the money until my next check came."

"For drugs?" Loviccio put the cross back into the paper bag and handed it to Duke.

"Hell, no." Emilio shook his head quickly. "I'm clean, man. Ask Father Xavier."

Duke nodded. "We will." He pointed at the bandage on Emilio's left arm. "How'd you cut yourself?"

"Some guy..."

"Bullshit." Loviccio dragged the boy closer. "Try again, Emilio, and the truth this time."

The boy nodded, rolling his head around his neck. "The door was locked, and I broke the glass with my pry bar. Father Xavier never locks that door. Why'd he lock it this morning?"

"Because the box you threw in the creek had nearly ten-thousand dollars in it. A gift from a wealthy parishioner that Father Xavier was going to take to the bank this afternoon." Duke fixed his tie. "Let's hope that box is waterproof."

They led Emilio, in handcuffs, back to Father Xavier's office. The boy stood silently while the priest wiped it down with a velvet cloth and replaced the crucifix in its original location. Lowering his head, the thief shook each time the priest raised his voice and lambasted him for showing so little faith.

"We've already contacted the Marine Unit and they're sending a team of divers." Shoving the boy into a chair, Loviccio glared at the priest. "Until we recover the box, there's no proof of a crime other than the stolen cross which has been returned, the blood on the floor, and the broken window." He shrugged. "All we know for sure is that the kid broke into your office."

"Then I have no intention of pressing charges." Father Xavier walked over and put his hands on Emilio's shoulders.

"Father, I'm not sure you understand." Loviccio sat down next to the boy and looked over his notes. "There's a record of the 9-1-1 call. We've been dispatched and arrested a likely suspect. This is just the beginning of the paperwork. If the dive team recovers the box, there won't be an opportunity for you to help Emilio, especially if there's as much money in the box as you claim."

The priest walked back around the desk and sat down. "Then I shall pray that the box is not found."

"And lose ten grand?" Duke expression was incredulous. His eyebrows went so high that they almost touched the front edge of his auburn cornrows.

"Money will never be more important than a human life." Father Xavier folded his hands on his desk. "Will you remove the handcuffs, please?"

Duke shook his head. "We can't do that, Father. You've already given us a verbal statement that a crime has been committed. We—"

"It's okay, Duke." Loviccio put his hand on Duke's shoulder. "Emilio isn't going anywhere and if the Father isn't going to press charges, there isn't much left for us to do."

"What?" Turning to face the senior detective, Duke searched for answers but found none.

Loviccio pinched the bridge of his nose. "As you wish, Father." Turning to Emilio, he pointed at the bloody bandage on the boy's forearm. "You'd best get that looked at before the divers find the cash box. Once they do, you're a collar for the robbery and it'll be hours before you get to an emergency room."

They released the boy in the priest's care and were walking back to the car in silence when a woman came running out of a building on the opposite side of Sutter. She screamed, "He's killing my son!" and ran past them, across the street toward the church.

Duke started after the woman, but Loviccio called him back. "No time. Let's get in there and see what's happening."

Together, they ran across the street, guns drawn, and into the three-story building. Sounds of a struggle came from an open door on the ground floor and the two detectives hurried over to it, standing on either side. Loviccio leaned in and snapped back quickly.

"There's a baby on the floor to the right. That's all I can see."

Duke repeated the movement from his side of the door. "I can see a man in a doorway to the left. He's holding a strap or a belt in his hand."

Loviccio nodded. "Okay. On three. One. Two. Three."

He went through the door, crouching low. Duke followed to the opposite side, his Glock aimed high at the man's back. "Police. Freeze!"

The man spun around to face the two detectives. In his right hand, he held a wide leather belt folded in half. In the other was a small silver-colored semi-automatic pistol, aimed at his partner. Duke took aim at the man's head and ordered him to drop the weapon.

"Screw you. Where's my bitch wife?"

Loviccio moved several feet away from Duke, making it impossible for the man to cover them both with his gun. "Put down the weapon, sir. Last chance."

"You bring that whore back in here so I can blow her brains out or I'll shoot one of you." Waving the gun back and forth between the detectives, a stream of spit came out with his words. "Miserable slut. Leaves the goddamn baby alone so she can get high upstairs with her bitch friends while I'm out tryin' to find work. Goddamn junkies."

"I'm not going to ask you again." Loviccio took another step away from Duke.

"And I'm not going to ask you again, either." The man lowered the weapon at Loviccio.

Duke fired once, hitting the man in the arm holding the weapon. The impact of the nine-millimeter round spun the man around and his shot went wild, slamming into the ceiling above Loviccio.

"Jesus!" Wiping several small bits of plaster from his head, Loviccio turned to Duke, shaking his fist. "Warn me before you do that again, junior."

"He was going to shoot."

The older detective picked up the small semi-automatic with his jacket sleeve. "Not with the safety on."

"Shit." Duke looked over at the man who lay shaking and cursing on the floor. "You'd better hope the baby is okay or the next round will be in your scrotum."

"Scrotum?" Loviccio shook his head. "Who talks like that?" He flicked the safety to the off position. The weapon was ready to fire. Clicking it back on, he pulled the slide and ejected the round in the chamber. Still with the tiny automatic aimed away from the child, he dropped the magazine out of the weapon and bent down to pick up the unused round. "As far as anyone is concerned, the safety was off."

Duke nodded. "Thanks."

Any kind of police activity in New York City brings out a crowd. This incident became an early evening circus within minutes of the first gunshot. From a flurry of 9-1-1 calls, dispatch sent out an "any available" and the four blue and whites closest to the scene rushed to assist. One of the callers said it was a cop that was shot, sparking the pace of the responding officers up a notch.

However, seeing Duke and Loviccio march the injured man out of the building in handcuffs, everyone caught their breath and put on the brakes. The uniformed officers moved the crowd back from the scene while an additional unmarked unit from Narcotics that was in the area assisted with the canvass.

EMS bandaged the man's arm and transported him, under police guard, to the hospital. His list of charges would start with the attempted murder of a police officer and end with the reckless endangerment of a child. At the low side of justice, he'd spend fifteen years in prison. Loviccio mumbled the word "paperwork" several times while paramedics were treating the man's forearm and slammed the back doors of the ambulance much harder than necessary.

Child Protective Services took charge of the infant. The mother came out of the church with Father Xavier and waited for the two detectives to cross the street. It was obvious from her slurred speech and bloodshot eyes that she was in no condition to care for a baby, much less herself. The priest convinced the mother to go to the hospital, agreeing to secure the couple's apartment and to look after her child once the little boy had been processed into the system.

According to neighbors, the couple had been fighting constantly since she'd given birth. It wasn't the man's child, but he paid the rent and handled the meals. One of the detectives from Narcotics knew the building as a crack house and had collared the woman's friend for minor possession a few months prior. The wounded man was unknown to the detective.

Along with the four sector cars, a supervisor arrived to begin the investigation into an officer-involved shooting. Duke sat in the passenger seat of their unmarked car with his feet dangling out the door. Loviccio slid into the driver's seat and slammed the door.

"Hell of a first day, junior." Stomping on the brake pedal, Loviccio pushed the button to start the engine and rammed the air conditioner switch into crisis mode. "You'll go before the shooting board in the morning, but it'll all be over in five minutes. It was a righteous shoot as far as anyone is concerned. Anyone asks me, the safety was off."

Duke looked up at the clouds and sighed. "I had days like this when I was in uniform. It's how I stopped drinking."

Loviccio laughed. "Hell, junior, it's days like this that require drinking."

The Ghost had left by the time Duke and Loviccio returned to the squad. Rita was at her desk, entering her notes into the system, and offered a box of crullers from the French bakery across the street. The senior detective looked down at the pastries and shook his head before he went out in the hallway to make a pot of tea.

"They were fresh this morning." Rita held the box open and waited until Duke had selected one.

Taking a bite of the pastry, he winced and dropped the rest of the stale cruller in the trash. "Yesterday morning, maybe."

"I hear you lost your virginity today." She smiled. "Good shoot?"

"Yes. But it wasn't my first."

"First as a detective. Still a busted cherry."

Loviccio came back in and sat down at his desk with a cup of tea. Sipping the hot beverage, he smiled. "Junior did okay out there. I think we'll keep him. Okay with you, honey?"

"Adding another man to our merry troupe? What happened to gender balance?" Rita saved the file she was working on and pushed back from the desk. "I thought the boss was going to put in for another female detective."

"Yeah, but the cop who was first in line decided to wait for that slot in Midtown." Loviccio put his teacup on Rita's desk and took a cruller out of the box. He dipped it into the hot tea and took a bite. "Day before yesterday." The hardened pastry followed Duke's chunk into the trash.

The night shift was wandering in. Loviccio put the box of crullers on the floor and kicked it under Rita's desk.

"You still working on the fives from the push in?"

She nodded. "Yeah. I'm on the last page of my notes. The couple was beat to shit. She's gonna have scars on both cheeks along with a broken jaw. The guy might not walk again."

"Same MO as the building next door?" Loviccio lifted the printout of Rita's entry from her desk.

"Uh, huh. Only this time, a cop saw them get in a blue van with a rusted roof." Flipping to the last page of her notes, Rita checked the name. "Sergeant Swinton, Midtown North supervisor, had just gotten home and was shaking out her tablecloth from her front balcony. She heard the shouts and saw two white males get into the van." Rita looked up at Loviccio and shrugged. "Too bad she lives on the top floor. Might have caught them or at least gotten a plate number."

Duke walked over and hopped up on Loviccio's desk. "You want to show me how to enter the DD5s?"

Loviccio checked the time. "Not tonight. Come in early tomorrow morning and we'll get them done. The boss rarely gets here before nine. Meet me here at eight and I'll bring fresh pastries. Then you've got the shooting board at ten."

"Pastries? Something vegetarian?" Duke wrinkled his nose.

"Cannoli from Ferrara's." Loviccio smiled. "Nothing but the best."

Leaving the squad, Duke walked the few blocks to the subway for his trip back to Manhattan. The car he sold five years ago had only been used to visit his mother in Jersey. It was a luxury for anyone living in the city and not worth the effort to commute to the job. He'd been riding the subway system for eighteen years and knew his way around the underground tunnels blindfolded.

The clattering subterranean journey from Brooklyn to Duke's apartment on East 34th Street and the FDR Highway was just short of half an hour. The unobstructed view of the East River from his fifth-floor balcony and the sprawling NYU Medical Center from his bedroom was a stark contrast to the rundown slums of Brooklyn where he'd spent his first day as a detective. He needed to wash the city away.

Juliana was waiting in the doorway. With a single glance as he stepped off the elevator in the middle of the hall, Duke could tell she wasn't wearing anything besides his robe. He pursed his lips and winked at her.

"You shot a bad guy on your first day on the job?" She loosened the terrycloth belt. "It was all over the radio."

Duke nodded. "Yes. In the arm." Slipping his finger into the knot on his tie, Duke pulled it off his neck and walked over to his girlfriend. "Do you want to go inside or have sex in the hallway?"

"Mmmm…" She smiled. "Let me think about that for a moment."

"No thinking allowed." Kissing her on the lips, Duke reached down and grabbed her butt cheek with one hand, giving it a squeeze. "Shooting someone has made me horny."

Juliana pushed him away. "Jesus, Garvey, you're supposed to investigate, not ratchet up the body count." She turned and padded barefoot into the apartment.

"Hey, he's still alive. Don't get carried away." Duke followed her, kicking the door closed. Slipping off his shoulder holster, Duke hung it in the coat closet next to Juliana's utility belt along with his jacket.

"Maybe I need to get carried away this evening." She let the robe fall off her shoulders. "Maybe I need a detective to investigate why *I'm* so horny. Is it the tie? Those sexy cornrows? The perfectly folded pocket square? Damn, Garvey, you really make an outfit shine."

Duke untied his shoes and took off the shirt. Leading Juliana by the hand, they walked into the bedroom. Her palm was warm, slightly moist, and she held him tightly.

He stopped next to the bed and turned toward her. "I had a really weird thing happen today."

Kneeling, she unbuckled his belt and dropped his pants to the floor. "You want something really weird this evening?" Juliana winked with a sly grin on her face. "I can get really kinky if that's what you need, Duke."

He stepped out of the pants but walked over to the window facing the river in his underwear. "Did you ever see something that you were sure you'd seen before?"

Juliana followed him over to the window, wrapping her arms around Duke from behind. "Yeah, but it's usually big, black, and hard like a hammer." Reaching down, she pressed her hand against his crotch. "Hmmm, not so hard right now."

"I'm serious." He lifted her hand and slid around to face his girlfriend.

"And I'm horny." She wrapped her fingers around his and smiled. "Glad to meet you. Wanna screw?"

"Now?"

"No. Let's wait a while. Maybe I'll practice with a banana while you stand there and shrink."

Duke pinched the bridge of his nose. "You're impossible."

Juliana folded her arms over her boobs. "No, just really, really aroused by what you were wearing." Taking his hand, she led him over to the bed. "Solve my problem, Detective Garvey, and I'll see what I can do to help you afterwards."

He pulled her close and held her shoulders. "Are you sure I have the solution?"

Snapping the elastic of his underpants, Juliana frowned. "Hard to tell with all this cloth in the way."

They had sex. It was a half-hearted effort by Duke, and Juliana could sense it. She got up from the bed when he was done and went into the shower, alone. By himself, in the fading warmth of his king-size bed, he rolled onto his side and gazed out the window at the lights of the huge medical center. He'd seen that black Jesus before. He knew it, but couldn't figure out where the image had first been imprinted on his memory.

When his mother had given up on the Catholic Church and adopted her country's only native religion, Duke had switched as well, not having much belief in God from the outset. The man who had raped his mother was certainly not a Rastafarian. Of that much, Duke was certain. Whether he was Catholic, Jewish, or Moslem was irrelevant. He'd never be referred to as "dad" or "father" in Duke's mind. But he was a member of some major religion that didn't give a damn who its followers impregnated.

Yet, without ever stepping foot into that particular church in Brooklyn in his life, the newly minted detective was certain that he'd seen the black Christ before. It was the cracked leg of the holy image that he remembered, and a memory of wondering why someone hadn't fixed it after all those years. Jesus was a carpenter. His wooden icon deserved much better treatment. Somehow, he recalled thinking that exact thought at some point in his past.

But that was the extent of his recollection. A cracked leg on a black Jesus. Nothing else in the church had been familiar, not even the neighborhood. Father Xavier was a stranger. Duke had met many people in his eleven years on the job and remembered most of them. This priest had never crossed his radar. He'd never met the man in the course of the job or otherwise. Duke was certain today had been his first encounter with the Father.

He reached for the pack of gum on his nightstand and unwrapped a stick. Shoving it into his mouth, Duke lay back with his hands behind his head. He wasn't a fan of mysteries and had no faith at all in the randomness of life. Each person's destiny was determined at birth. The choices people made, the roads they took, weren't some toss of a heavenly coin. He saw them as fate, plain and simple.

This statue was a piece of a puzzle that didn't belong. Memories were one thing. Déjà vu was bullshit in his mind. Duke made a mental note to go back to the church on his day off. Maybe Christ had an answer that he could hear if he listened hard enough.

Juliana came out of the bathroom a half hour later, wrapped in a large beach towel. "You obviously have something pinging around your skull."

"Christ with a cracked leg."

"Is that a thing or some new expression you picked up at the 84th?"

Duke smiled. "Eight-foot tall black Jesus with a long crack down the front leg, all the way to his foot."

"Part of a crime scene?" She grabbed a towel off the floor and tossed it into the bathroom. "Stolen goods?"

"No. For real. He's hanging over the altar at Saint Oda's Catholic Church on Sutter." Getting up from the bed, Duke brought up the photo of the fractured Christ he snapped before following Loviccio and the priest downstairs.

Juliana squinted at the picture on her boyfriend's cellphone. "Where's the crack?"

He expanded the image with his thumb and forefinger. "See it now?"

"Uh, huh." She took the phone from Duke and opened the image wider. "Looks to be almost an inch at the widest."

"I'm thinking about going back there on Sunday morning."

"I'm working three to eleven. Want company or is this official business?"

Duke looked at her and smiled. "I'm off the clock. Sure, you can come with me if I decide to go. But I might just let it wait until Monday."

"Is it important?"

He shrugged. "I doubt it."

Juliana let the towel fall to the floor. "Now that you've got this cleared up, can we get back to *our* business?"

"I was going to shower." Duke laid his cellphone on the nightstand.

"There's room for two, you know."

Picking up the towel she'd dropped, Duke wrapped it around her waist and pulled Juliana close to him. Kissing her, he tilted his head back and grinned. "Is it still me, or do I need to put the tie back on?"

She slid her hand over his growing erection. "It'll always be you, Garvey."

Chapter Seven
Seeing The Past

Loviccio was at his desk when Duke walked into the squad on Tuesday morning. His partner's keyboard was resting on his chair along with most of the office supplies he used on a daily basis. An array of pastries in small white boxes covered the open spaces on the desk, sharing the rest of the surface with napkins, plastic knives, paper plates, and a gallon of whole milk.

"Before the rest of the *gavones* get here, grab a cannoli and a big chunk of rainbow cookies."

"With milk?" Duke shuddered. "No coffee?"

"Junior, I'm not even drinking tea." Loviccio smiled. "Grab your coffee mug and fill it with milk. This'll take you back to your childhood."

Duke hung his sport jacket on the back of his chair. "What about the DD5s?"

"Done twenty minutes ago."

"Really?"

"Hey, you wanna eat or type?" Snatching a cannoli out of one of the boxes, Loviccio bit off the end and pointed it at Duke. "You saved my ass yesterday. Now we're even. You can enter DD5s any time you want. But right now, eat some of the finest Italian pastries in the known universe and have a big glass of milk. Didn't your moms always tell you that you need to drink milk to grow up big and strong?"

"No." Duke shook his head as he twisted the top off the gallon jug. "We drank Red Stripe and orange juice for breakfast. Red Stripe and soursop juice for lunch. And Red Stripe with a big glass of water for dinner." Blowing out a breath, Duke smiled. "For all I know, I may have been drinking that shitty beer in my baby bottle."

Loviccio came close to passing a mouthful of milk and cannoli through his nose. "Jesus, Duke, no wonder you stopped drinking."

"Are you going to insist The Ghost have a glass of milk with his cannoli?"

"Even if there were any left, by time Frank got here, he wouldn't ask and I wouldn't offer." Loviccio stuffed the rest of the cannoli in his mouth and looked over at The Ghost's desk. "Don't even think about it."

Duke followed Loviccio's gaze. "What do you think he'd do? Shoot you?"

"Nah, The Ghost's weapon hasn't been loaded for years. He keeps it in a holster on his desk so everyone will think he's a threat. Doesn't talk to anyone. Just sits there and goes through those books and newspapers over and over again."

"Anyone ever try to help him solve the murders?"

"Yeah, me." Finishing his milk, Loviccio pulled out the bottom drawer of his desk and put his feet on it. "I spent two years going through the material with no results. Whoever killed The Ghost's father left no trail, no clues, and nothing but useless bits of trash that he tried to turn into evidence."

"What about the Smith and Wesson that was left at the scene?"

"The serial numbers had been ground off. I told you about the gloves. So there were no fingerprints anywhere on the weapon. We even pulled a glove inside out hoping to lift a print off the inner surface." Loviccio took two large chunks of rainbow cookies from a box on his desk and split them in half. "The FBI also tried to pull fingerprints from the inside of the gloves with some new technique, but were unsuccessful. And even if we did get fingerprints, what were we going to match them to? If the shooter had never been fingerprinted before, they wouldn't be in the system. Just another waste of time." He stuffed the larger of the two halves in his mouth and added a gulp of milk. "I did my best to convince Frank that it was hopeless, but he wouldn't hear it."

Duke shook his head. "A blind man always hopes to see the sun. A fool will never open his eyes."

"And if I find out who's parked in my spot, that fool is going to walk around all day with my foot up his ass." Rita, who neither of the two men heard walk into the squad, threw her windbreaker on her desk and walked over to Loviccio. "You went to Ferrara's and didn't buy bowties?"

Loviccio reached into a bag on the floor and pulled up a small white box tied with string. "Of course I did. Just keeping them safe for you, honey."

"You're the best, sweetheart." She snatched the box out of his hand and pulled a switchblade from her back pocket. Snapping it open, Rita slit the string and closed the knife in one motion.

"You two been partnered long?" Duke looked over at the box Rita had just opened. "Bowties?"

She took one out of the box and handed it to Duke. "Best cookie ever invented."

Duke took a bite and washed it down with some milk. "Too sugary."

"Not if you've got a sweet tooth." Rita broke a bowtie in half and dipped it into Loviccio's cup of milk. "Now they have ones with chocolate filling or dipped. Those are too sugary."

"Five years as partners, to answer your question." Refilling his cup, Loviccio ate the other chunk of his rainbow cookie. "But she'll figure out the job, eventually."

Rita blew out a laugh. "Mister Paperwork will eventually figure out how to shoot straight."

"Hey, at least I can hit a moving target." Loviccio leaned over toward Duke. "Ask her about the traffic light she shot while aiming at an armed suspect who was attempting to escape."

"No. Wait. Ask Ronnie about the three rounds he put into the ceiling at the police range." Rita cracked up with laughter. "And that was after he shot out the fluorescent lamp."

Lieutenant Moscowitz walked into the squad, talking on his cellphone. He waved at the three detectives and went into his office, slamming the door closed behind him.

"His wife." Loviccio looked up at the ceiling and sighed. "The woman has developed henpecking into an art form."

Singing loud enough that the group heard him coming down the hall, Peter Cheng marched into the squad. Rita applauded. "Don't give up your day job, PC."

Loviccio leaned over toward Duke and stage-whispered, "He got laid last night."

"Twice." Cheng bowed. "And she bought dinner."

"On a Monday night? How you gonna top that for the rest of the week?" Rita took another bowtie and shoved the box into her desk drawer.

"Hey, I'm just getting warmed up." Cheng hung his sport jacket on the back of his chair and walked over to the pastry collection. "Who went to Ferrara's?"

Loviccio smiled. "The only pure Italian in the squad."

Cursing in Spanish with her phone to her ear, Kelly Tang stomped into the squad, continued her tirade all the way to her desk, and then back out the door. Rita followed her to the doorway and watched as the woman hip-checked the door to the restroom.

"She's pissed." Rita looked back at the three men. "Boyfriend trouble, I'll bet."

"I thought they broke up on Friday." Cheng snatched a cannoli out of the box and poured himself a glass of milk.

"That was four days ago, PC." Walking back to her desk, Rita tapped her keyboard and took her screen out of sleep mode. "But I thought he was French Canadian."

Cheng shook his head. "That was two weeks ago, right after she broke up with the Dutch kid."

"She's working her way around the globe." Duke laughed. "Nothing like diversity."

Loviccio looked up at the digital clock on the wall. "Don't you have the shooting board in ten minutes?"

"Yes. Downstairs in the Captain's office."

"You'll be in and out in under five." Rita logged on to the NYPD system and grabbed another bowtie from the box before pushing the drawer closed with her thumb.

Lieutenant Moscowitz came out of his office with a slip of pink paper in his hand. "Jankowsky, Loviccio, multiple victim shooting, 872 DeKalb Avenue. Albertini and Jackson are already on the scene. Take Garvey with you. He can deal with the shooting board when you get back." He walked over to Loviccio's desk and raised an eyebrow. "You went to Ferrara's?" The lieutenant turned to Rita. "Where are the bowties?"

Three bodies blocked the westbound lanes of DeKalb Avenue in front of number 872. Two more live ones were sitting in a pair of ambulances, awaiting transport, when the trio of detectives arrived. Moe Jackson met them as they got out of the unmarked car.

"What we have here is your standard Tuesday morning shootout at the DeKalb corral." He pointed at the three corpses. "The two dead brothers are Omar Vasquez and Snooky Colon."

"Snooky?" Loviccio shook his head. "Really?"

Jackson continued. "Yeah. It's on his driver's license. I don't make this shit up, Ronnie."

Rita nodded toward the third body. "Who's the female?"

"Snooky's wife, Luscious."

"No." Loviccio erupted with laughter. "Snooky and Luscious? What happened to Omar? Couldn't get a clever name?"

"Not in this life." Returning to his notes, Jackson laid out the events. "Snooky and his wife were coming home from a late night party. They were met on the street outside 872 DeKalb by Omar and his two companions in the ambulances, who attempted to rob them."

Duke looked over at the two wounded men. "Why two ambulances?"

"Well, that's where this gets weird." Detective Jackson smiled. "According to Ulysses, in ambulance number one, Luscious pulled a small semi-automatic from her purse and shot Omar. His brother, Apollo, in ambulance number two, shot the woman, but as she went down, she fired again and struck her husband center mass by accident. Ulysses panicked and ran, but Apollo shot him in the leg to stop him. Ulysses returned fire and hit Apollo in the knee."

Loviccio spun around twice, looking at the bodies and the injured. "Is that it? Nobody else wanna get into this? Christ, Moe, you couldn't get the two Greek gods to take each other out before we got here?"

"Relax, Ronnie. We'll handle all the paperwork. Just get the canvass done. The Medical Examiner is on his way, and Crime Scene will be here as soon as they finish with another call." Detective Jackson reached over and flicked some crumbs off Loviccio's tie. "Your momma lets you go out in public dressed like that?"

It was almost one o'clock by the time the detectives returned to the squad. The Ghost had arrived and was seated at his desk, poring over the pages of a book. Lieutenant Moscowitz had put the remaining pastries in the small refrigerator shared by the squad and Duke retrieved a box, not having had anything for lunch.

In order to walk from the refrigerator to his desk, he had to pass The Ghost in both directions. On the way back, he stopped and opened the box while standing next to the ancient detective's desk.

"Want one, Frank? They're fresh this morning." He offered the open box and smiled.

The Ghost turned slowly and brought his face up to look at the young detective. Words seemed to be coming in spurts from

Nussbaum's mouth, but Duke couldn't hear them if they were indeed spoken. The man's cheeks were moving, but they could have been spasms. To Duke, it was as though all the sound in the room had been sucked into a black hole. The air around him stopped moving even though the ceiling fan above his head was still spinning.

His feet glued to the floor, Duke stared at Detective Nussbaum's concave cheeks and liver-spotted forehead as the ancient man's tiny muscles quivered. A few wisps of gray hair that had drifted over one long ear were fluttering as the aged man's face hardened to stone. At the moment that their eyes made contact, Duke's body stiffened. His neck locked and his teeth ground against each other as his jaw muscles tightened.

All he could see of The Ghost were the man's pupils. Nussbaum's green, almost turquoise eyes were open windows to the past. Duke peered into them, into an emerald depth that had no bottom. In the cold, hideous silence, the balance of Nussbaum's face melted and transformed into an old wine bottle candle with two glowing green marbles stuck into the cooled wax on one side.

Duke couldn't blink. No words came from his mouth. Finally, he took a long deep breath, but the air in his lungs was frozen. His throat hurt when he swallowed. The more he looked at The Ghost, the more impossible it became to force his gaze in another direction. He'd seen those eyes before. He knew it in a place so deep inside that the feeling was without question. The Ghost wore an expression that no one could ever forget. It was the face of death. Duke Garvey was seeing the eyes of a nightmare from some time long before he was born.

Their riveting gaze was unchanged for several long breaths before Loviccio dashed over and took Duke around the shoulders. No one spoke. Even the radio was silent as the senior detective led him away from The Ghost. The air in the room was heavy with the silence. Kelly Tang, her desk closest to the scene, got up and walked over to her partner's desk. Peter slid his chair to one side so that she could sit next to him, facing away from The Ghost.

In reality, Frank Nussbaum had not said a word the entire time. Frozen in his seat, he watched as Duke stumbled away from him with Loviccio's assistance. Lieutenant Moscowitz had come as far as the doorway of his office and was still standing there, staring at the tableau of statues that made up his squad.

"Frank, are you okay?"

The volume of the lieutenant's voice shook the detectives out of their trances...everyone except Duke. He'd made it as far as his desk, but couldn't bring himself to sit. Loviccio pulled Duke's chair out from the desk and spun it around for the junior detective, but couldn't convince him to use it for anything beyond a handhold.

Jackson and Albertini, who had reached the doorway of the squad just before Duke's offer, stopped for a moment and then walked single-file to their adjoining desks to stand next to them.

Moe put his notepad on the desk and leaned over to ask Peter Cheng if The Ghost had made a move.

"No. He was just sitting there, staring at Garvey." Peter glanced back over his shoulder toward The Ghost. "I'm not sure he's still breathing."

Duke finally regained his composure and slid into his desk chair. His shirt was soaked with sweat on the front and back. He loosened his tie and bent over to stare at the floor for a few moments. The bile in his throat took some serious effort to swallow.

Loviccio knelt and put his hand on Duke's shoulder. "You okay?"

"No." Duke took several quick breaths and sat back hard in his chair. "No, I'm not okay. I don't know what I am right now, but it's miles away from okay. I think I'm going to puke."

"What's wrong? What did he say?"

Duke shook his head. "Nothing. Not a word. It was all in his eyes."

Loviccio turned to look at The Ghost who was still staring across the squad at Duke. "His eyes?"

"Yes. I've seen those eyes before." Duke took a deep breath and steepled his hands over his nose and mouth. "It was as though I was looking through a pair of binoculars and I could see another face beyond his. A man's face with those horrible glowing eyes."

"Another face? Who was it?" Sliding his chair over, Loviccio sat down and folded his arms across his chest.

"I don't know, but it was like I could see right through Nussbaum's head and out to another set of eyes the same color." Duke reached for the lukewarm mug of milk he hadn't finished earlier and took a sip. "And in that moment, while I was looking through those eyes, all I could see was death." He gulped. "A horrible death and so much fear."

Rita scratched her ear. "You saw all that in The Ghost's eyes? Damn, Garvey, how many cannolies did you eat? I think you've overdosed on the cheese and sugar."

Duke started to get up from his chair, but Loviccio held him back. "Don't go over there, Junior. Leave him be for now."

A phone rang, and the lieutenant ducked back into his office to answer it. He was gone for a few seconds and then came out with a hastily written note. "Moe, a sector car is bringing in a woman from 872 DeKalb who has information about the shooting there this morning."

"Good. We'll set up interview two. Have the uniforms put her in there." Detective Jackson shifted around toward his partner. "Better idea, let's meet her downstairs." He lifted his sport jacket from the back of his chair and threw it over his shoulder. "It's a little weird up here right now."

The two detectives hurried from the squad. Albertini snatched the last chunk of rainbow cookies as she walked past Loviccio's desk.

Grabbing Duke by his shoulders, Loviccio pulled him up from his chair and handed Duke his jacket. "Let's get some fresh air." He took a cannoli and yanked a portable radio from the rack by the door. Looking over at Lieutenant Moscowitz as they left, he shrugged. "We'll be on the air if you need us, but I think junior needs to chill out for a bit."

Loviccio managed to push and drag Duke across the boulevard and over to a park bench. With the younger detective's legs sprawled out, Loviccio walked back and forth, stepping over Duke's legs as he spoke.

"Are you friggin' nuts? I told you to stay away from The Ghost and you march over there with a box of cannoli in your hands like he's your best friend. I'm amazed EMS hasn't responded to the squad. Sure as shit, Frank's heart is running out of beats and you just put it into overdrive."

Duke stared past Loviccio at the leaves fluttering in the trees. He saw the detective's lips moving, but there was only the sound of the wind in his ears. A sector car roared through the intersection, hitting its siren just as it passed the park. Loviccio stopped talking until it was across the next boulevard. Duke heard nothing but the breeze.

"I don't know what came over you. Maybe you spent too much time helping homeless people on your beat. Maybe you see The Ghost as an old man in need of your help. Are you a friggin'

Boy Scout?" Leaning over, Loviccio nudged Duke's shoulder. "Yo, are you listening to me?"

With a long sigh, Duke returned to the present. "Yes, I hear you."

"Good. Because for a minute there, I thought you'd zipped off to another dimension."

"Jesus, Ronnie, I may have just seen one." Duke put his head between his knees and stared at a line of ants marching from the sidewalk to the grass. Picking up a twig, he interrupted their procession, knocking several of the bugs to the left and right of their path.

Loviccio took a seat next to Duke. "What do you think you saw?"

"Murder. Cold, calculated murder. A bullet smashing into a face with greenish, almost turquoise eyes identical to Nussbaum's." Kicking the ant platoon into disarray, Duke jumped up from the bench and stood with both hands on his hips. "The bullet was moving away from me in slow motion. I could see the front sight of a pistol and there was a puff of smoke still coming from the barrel."

"Were you holding the gun?"

Duke shook his head. "I don't know. I think so. How else could I see the front sight or the bullet?"

"You killed someone?"

"Not me." A puzzled expression filled Duke's face. "But another me." The junior detective got up from the bench and walked several feet away before turning around and shaking his head. "From another life."

Loviccio slapped his knees. "What the hell are you talking about, Garvey? Another you? Like in another dimension? Screw that shit. We don't do science fiction in the 84th. Robbery, homicide, home invasion, even screwed up priests who want to give every poor slob a break because it pleases some heavenly Father."

Duke stared at the clouds. "My mother thinks everyone has lived many lives. They die and come back again and again."

"Until they get it right?" Loviccio laughed. "Some of us will be here forever."

"No. It's not about getting it right, according to her. The quality of each existence has to do with how the universe affects your life and what happens in the moments between the life that's ending and the next one that's about to begin."

"Horseshit." Stretching out his legs, Loviccio shook his head several times. "When you're dead, you're dead. That's it. Worm food. If we're coming back, we're all coming back together with JC in the lead."

Smiling, Duke walked over and put one foot up on the bench, leaning over close to Loviccio. "And you find that easier to believe than one-at-a-time reincarnation? It's going to be a mass return of the dead? Where will they live? What will they eat? Hell, we're running out of food and fresh water every day. Imagine what will happen when several billion angels fly down from heaven and try to buy Metro cards at the same time."

Loviccio grinned. "It'll be crowded. That's for certain."

"Believe what you want." Duke shrugged. "I don't buy any of it. Your version or my mother's. But I saw something today. Something in The Ghost's eyes that scared the shit out of me."

"Let's hope you didn't put the old man in cardiac arrest with your performance." Loviccio checked the time. "Another half hour and Nussbaum's gone for the day."

"What about the shooting board?"

"I'll go with you to O'Malley's office and explain that we got tied up with the canvass on DeKalb and you were working with me on the DD5s when we got back." He smiled. "The Captain's gonna be pissed off either way, but he'll have to outlive the Energizer Bunny to pay off all the favors he owes me."

Duke turned and walked over to the grass, plopping down in it and staring up at the passing clouds.

"What are you doing?" Loviccio followed him but stood, looking down as Duke smiled at him.

"All those years that I waited to get out of the bag and into plain clothes. Now, I'm wondering if there's some reason for me to think I wasn't ready."

"Ready to be a detective?" With a laugh, Loviccio reached down and offered Duke a hand. "Come on, junior. You're ready. You're more than ready."

Taking Loviccio's hand, Duke got to his feet and dusted himself off. "So, all the new detectives have a freak-out moment?"

Loviccio shook his head. "Only the ones who dare to mess with The Ghost."

Chapter Eight
A Mother's Intuition

Captain O'Malley began to read the riot act to Duke, but stopped when Loviccio walked into his office. It was a simple shooting, and no one died, so the captain was handling the investigation on his own. Loviccio took a seat next to Duke and stretched his legs with his hands locked behind his neck.

"You're satisfied it was a good shoot?" O'Malley pointed at Loviccio. "There was no other way to disarm the hostage taker?"

Loviccio frowned. "Who said anything about a hostage? The baby was on the floor, at least twenty feet away from the guy who was about to shoot me."

"He told one of the paramedics that the gun was unloaded."

"Bullshit." Duke shook his head. "I cleared it. The clip was full and there was one in the pipe."

Captain O'Malley wrote their comments on a yellow legal pad and then laid the pen down next to it. He got up from his desk and walked over to the gritty window with a dusty view of the alley between the buildings. Without turning, he asked, "Was the safety off?"

"Yes." Duke looked at Loviccio and pursed his lips.

"Yeah. I checked it after Duke shot the guy in the arm. Probably saved my life." Blowing out a shallow breath, Loviccio stood from the chair. "Anything else, Captain?"

O'Malley, still staring out the window, shook his head once. "No. I'll sign off on it. Good job, detective."

"Thank you, sir." Duke got up and walked to the door. "Have a nice day, Captain."

Loviccio grabbed him by the elbow and led Duke into the hallway. "Have a nice day? What the hell, Garvey? Who talks like that?"

The Ghost was gone when the two detectives walked into the squad. According to Lieutenant Moscowitz, he'd gotten up from his desk about five minutes after Duke and Loviccio left. At first, everyone thought The Ghost was headed to the restrooms. The lamp was still lit on his desk and there were several books open from the stacks. But Nussbaum walked out the door and down the stairs without his coat or hat.

Sergeant Williams saw The Ghost coming down the stairs an hour earlier than his standard departure and did his best to clear people out of the lobby. A uniformed officer held the door for the old man and was hissed at for her kindness. Another cop, coming in from the garage, said that The Ghost sat in his car for almost ten minutes before starting the engine and ripping into traffic.

The lieutenant told Duke that no one had spoken to The Ghost in so long that he figured the old man just didn't know how to react. Loviccio said The Ghost was just nuts and packed up the rest of the pastries and milk.

A bar fight in the Greenpoint Section of Brooklyn had broken out while Duke and Loviccio were chatting with Captain O'Malley. Two patrons had been stabbed, and the bartender was on his way to the hospital with a pool cue protruding from his abdomen. All the available detectives were on the scene but needed more help with the canvass. Moscowitz asked Duke if he was okay and, hearing a positive response, sent the two remaining detectives off to assist.

Kelly Tang met Loviccio and Duke as they parked across the street from the Suds & Buds. She leaned against their car and pointed at the tavern. "This started on the street and worked its way into the bar."

Loviccio scratched his head. "Isn't that backwards?"

"Yeah, but that's only the beginning." She pulled her notepad from her back pocket and flipped it open. "Mrs. Yazmeen Asghar came here looking for her husband, Malik. The husband was playing pool with a young lady who claims her only name is Jasmine. When Mrs. Asghar arrived at the bar where she knew her husband usually hung out, Malik saw her walking across Clay Street and went outside to meet her."

"What about Jasmine?" Duke leaned around Detective Tang to watch two paramedics load a stretcher with a female into a waiting ambulance.

Kelly turned around and nodded. "That's her. One stab wound to the upper right chest. She's stable and pretty pissed off."

"And the Mrs.?" Loviccio found an itch on the back of his scalp and was working it with two hands.

"In the backseat of that patrol car." She pointed to her left. "Under arrest for two counts of assault."

"With a pool cue?" Duke smiled.

"Yep." Detective Tang continued. "And a steak knife. Mrs. Asghar pushed her husband to the ground and went into the bar. She confronted Jasmine, grabbing a steak knife from a nearby table and stabbing the woman she claimed was sleeping with her husband. The bartender tried to get between them and punched Mrs. Asghar in the face after she attacked Jasmine."

Loviccio, finally relieved of the itch, bent down and retied a shoelace. "Let me guess. Mr. Asghar tried to stop the bartender with a pool cue."

"No. That would be Isadore Cohen." Kelly nodded with her shoulder at a man in handcuffs sitting in the open door of a sector car. "Izzy, as he prefers to be called, has been sleeping with Mrs. Asghar. He followed her to the Suds & Buds and tried to stop her from beating on her husband, Malik."

Duke squinted at the man who had to be at least eighty-years-old. "With a cane or a walker?"

"Karate." Kelly smiled. "The man is a black-belt master something or other. Only his aim is a bit off." She pointed to the second ambulance. "His first swing grazed the wife and took out the husband. Broke his nose and jaw with a single punch to the face. Then, figuring that there were more people to beat on, Izzy went into the bar and saw the bartender leaning over the bleeding Jasmine with a pool cue in his hand."

"Jesus." Loviccio slapped his forehead. "The old man skewered the bartender?"

Kelly nodded. "You got it. He was ready for a spit."

"What do you need us to do?" Taking a pair of gloves from his back pocket, Loviccio unbuttoned his jacket.

"Tell me it's Friday and you'll take over so I can go home for the weekend." Detective Tang folded her notepad and stuffed it into her back pocket. "Better yet, tell me that Garvey didn't get in The Ghost's face this afternoon. Tell me it was some weird dream, and that Nussbaum isn't coming in tomorrow at noon with a shotgun."

Frowning, Loviccio tugged on the gloves. "Yo, I think we've had enough with the dream bullshit for one day."

"Fine. Help out with the canvass. Cheng and Jankowsky are inside the bar interviewing witnesses. I've got five or six uniforms talking to people on this side of the street. Start across, on the other side of Clay Street. Jackson and Albertini are working Manhattan Avenue." Kelly looked up at the darkening sky. "Oh, please, let it rain. I was hoping this would get worse."

Detective Tang got her wish. The skies opened up minutes later, dousing everyone in New York City with a summer evening downpour. The blood staining Clay Street in front of the bar was washed away. Those who hadn't been interviewed by the police took cover, many hopping into cars and leaving the scene.

EMS removed the wounded. The Medical Examiner's black van took the deceased. With life in Greenpoint returned to the normal thrum and pace of the city, the detectives of the 84th Squad filed into their office to begin the arduous task of documenting the incident.

It was after eight when Kelly Tang finished reviewing everyone's DD5s. Not another word about The Ghost was spoken.

Duke had called Juliana to say he was going to be late and gave her the basic details of the incident with The Ghost. Sitting in a subway car on his way uptown, he stared at the graffiti and advertising but couldn't focus on any of the words. An attractive woman seated across from Duke was humming a tune that she was listening to via earbuds, and he strained to recognize the music.

Suddenly aware that a strange man was staring at her, the woman got up and walked to the end of the car. She hissed the word, "pervert," as she passed him. Duke closed his eyes and said nothing in response.

A man in tattered clothes, stinking from cigarette smoke, sat down next to the detective and opened a paperback. Out of the corner of his eye, Duke saw the book was written in Spanish. He looked at the man and tried to discern whether or not he was Hispanic. To Duke, the man appeared to be just another white guy on the train. Nonetheless, Duke kept his hand on the butt of his Glock until the man got off at his stop.

Juliana was waiting downstairs on the stoop when Duke walked up East 34th Street. The blue network had already spread word of the encounter with The Ghost. "You look like a man who thinks he's being followed. If you snap your neck around one more time, you're going to need a chiropractor to put it back in place. Loviccio called me about twenty minutes ago and told me that you had taken a trip into The Ghost's brain."

"I can't get those eyes out of my head." Duke dropped his hands to his sides and rolled his head around his shoulders. "The image of a bullet almost floating in slow motion away from the barrel of a gun." He shuddered. "It was like watching a movie, except I was in it, not part of the audience."

"Your mother called an hour ago."

Duke looked at her in surprise. "Why didn't you tell me that first? You know she gets crazy if I don't call her back immediately."

"She said not to bother, she'd call you in the morning, but you shouldn't worry."

"Worry about what?" Duke's expression matched his confused tone of voice.

Sitting down on the stoop, Juliana shrugged. "She said there's no such thing as ghosts. And even if there were, she knows you can put them to rest. Her words exactly were, 'Don't be makin' no worry 'bout no ghosts.' And that I should let you get a good night's sleep once in a while."

"My mother said this?" Duke furrowed his brow. "She specifically mentioned ghosts?"

"And that you shouldn't worry about them." Juliana stood and took Duke's hands. "What's she talking about, Garvey?"

Duke pushed out his cheek with his tongue. His mother had visions for as long as he could remember. Usually, they came from smoking ganja. "Some Rastafarian bullshit. Maybe she hit the pipe a few times too many before dinner." He got up on the same step as Juliana and gave her a long, passionate kiss. "A ghost named Frank Nussbaum? Now that's some funny shit."

Chapter Nine
Cookies

Detective Nussbaum failed to show for his shift on Wednesday. A woman called on Thursday morning and said that Frank wasn't feeling well, but she expected him to be in on Friday. At half past noon on Friday, and no Ghost, all the detectives in the 84th Squad were certain that Nussbaum had died. No one shed a tear.

The storm that dampened the investigation in Greenpoint lingered until Friday afternoon. Between the strong winds and pouring rain, crime in the city had slowed to a more manageable pace. Everyone hunkered down to ride out the remains of an early season tropical storm that had crept up the eastern seaboard. According to the forecasters, the city was going to get two inches of rain before it was over.

A pair of witnesses had come forward in the homicide at 1070 Park Place. Loviccio and Duke were in Interview Room Three talking to one of them, a black male who called himself Zipper. Zipper's first question to the desk sergeant had been about a reward.

Loviccio stood by the door and let Duke handle the interview. Zipper wasn't a suspect...yet.

"The man you saw coming out of the building," Duke paused to check his notes, "you say he was dark-skinned but not black?"

"Wasn't no brother. Not dressed like that." Zipper chuckled. "Looked like some European tourist, 'cept for the Mets hat. Dude be boppin' and shuckin' like he got music playin' in his head. I was gettin' into a cab to go see my woman. I smiled at him but he don't give me no never mind. Don't even look back."

"You'd seen him there before?"

"Couple a times. Always leavin' in the early mornin'." Zipper adjusted his dew-rag. "Faggoty lookin' dude. Comes out skippin' and shit. Almost thought he was whistlin' one time. Ain't never seen no boy that happy all a time."

Duke sat back and folded his arms across his chest. "Did you know Vincent Marsden?"

"I seen him round." Zipper smiled. "Boy likes his sweets. All them skinny ass junkies need them sweets. Most ain't got no teeth. Got a mouth make a dentist wanna retire his lazy ass after drillin' all that junkie shit outta there."

The image of a dentist with a jackhammer crossed Duke's mind, and he winced. "How do you know he likes sweets?"

"I seen him in the bodega over by Kingston and Saint Marks. I works there occasionally, emptying boxes and filling shelves and shit. I got a girlfriend in the Bronx that I takes care of."

Loviccio muttered, "Honest work and a family. Who'd a thunk it?"

"Yo, not every young black man is a criminal." Zipper looked at Duke for support.

Duke held up his hand. "No one's saying you're a criminal, Zipper."

"And you, Detective 'I'm too well-dressed for this job,' you talks more like a white boy than a brother. I ain't never seen no brother with red hair. What's up with that?" Frowning, Zipper took a toothpick and worked at a piece of food in his back tooth. "Got some college. Got the badge and gun. Shit, you almost white." Zipper leaned toward Duke and squinted. "You a Oreo?"

"Oreo?" Duke shrugged. "What's that?"

"Black on the outside and white where it gets creamy." Laughing, Zipper pushed back from the metal table and pointed at Loviccio. "And you is just the reverse. I seen old detectives like you afore this. You spend so much time on the street with the brothers that you think you are one inside. Damn, that's some sick shit. But you just some old white asshole with a bad attitude. Shit, thinking all brothas is criminals then trying to get inside them with that friendly bullshit talk."

Loviccio looked down at the floor and shook his head. "That's a first. Most people like my attitude."

Duke brought the conversation back on point. "Did Vincent ever come into the bodega with the man in the Mets hat?"

"Uh, huh."

"Did he ever come in there with anyone else?"

"No, man. Vinnie was a loner 'cept for this dude. Boy come in, buy his candy, soda, whatever, and leave. I ain't never seen him with no one else. But they's a lot of bodybuildin' type mens that be comin' and goin' from 1070 Park Place. And all the time, Vinnie be lookin' down from that balcony and blowin' kisses like they's some Romeo and Juliet shit goin' on."

Duke looked over at Loviccio and shrugged. "I think Zipper was one of those Romeos."

"Bullshit, man." Zipper jumped up from the chair. "Dude try that shit with me and I bust a cap in his white ass."

"But he tried, didn't he?" Duke motioned for Zipper to take his seat. "He tried, and you got pissed off and shot him."

"No, man. That's bullshit. I ain't never been in Vinnie's apartment."

Loviccio walked over and dropped a fingerprint card on the table. "So how'd your thumbprint get on his nightstand?"

Zipper grabbed the card and spun it around. "This is bullshit, man. I ain't never been inside that dude's place and that ain't my thumbprint."

"How do you know?" Loviccio lifted the card off the table and stuffed it into this shirt pocket.

Holding his thumbs up so that both detectives could see them, Zipper smiled. "Cause they ain't got these big-ass scars on 'em."

Both of his thumbs had deep caverns running their length. Zipper explained that he'd cut his hands on a broken window when he was a teenager. "We was tryin' to get into my aunt's house and we didn't have no key. I busted a little window in the back door with my elbow, but ripped up my damn thumbs pulling the glass out the way."

Duke looked at Loviccio and grinned. "Nice try."

"Look, man, I gots shit to do, so if you done with all this bullshit, I'm outta here."

"Thanks for coming in, Zipper." Duke stood and folded his notepad closed.

Loviccio opened the door. "Stay available, okay?"

Zipper winked. "I'm as easy to find as a piece of ass on Saturday night."

Their second witness, a newspaper delivery van driver, had rushed into the restroom moments before Duke went out to get him. He asked Rita to send the man in when he was done and went back inside the soundproof room.

Loviccio sat on the edge of the metal table, cleaning under his fingernails with a pocketknife. "Zipper's got a point."

"Which is?"

"The Oreo thing. I'm mean, not for nothin' but you sound whiter than me. You don't have a Jamaican accent...mon."

"My mother sent me to a school for American ex-pats in Montego Bay. Everyone I heard as I was growing up spoke like a white person. I can speak Patois if you like, but you probably won't understand a word I'm saying." Duke grinned. "It would be the same thing if you started talking Italian."

"Sicilian."

"There's a difference?"

Loviccio nodded and closed the knife. "Italy is one country with many tongues. Sicilians consider their island to be a separate country with better food and a much more interesting choice of words."

"Better food?" Duke smiled. "I cook Italian. What's the difference?"

"Your sauce comes out of a jar?"

"Yes."

"That's the difference." Loviccio looked out the window on the door and saw the deliveryman approaching. "When you start makin' your sauce from scratch, you'll be cooking like a Sicilian. Until then, you're just another New Yorker who thinks he can cook Italian food."

Rita led the delivery truck driver into the interview room. "Here's Johnny."

John Vanderbrock, pale and sweating, slid onto a metal chair and threw his head back. Gulping several deep breaths, he wiped his forehead with his sleeve and folded his hands on the table.

"I'm sorry, officers, but I must have eaten something last night that didn't agree with me." Vanderbrock blew out a long, ragged breath.

Duke opened his notepad to a clean page. "Detective Jankowsky tells us that you were parked in front of 1070 Park Place early Monday morning."

"Yeah. I'd just finished my route and there's a bodega on the corner of Saint Marks that has hot coffee and fresh baked chocolate chip cookies all night long."

Loviccio leaned over and whispered, "Same place where Zipper works."

"Can you be more specific as to the time?" Duke raised his eyebrows.

"Seven minutes after five." Vanderbrock smiled. "I got one of those new Apple watches for Christmas. First digital watch I've ever owned. I keep a logbook so's I can record my finish time. Best so far is four-fifty-one. And I get paid until six. So every minute ahead of six is me gettin' paid to do nothin'."

Duke wrote the time in his notepad and looked up at the delivery driver. "And you saw someone come out of 1070 Park Place while you were parked there, marking time?"

"I've been stopping at that same bodega for five years. It's only in the past couple of months that anyone has been awake in that building before the sun comes up. I think they're all old folks, retired, right? Anyhow, Monday morning, around five minutes after I parked and made my logbook entry, this guy comes out the door spinnin' a cane like he's just got laid and he's lookin' for someone to tell about it."

"Did you see his face?" Duke held his pen over the paper, waiting for an answer.

"Just for a few seconds." Vanderbrock squinted with his nose wrinkled for effect. "He looked at me and then ducked around a taxi, heading toward Saint Marks. The wind caught his Mets cap, and he almost spun around, but he grabbed it and walked on."

Duke looked up at Loviccio, who smiled, nodding his head. "Do you think you would recognize the man if you saw him again?"

"With the cane and the Mets hat? Sure, no problem." The delivery driver shrugged. "I got an eye for faces."

The two detectives met with Lieutenant Moscowitz after Mr. Vanderbrock left. They had asked him to sit with the department's sketch artist, but his roiling guts would only allow seating on a toilet and he was headed home. The delivery driver promised to stop by the squad tomorrow if he was feeling up to it.

A man with a cane and Mets cap shouldn't be as hard to find as Zipper or a hooker on Saturday night, but then again, detectives were still searching for the body of Jimmy Hoffa after all those years. It was the slimmest of leads, and neither Loviccio nor Duke had anything to attach to it.

Duke, still freaked about what he'd seen in The Ghost's eyes, asked if there was any word about the man's condition. Moscowitz told him no, but the unidentified woman had called again and said that The Ghost would be in on Monday. She asked the lieutenant for the name of the detective who had attempted the interaction but was unresponsive to any of his questions.

"Why would she want to know me?"

Moscowitz shrugged. "Maybe The Ghost wants to send you a letter of apology for freaking you out."

Chapter Ten
Carpenters

Stars still twinkled in the night sky when Duke awoke covered in sweat. It was Sunday morning and the fourth night in a row that he'd only been able to fall asleep with the assistance of whiskey and a shotglass. The image of the bullet coming out of the barrel and toward those frightened green eyes was too powerful to sleep through.

    Juliana had done her best to assuage the devils that were keeping her boyfriend awake and sexually repressed. They'd gone out for Chinese food on Friday night. It was one of his favorite restaurants. Halfway through eating an eggroll, Duke had gotten up from the table and stared at a man who'd just sat down. The anxious detective had walked over to the hostess station and made a fuss about cold soup and the long wait for their appetizers, just so he could stroll back to their table and look at the man's wrinkled face. They left without waiting for the rest of the meal.

    Despite a break in the humidity, Duke insisted on staying indoors the previous Saturday, searching the internet for information about the murder of Frank Nussbaum's father. Everything Loviccio and Rita had told him was available to be read on a variety of websites. The list of victims, in order by date and location, had links to their biographies as well as dozens of additional websites dealing with serial killers, military murders, and even one to an online store selling sex toys with camouflage coloration.

It wasn't until late that previous afternoon that Juliana had managed to drag Duke out of the apartment and down to a bar alongside the East River. He ordered a cold beer in a frosty mug with a Jack Daniel's chaser, drank the shot, but never even sipped the beer, holding the mug until the tablecloth was soaked from condensation.

Standing on the balcony in his sweatpants, Duke dried his face with a towel and tossed it onto one of the loungers. Sunday was the quietest day of the week and he relished the peace. With a contented sigh, he leaned over the railing and stared at the tiny people and toy cars, five floors down, that were creeping about the empty streets. Dawn was still an hour away.

Juliana heard him open the French doors and followed him out several minutes later, barefoot and wrapped in her bathrobe.

"Are you up for good this time?"

He shrugged. "I could get back in bed, but I'm not going to fall back to sleep."

Reaching around him, Juliana slid her hand into his sweats and gently worked her way down to his crotch. "Good. I don't want to sleep."

Duke turned around slowly, giving her hand better access. "I'm going to the church this morning."

"You decided to go? I thought you said it was just a hunch, something unimportant. You searching for God all of a sudden, Garvey?" She reached lower and tickled his inner thigh.

"You could make me believe in God, baby." He let out a soft moan. "Right there."

She brought her other hand into action, untying the bow he'd made in front and letting the sweats fall to his knees. "I can make you pray, Garvey, but we better be singin' in perfect harmony."

Stepping out of the pants, Duke reached down and loosened the cloth belt of Juliana's robe. He tugged it gently off her shoulders and led his girlfriend back into the bedroom.

They kissed again. Much longer this time, and then Duke walked over and closed the curtains. Turning, he grinned. "I'm going to see Jesus and ask him why he's got a broken leg."

Juliana lay down on the bed and held out her hand. "Just remember, if you interrogate him, you better have probable cause." She pulled Duke down next to her, stroking his erection. "And you'd better get all those impure thoughts out of your head before you leave. Jesus knows."

"According my lieutenant, Jesus saves but Moses invests."

"What the hell does that mean?"

Duke shrugged and pulled his girlfriend closer. "I really don't know, but he laughs like a little girl every time he says it."

Not wanting to ride the subway on his day off, Duke summoned a ride-share car and rode in style to Saint Oda's Catholic Church on Sutter. A street festival had closed off Sutter between Cleveland and Jerome. Reggae music was pulsing from a wall of speakers and the smells of cooking tickled his nose. Duke got out of the car on Jerome and walked the two blocks to the church. As much as the allure of home summoned him, the job was on his mind this morning.

Father Xavier, who had just finished morning Mass, was waiting at the top of the stairs. Several of his parishioners were gathered around him, taking in the sunny day and fresh air. Duke strolled up the stairs and shook hands with the priest.

"Emilio was released from the hospital late yesterday."

Duke nodded. "And you're still not pressing charges? I understand the divers were unsuccessful in finding the cash box."

"No, my son. Emilio has apologized for his error. And if the money is lost, then it is God's will." The priest sighed with a shrug. Slowly, he walked over and held the door open. "Come in, my son. Jesus awaits you."

With Duke at his heels, Father Xavier marched into the church and straight to the altar. He knelt, genuflected, and then stood with a flashlight in his hand.

"It's a bit too dark in here to see all the details." He handed the torch to Duke. "I can't let you climb up there, but this will help."

"Thanks." Duke took the light and flicked it on. He walked as close as possible to the statue and began examining the crack, starting at the nail in Christ's left foot.

Even from the floor of the church looking up, it was easy to see the dust that had accumulated in the crack using the flashlight. Decades of debris had formed a soft, rounded mass at the bottom of the fissure. Going up the sides, Duke was able to spot several spider webs and wondered if they were blessed insects by virtue of their home.

The fracture widened from less than a quarter of an inch at the knee to nearly a full inch by the time it reached Christ's left foot. Duke squinted to see if there was anything in the opening other than dust and spider webs. But that was all that was visible from down below.

He handed the flashlight back to Father Xavier. "You said the other day that the crack has been there all the years you've preached at this church. Is there any record of the crack before your arrival?"

The priest shook his head. "No, but after you mentioned it, I went back through the church records." He motioned for Duke to follow him. "In my office, I've got some papers that may help."

They headed toward the stairway, and Duke noticed a small wooden statue of a woman dressed in a nun's habit standing in a darkened nook. He hadn't spotted her before and walked over to take a closer look.

"Who's this?"

"Saint Oda." The priest flipped on a spotlight, illuminating the church's namesake. "She was born blind but then found Jesus and her sight returned. Notice the book she's carrying in her left hand. It's a symbol of her sight having miraculously come back."

Duke bent down and looked at her legs for signs of a crack. "She's in better shape than Jesus."

Father Xavier laughed. "She doesn't have to work as hard."

"Is that a bird in her other hand?"

"Yes. A magpie. Legend has it that she was always protected by magpies. They kept suitors at bay. She was a most beautiful woman and even after she'd dedicated her life to God, men still pursued her."

"A hopeless goal. A prize that can never be won." Shaking his head, Duke looked at the priest. "I dated a few women like that."

Downstairs on Father Xavier's desk were several yellowing sheets of paper. Duke walked over and looked at them without touching. The first one was a handwritten proposal in carefully penned cursive from a Nunzio Hernandez who had printed the word "carpenter" after his name. It was dated twenty-nine years ago and for the sum of one-thousand dollars, Nunzio was going to repair the crack in Jesus' leg.

Duke looked up at the priest. "He was never hired?"

"Not that I can remember."

Lifting the next piece of paper, Duke read the name and address at the top out loud, "Cynthia Carson, 284 Ashford Street, Brooklyn."

"A five-minute walk from here." Sliding into the chair behind his desk, Father Xavier looked out the window. "I don't remember her, but she must have been a regular here." He paused and turned around to face Duke. "But to tell you the truth, my memory isn't as good as it once was. I've met so many people over the years that sometimes I'll remember a face but not the name that goes with it. In Mrs. Carson's case, I'm drawing a blank."

Duke read the first paragraph of the letter. "I wish to see the statue of our Lord repaired as quickly as possible. It's a sin and an affront to the church to have that kind of damage on display. To that end, I have enclosed a check for one-thousand dollars to cover the repairs. If more is needed, I will be glad to provide additional funds." He looked at the priest. "Was there a check enclosed?"

"I can't honestly say." Scratching his chin, the priest shrugged. "It was almost thirty years ago. Who could remember that far back?"

The last sheet of paper was from another carpenter. Omar Issanor was offering to do the work for free, as long as Father Xavier would help with his conversion from Islam to Catholicism. The priest said that Omar was a refugee from somewhere in the Middle East. He clearly remembered the man coming to the church and offering to do anything if the priest would help with his new faith.

"He did odd jobs, but no carpentry."

"And so, thirty years later and the statue is still cracked."

The priest nodded. "I doubt it will ever be fixed. It seems to be God's will that this imperfection be permanent."

Duke went back to the letter. "Have you had any contact over the years with Cynthia Carson?"

"Again, not that I can remember. We have around forty regular parishioners and I know their names and faces. Mrs. Carson isn't one of them."

"You mind if I take these?" Duke looked hopefully at the priest. "I'll get them back to you next week."

"Certainly." Handing Duke a large envelope from one of the desk drawers, Father Xavier hesitated. "Why the interest?"

Duke shrugged. "I'm not sure, but I've been here before. I had this weird feeling the other day that I'd seen that cracked Jesus."

"A previous life?"

"Don't buy into that sh...sorry, stuff."

"Neither does the church." Father Xavier slid the three documents into the envelope and folded the flap closed. "You think there's something in these letters that will expand that memory?"

"One can only hope." Duke smiled and took the envelope from the priest. "Maybe Cynthia Carson can shed some light on the subject."

The priest's eyebrows went up. "If she still lives in Brooklyn."

Duke tucked the envelope under his arm and turned toward the door. "From what I hear, no one ever leaves Brooklyn for good."

284 Ashford Street may have been a residence in the past. Currently, it was a vacant lot filled with discarded tires, broken pallets, and rats. According to the neighbors on either side of the lot, no house had existed there for at least twenty years. Duke took their names and shot a photo of the lot with his cellphone.

He would have to wait until Monday to check with the tax collector to find out who had lived there, but an elderly man who was sitting on his porch across the street offered some historical data.

"Late sixties, there was a young couple who bought the house on a rainy afternoon. Pouring so hard that they all sat in the realtor's car for half an hour before they could get out and walk into the house." The man spit a wad of chaw into a bucket at his feet and reloaded his cheeks from a small tin. "No kids and the guy up and left her in the summer, as I recall. Pretty lookin' woman. A bit too tall for my tastes."

Duke wrote the information in his notepad, standing on the first step of the tobacco-stained stoop. "You remember their names?"

"Nah. Never met 'em." He pushed the goop in his mouth around to the opposite cheek with his thumb. "My wife went over there when they first moved in with a pie she'd baked."

"Can I speak to her? Perhaps she remembers."

"Nope. She died five years ago." The man spit and looked up at Duke. "Lung cancer. Took her out in seven months." He spit again and reached for the tin. "I stopped smokin' the day they lowered her into the ground. Use this shit instead."

Duke folded his notepad and stepped down from the wooden stairs. "Thanks for your help."

"No problem, junior." Gazing up at the sky, the man shook his head slowly. "Too bad ghosts don't talk."

Chapter Eleven
Digging Up A Grave

Loviccio assured Duke that The Ghost hadn't worked a weekend shift in twenty years. Logging in with the desk sergeant, Duke asked who was upstairs, just to be sure. The sergeant said not to worry. The Ghost was still among the missing. He complimented Duke on having the guts to speak to the ancient detective, but assured him that Frank Nussbaum hadn't said a word to anyone in the police department for decades.

Two detectives, unknown to Duke, were in the squad when he walked in. He introduced himself to Sean Collins and Jake Vargas, both seasoned investigators, both deep into paperwork.

Vargas nodded toward the door. "If you're gonna be here a while, make a fresh pot of coffee. There's only a couple of cups left and we're heading out on a robbery call in a few minutes." He paused and squinted at Duke. "Unless you drink tea."

"You the kid that chased The Ghost out of the squad?" Collins folded his arms across his chest. "That took some balls."

"I didn't chase him out." Duke laughed. "I just offered him a cannoli."

Collins got up from his seat and held out his hand. "Congratulations, Garvey, everyone's been trying to get the old man to retire for years. You may have done it with a single pastry."

With the two detectives out of the squad, Duke sat down at The Ghost's desk and opened his notepad. From what he could tell, the piles of books were divided into three sections. The stack to his left had titles relating to serial killers. Most of them were fiction, but a few were written by authors with "PHD" or "Esq." after their names.

The pile on the other side of the desk was a combination of military history and police procedural manuals. Duke remembered reading most of the manuals in depth while he was in the academy. Why The Ghost needed a refresher was just another piece of a puzzle that Duke was itching to solve. The statue of Jesus with the cracked leg was a small twig compared to the vision he got from Nussbaum's eyes. No matter how hard he tried, the detective couldn't erase it from his memory.

What sat along the front edge of the desk was a collection of folded newspapers, tattered magazines, and folders of DD5s carefully stacked in date order. Duke started with the DD5s to see if any of them mentioned Saint Oda's or Cynthia Carson at 284 Ashford Street.

He got as far as two years in the past when Rita Jankowsky walked into the squad.

"Yo, you gotta put in for overtime during your shift."

Duke smiled. "I'm on my own dime here."

"And you're going through Nussbaum's shit? You really are crazy, Garvey."

"Trust me, after what happened on Tuesday, I'll make certain that every piece of paper is back where it belongs."

Rita strolled over and lifted Duke's notepad off the desk. "Who's Cynthia Carson?"

"A woman who tried to get the crack in Christ's leg repaired."

"Christ has a broken leg?"

Chuckling, Duke showed Rita the photos he'd taken with his cellphone. "According to Father Xavier at Saint Oda's and the letter she'd written, Mrs. Carson was concerned about the cracked leg and sent the church a sizeable amount of cash to cover the repairs."

"And they didn't do the repairs? That's fraud." Rita grabbed the phone out of Duke's hand and enlarged the picture. "Mrs. Carson has a case against the church."

"Assuming she's still alive and wants to press charges after thirty-something years."

"You do an internet search?"

"Yes. No results." Duke took the cellphone from Rita and thumbed through the pictures until he found the one of Saint Oda. "They named the church after a saint who liked magpies."

"Mud pies?"

Duke looked down at the floor and laughed. "No. Birds. Remember from the song, four and twenty magpies baked in a pie?"

"That's blackbirds." Rita coughed as she laughed. "Saint Oda is the patron saint of magpies?"

"No. It's just part of the legend." Closing his phone, Duke leaned back in The Ghost's chair. "I'm reading this stack of old DD5s and don't see anything that relates to his father's murder."

Rita picked up one of the reports and scanned the detective's comments. "This one's a robbery at Fort Hamilton. That was his father's last command. Nussbaum probably went through every crime committed at the barracks looking for a suspect."

"I'm guessing he never found one."

"Oh, he found plenty of them. Followed leads that went nowhere." She laid the report carefully on the pile it had come from and took a step back. "You're looking at nearly thirty years of dead ends. A detective's career that failed to solve a single crime." Rita pointed at Duke's phone. "You think this Carson woman is someone he hasn't investigated?" She laughed. "Dig around in this paper graveyard long enough and you'll find a file with her name on it."

Duke slid forward in the chair. "I don't get it. Why didn't Nussbaum ask for help? One detective isn't going to close a serial killer with that many murders by himself."

"Pride." Rita shrugged. "Pure and simple. The man has too much pride to admit he couldn't solve his father's murder. Think about it. Is there any case more dear to a cop's heart than where his family is involved?"

"Regardless, there has to come a time when even the most stubborn investigator will accept that they can't do it alone." Leaning back in The Ghost's chair, Duke held his hands out. "There's just too much shit here for one person to sift through. The answer could fall through a crack and he'd never know it."

"Well, in Nussbaum's case, that time isn't going to come until he's dead and in the ground."

Restacking the DD5 folders and straightening all the books so they looked the same as when he sat down, Duke got up from The Ghost's chair and surveyed the parchment landscape. He was about to walk away when he noticed a small Plexiglas cube with a chunk of mashed bullet inside, sitting behind a pencil cup.

"Tell me that's not the bullet that killed Nussbaum's father." Duke moved the pencil cup out of the way. "Holy shit."

".357 magnum, full metal jacket." Rita knelt down next to Duke and moved the tiny cube with her index finger. "Nussbaum waited years to get a hold of the bullet that killed his father. After everyone else had given up on finding the killer, he walked into the evidence room and demanded they hand over the spent round. For months, he carried it around in his shirt pocket. He'd spin it around on the desk and mutter to it. Made everyone crazy. The Plexiglas thing was done by our previous boss after almost a year of us putting up with the racket of the metallic marble."

"Nussbaum let him seal it up?"

"Yeah. The DA was still claiming it was evidence. Even after all those years. The boss told him that he should sit next to The Ghost and listen to the noise for a few hours. It was enough to shut him up." Pushing the bullet back into its original position, Rita stood and folded her arms over her chest. "By sealing it in plastic, no one could ever examine the bullet as evidence again. Thus, its evidentiary value became zero. Frank agreed to the encasement rather than have the bullet seized by the DA and put back in the evidence locker forever."

Duke reached over and lifted the Plexiglas square up to eye level. It felt warm to his touch, and he put it back down and wiped his hands on his pants. Raising it a second time, the temperature of the little display had gone up significantly. Duke's palm began to sweat, and he switched hands to see if it made a difference. It didn't.

With the heat from the cube increasing, he was going to put it down, but decided to take a closer look at its contents. Duke held the corners with his fingertips, making as little contact with the object as possible. He brought it up to eye level, close enough to see where the copper jacket had been compressed into the lead.

Squeezing his eyes closed for a second, Duke thought he could see a foggy image of fingers sliding the bullet into the cylinder of a pistol, and tried to focus. But then a flash forced them open and in the next instant, the heat coming from the cube became too much for his fingers.

Duke dropped the cube onto The Ghost's desk. "Ow!"

"What?"

Duke licked his fingertips. "Damn thing got hot. Burned my fingers." The tips of his index finger and thumb looked as though he'd grabbed a hot skillet without an oven mitt.

Rita touched the top of the cube with her index finger. "Ice cold." She picked it up and tossed it from one hand to the other, dropping it into Duke's open palm when she was done.

"It's cold now." Duke shook his head. "It was as hot as a frying pan a moment ago. Look at my fingers." The burn marks were fading as he held them up close to her face.

"It's The Ghost." Stepping back from Duke, Rita put her arms overhead and waved her hands as though the squad had floating spirits above their heads. "Woo, I'm the spirit of the bullet. You should never have touched me. Woo!"

"Very funny." Duke put the cube back behind the pencil cup and slid the chair under The Ghost's desk where he'd found it. He took a long, hard look at the desk and its contents and, satisfied that everything was in place, walked over to his desk and logged on to the NYPD's database.

Despite Rita's insistence that The Ghost would have already done the search, he typed in Cynthia Carson and clicked the search icon. Hopefully, the NYPD had a deeper well of data than the public internet. Four pages relating to the name "Carson" came up, including a couple of listings describing how to cook a Thanksgiving turkey. None of the females had an address in

Brooklyn. A Bowson Carson lived in Greenpoint. Kyle Carson was from New Jersey but had been busted for buying cocaine from a dealer on DeKalb by the subway entrance. He was currently doing eight years for possession upstate. The closest match was for Clyde Carson, but he was a teenager who was shot and killed in a robbery twenty years ago.

Rita walked over and stood behind Duke, reading the screen as he scrolled. "I told you. Nussbaum has probably read these a hundred times. None of them have any connection to his father's murder."

"One of them does." Duke sat back in his chair and folded his hands in his lap. "I know it. I can feel it."

"The only thing you're gonna feel is Nussbaum's wrath if you haven't put everything on his desk back where you found it." Turning toward the doorway, Rita grabbed her coffee cup. "You want a cup of coffee?"

"You're not going to make tea?"

She smiled. "Only when Ronnie's around."

Duke nodded. "Sure. It's hot. I made it a few minutes ago."

Rita walked out the door and leaned her head back in a moment later. "You made this a few minutes ago?"

"Yes. Why?"

"It's ice cold. What's a few minutes ago?"

Duke looked at the time on the computer screen. "Holy shit. I've been here for two-and-a-half hours?"

Rita smiled. "Time flies. Especially when you're chasing ghosts."

Chapter Twelve
Searching For Answers In The Dark

It was almost nine o'clock at night when Duke left the squad. Juliana had texted him several times after her shift ended. Based on their suggestive content, most of the messages weren't meant for anyone's eyes but his. Collins and Vargas had returned with a suspect in custody on their case just before eight and were still in the interview room taking his statement when Duke logged out.

    The name, age, and sex of the killer were still a mystery, but there was nothing that the detective didn't know about the murder of Frank Nussbaum's military father. He'd read newspaper articles, DD5s, and dozens of witness statements. The only commonalities were the fake camouflage outfit and the caliber of the weapon. All twenty murders were committed with the same .357 magnum revolver. Ballistics had matched every bullet that was removed from a corpse to the same gun. These two facts were undisputed.

    The killer hadn't traveled very far. All the dead were in three states. New York had the majority at eleven. Four people were murdered in Groton, Connecticut, not far from the state line. The rest were shot in New Jersey. Fort Dix accounted for one of the bodies. The remainder were killed in two separate incidents, a year apart, at McGuire Air Force Base.

The consensus was that the killer was a woman although several witnesses insisted they could see an Adam's apple on the shooter's throat. This purely male trait along with the "man's" gait was reported in three of the murders. A range of late teen to retiree was in the DD5s. The ancient end of the age scale came from a group of seniors who had the bad luck to be in the same diner when a Master Sergeant in full uniform was shot in the back of the head.

Fifteen different suspects had been interviewed. All had legitimate alibis. One of the suspects, a retired Naval officer, shot himself in the head hours after he'd been questioned. It turned out the midshipman had nothing more than a guilty conscience. Three more murders, including Nussbaum's father, took place afterwards.

A gas station attendant on the New Jersey Turnpike was shot, along with a buck private from Fort Dix. The civilian lived for over a week in the intensive care unit. His description of the killer was sufficient for a sketch artist to draw a likeness of an acne-faced boy in his late twenties with a scar below his left eye. It was the only mention of a scar by any of the witnesses.

Detectives from the tri-state area had canvassed the murder scenes in detail. Tire tracks were photographed, footprints were cast in plaster. What little surveillance video existed was grainy black and white footage. Duke watched several of the tapes on one of the many websites that had sprung up to document serial killers. He wasn't sure if it was the Loch Ness Monster, Sasquatch, or a childhood friend from Jamaica that was moving across the screen.

An in-depth search of the obituaries from all newspapers in the three states was done after the killings ended. Most of the detectives who'd worked the case agreed that the only way the spree would stop would be if the murderer either died of natural causes or was killed in the act. Over one-hundred of the recently deceased were investigated. None of them had any ties to the murders, and all of them were somewhere else when the crimes had taken place.

A copycat killer had taken up the slack two years after Nussbaum's father was shot. He was a retired Marine who'd returned from a second tour in Iraq and held a grudge against a trio of officers he'd served under. The faux camouflage he'd sewn together had a large group of detectives convinced the original killer was alive and still shooting. But the police had held back the details about the caliber of the weapon used in the murders. The Marine took out his victims with a .45 caliber semi-automatic. He was shot and killed by an off-duty cop who saw him shoot the third Marine officer at a gas station.

Psychics had been consulted. Professionals who studied the normal, the abnormal, and the paranormal offered their opinions. Sightings of a person in sewn together military togs were as common as clouds. Every one of them was documented by a police report. Duke was sure that The Ghost had read them many times.

Duke was staggered by the sheer volume of dead ends. How someone had managed to shoot and kill twenty people and then vanish off the face of the Earth seemed to be a magic trick worthy of

Houdini. The killer had run his spree and then stopped for whatever reason. Finding a retired murderer with no clues was an impossible crime to solve. It would remain a cold case forever. How The Ghost had taken the better part of thirty years to study this case and not reached that same conclusion was the genuine mystery as far as Duke was concerned. Why Frank Nussbaum continued his quest after every avenue turned out to be a dead end was an even greater unknown.

Duke understood what it meant to be driven, to have a goal that would be reached regardless of the odds. Growing up in Jamaica with boys who saw mischief as the norm, Duke was already sliding down a slippery slope. However, with a mother who would grab a switch of sugar cane to keep him in line, Duke saw his future in his mother's eyes, and halted his decline. The boy knew that she was going to raise him on the right side of the law, even if it meant locking her son in his room without food for a day.

However, this was not pure drive. Nussbaum's search had no end. Duke was certain that The Ghost realized that fact. The only possible conclusion was that the quest had emptied the old detective's brain of usable space. There was no more room for logical thought. Nothing but the same useless conclusions had stifled his ability to think. Detective Nussbaum had become an empty shell.

The killer's apparent goal was to murder as many soldiers as possible. Reviled as he was, Duke understood how it could be someone's lifelong ambition and slowly began to comprehend the killer's plan. Getting inside the head of a serial killer took years of constant interrogation. The Ghost had never found a way in. Duke was starting from the ground floor and had no idea where to go from there, but he was raised to take challenges to a personal level. To solve the murder of Nussbaum's father became a moral imperative for the young detective. With or without the help of the squad, Detective David Garvey was going to find the killer...dead or alive.

He was still troubled by the preserved bullet and damaged Jesus. The feeling in his gut that he'd seen the statue before was so strong that he knew he'd been in Saint Oda's at some time in his life. Perhaps his mother had taken him there when they first arrived in America. He'd call her in the morning to ask.

The mysterious Cynthia Carson had an interest in the broken Jesus. Reading her letter again, Duke felt anxiety in her choice of words. Was she responsible for the damage to Christ's leg, or was she just a wealthy parishioner who felt the urge to make the idol whole again? Was she the only person in thirty years who had donated toward the repairs? He'd have to question the Priest again.

The bullet in the Plexiglas was even more of an anomaly. He had no doubt that the little cube had thrown off enough heat to cause pain. Looking at his fingertips, Duke thought they still looked a bit redder than the other hand. But again, it was as though the bullet sensed his familiarity and warmed to the touch in remembrance.

Duke shook his head. Bullets were inanimate objects that killed people and punched holes in paper targets. To think that it had even the minutest sentient ability was moronic.

Nonetheless, the image in Nussbaum's eyes remained. Closing his eyelids as tightly as possible on the subway, Duke could see the green glow of The Ghost's pupils. Over and over, he watched the bullet slide out the barrel of the gun. It moved forward toward those eyes without wavering, without slowing, without a conscience.

He was so engrossed in the images that Duke went two stops past his exit and had to walk fourteen blocks back to his apartment.

Juliana was waiting in bed for Duke. She'd lit a dozen candles and poured two glasses of wine. That was at eight o'clock. When her boyfriend stumbled through the door at ten-thirty, only one candle was still lit and both wineglasses were empty. She'd started out naked, on top of the covers, but as the air conditioning had lowered the temperature to near freezing, Juliana had put on one of Duke's t-shirts and was now under the blanket.

"You called an hour ago. Did you walk here from Brooklyn?"

"Missed my stop."

She frowned. "You fall asleep on the train?"

"No." Duke sat down on the edge of the bed and kicked off his shoes. "Deep in thought."

Juliana flipped the covers back and smiled. "You wanna get deep into me?"

Loosening his tie, Duke lay back with his arms splayed out to the sides. "Unwrap me and I'll drill for oil."

"I was hoping you'd dig for gold."

Duke rolled over and planted a sloppy kiss on her lips. "I think I've already found my treasure."

The city was awakening when Duke walked out on his balcony with a cup of coffee. Juliana was in the shower, getting ready for her seven o'clock roll call. She had the next two days off and was going to drive out to Pittsburgh to see her father. Duke planned on spending the evenings in the police archives, reading the material that Nussbaum didn't have sequestered on his desk.

His girlfriend came up behind him, wearing his terrycloth robe. "My dad was expecting to meet you."

"He will. Listen, it's only been three months."

"For a pair of cops in a serious relationship, that's an eternity." Juliana pursed her lips. "And you're not counting the nine years we were partners."

Duke spun around and put the coffee cup on the glass patio table. "I wish you'd stop using that word."

"Serious or partners?"

"Serious." He put his hands on her shoulders. "We're having fun. We do things that a couple does. We go to restaurants together.

We go to movies. Is this our future? I don't know. No one knows. But each time you use that word, it puts a certain stigma on our relationship. It's a rope that we don't need to tie right now."

Juliana pushed him away. "I'm not talking about marriage, you idiot. But it's not like we're jumping from bed to bed. We're a couple. We're not goddamn swingers, Garvey. This isn't some casual relationship where you forget my name in the morning."

"You know, every time you've gone to see your father, you get uptight before you leave and come back with a dark cloud hanging over your head. You start talking about the future like there isn't one."

"He's dying, Garvey." She flopped down onto one of the loungers. "He doesn't know it. To him, everything seems the same, except it's still 1970 in his mind. Time has stopped for him. He doesn't remember my mother. He doesn't know who I am. As far as he's concerned, he's living in his college dorm. There are textbooks piled all around his bed. He doesn't read them. Doesn't even know which ones are there."

Duke sat down next to her. "It's a horrible way to die, but at least he's not in any pain."

"Small solace."

Duke sighed, "Sometimes that's all you get."

Chapter Thirteen
Links To The Past

Detective Francis Herman Nussbaum walked into the 84th Detective Squad on Monday morning at nine o'clock, dressed in his official NYPD blue uniform. It was obvious from the way the jacket was draped over his shoulders and the bunched up extra fabric that The Ghost had been significantly more muscular thirty years ago. The pants had been carefully cuffed, clearly a departmental violation, and the end of the too long belt was through all the loops on the opposite side, but the man wore the beat cop's uniform with a look of pride on his face.

Peter Tang was on the phone when The Ghost marched in. He dropped the receiver on his desk. For a moment, he thought it was the Chief of Police. His partner, Kelly, was in the restroom, and walked into the squad, speaking to someone on the phone in Spanish. She ended the call without a word and stood in the doorway, whispering, "*Madre dios*" over and over.

Not sure who had just walked into the squad, but certain it was a ranking officer, Lieutenant Moscowitz adjusted his tie and stood at attention by his desk. When The Ghost failed to stop at his office, Moscowitz rushed over to the door and yanked it open. He was about to call out to the unknown officer when The Ghost stopped several feet from his own desk, spun on his heel, and saluted.

Loviccio and Duke came into the squad, each carrying empty cardboard boxes. Rita followed behind them with a large, metal trashcan.

Duke turned to the lieutenant and was about to speak, but The Ghost beat him to the punch. "I have put in my papers. Today is my last day on the job. These detectives will help me carry my belongings down to my car." Nussbaum's voice was filled with gravel and as deep as an elevator shaft, but the words were clear and spoken without hesitation.

"Frank, you're really retiring?" Lieutenant Moscowitz walked over to The Ghost and offered his hand. "But what about the case?"

The Ghost looked around the room and stopped with his gaze on Duke's face. "There are other detectives here who are better prepared to solve my father's murder." And for the first time anyone in the squad could remember, The Ghost smiled.

The detectives stood at their desks for the next thirty minutes while Frank Nussbaum loaded the books, newspapers, and file folders that had been stacked on his desk into the boxes. No one helped. No one even offered to help. They all remained standing while one detective's career disappeared forever.

Nussbaum opened each drawer in his desk once the work surface had been laid bare. He placed the contents into the last empty box, sorting them as they were loaded. Office supplies, manuals, and a pair of clean shirts with ties already knotted around the collar, went into the box with measured deliberation. Satisfied that the drawer had nothing left to offer, he pushed it closed with his fingertips, wiping his hands on a handkerchief he'd pulled from his shirt pocket, before he went on to the next one.

Sergeant Williams came upstairs with two uniformed officers to help carry The Ghost's boxes to his car. Duke offered, but Lieutenant Moscowitz wanted all his detectives where he could see them while this event unfolded. On the stairway, the balance of the 84th Squad–uniformed and plainclothes–stood at attention while the procession of cardboard boxes moved past them. The Ghost followed the boxes with long, confident strides, stopping in front of Duke where he reached into his pocket and retrieved the Plexiglas cube with the fatal bullet.

He handed the tiny plastic box to the startled detective and nodded slowly. "It's the only clue, but I think you'll know where it leads." And with that said, Frank Nussbaum put on his hat and left the 84th Detective Squad as a civilian.

A stunned silence blanketed the squad for several minutes after The Ghost's final exit. Telephones were ringing, but no one answered them. The lines of cops on the stairway dispersed and nothing but soft murmurs were heard in the building.

Duke had gone downstairs, just a few steps behind Nussbaum, and watched him get into a late model Cadillac. A woman was driving the car, but she wore a wide-brimmed hat that covered most of her face. Grabbing a pen from his shirt pocket, Duke wrote the license plate number on the palm of his hand as they pulled away from the curb.

He didn't realize that Loviccio had also come down the stairs and was standing behind him. Duke almost knocked him over when he spun around.

"Jesus, Ronnie. I thought the only ghost in the squad just left."

"Did you see the woman behind the wheel?"

Duke nodded. "Yes, but not her face."

"No one has." Loviccio shook his head. "We know she's old. Albertini was late one morning and took The Ghost's parking spot. She got into it with the woman and had to move her car, but got a good look at the woman before she rolled up the driver's window. It's only in the past few months that The Ghost has been driving himself to work."

"Anyone ever trace the plates?"

"Registered to Nussbaum LLC."

"The Ghost has a corporation?" Duke chuckled. "What's he hiding?"

Loviccio shoved his hands in his back pockets. "No one knows. Years ago, I tried to get some information about the corporation, but other than what's in the public records, there's nothing. At least, I think there's nothing. I traced the corporate address and came back to a vacant lot on Ashford Street."

Duke's feet froze in place. "284 Ashford Street?"

"Maybe." Loviccio shrugged. "I have some notes in a private folder on my computer upstairs. Why?"

"The name Cynthia Carson ring a bell?"

"Not off the top of my head. Who is she?"

Clasping his hands together, a smile brightened the younger detective's face. "A friend of Saint Oda's who might just be the first link in a very long chain."

The password-protected folder on Loviccio's computer had copies of every DD5 that pertained to the murder of Frank Nussbaum's father. He'd sorted them by date but remembered that the Cadillac had been a recent acquisition and opened the correct sub-folder on the first try.

Number 284 was the correct address on Ashford Street for Nussbaum LLC. However, nowhere did the name Cynthia Carson or any variant appear on their corporate documents. Loviccio had done a search through the tax assessor's database to find all the previous owners of that lot and had found only two.

The City of New York had real estate records going back to the 1700s. The borough of Brooklyn, however, had lost most of their data in a fire just before World War II. The information for 284 Ashford Street began with a sale on August 4, 1951. George Tabor and his wife Helena purchased the property from his parents–Victor and Spraska Tabor–for the sum of one dollar. They sold it in 1965 to the Zarelski family, who lived there until 1998, when the two-story house was bought by the Nussbaum Corporation. According to the last entry, the house was demolished six weeks after the purchase was recorded.

"But no mention of Mrs. Carson." Duke slammed his hand on the desk. "Shit."

"Did you search birth records and obits?"

"Yes." Hopping up onto Loviccio's desk, Duke looked up at the ceiling, counting on his fingers. "Birth records, the obituary columns of all three newspapers, every online place where she could hide. The only proof that Cynthia Carson ever existed is the letter to Father Xavier."

Loviccio slid the chair back from the desk and cocked his head to one side. "I don't get it. Why is this Cynthia Carson so important? And what does the cracked leg of a statue have to do with the murders?"

"I don't know yet." Duke jumped off the desk. "Remember, I've only been a detective for a week. The answer could be right in front of my nose and I'm too new to the job to smell it."

"You said you'd been in the church before—"

"Thought I'd been in the church before."

Loviccio conceded. "Okay, you *thought* you were in the church before. And the thing with Nussbaum's eyes, did you *think* he was in the church, too?"

"Maybe." Duke paused and looked out the window. "He's an old man. Lots of churches in Brooklyn and according to his jacket, he's lived six blocks from Fort Hamilton ever since his father was shot."

"Garvey, the man's last name is Nussbaum. Did you happen to notice the Jewish star hanging around his neck?" Loviccio laughed. "If The Ghost has ever been in a church, it would be on a job."

Moe Jackson sauntered over and looked at the report on Loviccio's screen. "There's an old guy who lives across the street from 284 Ashford. His wife got beat up pretty bad around six or seven years ago. I was primary on the call. We collared a neighborhood punk for the assault. Maybe the wife was friendly with the people who lived there. The old man was a real grouch."

Duke shook his head. "The wife is dead and the old man must have found true happiness. I spoke to him yesterday, and he was as friendly as any other New Yorker."

"In other words, you didn't get shot." Jackson looked over his shoulder at The Ghost's empty desk. "He took everything?"

Pulling the bullet encased in plastic from his pocket, Duke held it close to his eyes. "Everything but the questions."

Lieutenant Moscowitz came out of his office and handed Duke a slip of paper. "Caribbean Bakery, corner of Albany and Union Street, was just robbed at gunpoint. Sector cars are on the scene. One shot, but not critical. Garvey, you're primary. Take the Italian stallion and get over there. Jackson, you and Albertini handle the canvass."

The scene in front of the Caribbean Bakery reminded Duke of Negril on a busy afternoon. Union Street was filled with former residents of the West Indies. Every island from Jamaica to Trinidad was represented with men and women shouting in Patois and pointing at the police while reggae music pumped from open windows above them. The fragrance of fresh-baked coco bread permeated the sidewalk, and smoke from rooftop cooking fires drifted down to mix with the illegal odors that would occasionally waft across the street.

Duke got out of their unmarked car and clipped his badge onto his sport jacket. Standing by the door, he closed his eyes and saw the cliffs in Negril where, on a dare, he'd jumped off a four-story-high cliff into the sea. He remembered the sounds of friends and tourists cheering him on and a girl who he'd been dating saying he was a coward if he backed down. He jumped and hit the water belly first. The pain was so excruciating that Duke almost drowned.

Undaunted, he swam to the surface and waved at the top of the cliff, but the girl was gone. Shaking his head, Duke closed the car door with his hip and headed across the street.

A uniformed sergeant met him halfway. "One male assailant, approximately fifteen-years-old, armed with a small caliber handgun pushed through a group of patrons waiting to be served. He fired one round into the ceiling of the bakery and everyone inside hit the floor. Mrs. Colony, sitting over there on the curb, refused to give up the money in the cash register and took a bullet in the foot for her stubbornness."

"Anyone else injured?"

"Negative. The shooter grabbed a loaf of bread off the counter and ran out the door. Several witnesses saw him round the corner and disappear, but they also heard the sound of tires screeching."

Loviccio took out his notepad. "Make sure Crime Scene checks for tire tracks and let's hope the fifteen-year-old knows how to drive."

The sergeant nodded. "They're on the way. I've got several officers working this side of the street to interview witnesses."

"Good. Jackson and Albertini will talk to the customers who were in the store." Duke looked over at Loviccio. "Let's see what Mrs. Colony has to say."

Mrs. Colony was pissed. Despite the blood soaking through the bandage on her right foot, she refused to go to the hospital. Her answers to Duke's questions, in Patois heavily laced with profanity, were punctuated with a large mixing spoon she kept waving in the air.

"Damn, stupid, rude boys." She spit at Duke's feet. "Jah strike down de evil. Send dem straight to hell. When de fruit fall from de tree an rot, den it time to trow away not come an shoot. Me ten years younger and me split his head wit dis spoon. Come round here stealin' and shootin' and scarin' me customers."

Stepping back from the pile of spittle, Duke pulled out his notepad. "Tell me what happened, Mrs. Colony."

"Babylon, me already tell dem odder cops. What wrong wit you, mon? Me a come here too many years, Jah protect. Maybe time go home? Maybe time a go where people have ears dat work. You ras clot."

Duke closed his eyes for a second and took a deep breath. The last time his mother had called him a "ras clot" he'd been with some friends in Jamaica who'd stolen a car. His friends had all been captured when they wrecked the car and were trapped inside, but he'd been thrown free and managed to get away. When he walked into the house, bleeding and shaken, his mother had given him enough time to explain what had happened. She wasn't interested in why and spit out the words as she sent him to his room without dinner.

Softening his voice, Duke tried to staunch her anger. "Why don't you tell me so I don't have to get it secondhand?"

"Secondhand? Don't you damn cops talk each odder? What wrong dis country when no one speak to no one?"

"We do, ma'am, but it's best I hear it from you rather than from someone else."

Mrs. Colony spit again, missing Duke's feet, but only by an inch. "Mon, dis rude boy come in me shop wit de gun wavin' in de air like he some wild child come down from de mountains wit fire burnin' his toes. Mash de gun in me customer's face and be screamin' and shovin' people like dey deaf and don't hear him." She pointed the spoon at Duke. "Ain't safe no more. Can't make a livin' when de customers need de bulletproof jacket jus to buy me bread."

Duke pushed the spoon out of his face. "Had you ever seen the boy before?"

"You think me know every face? No, mon. Me don't go lookin' for trouble dis morning. It come lookin' for me." Mrs. Colony switched the spoon to her other hand. "Rude boy come in an mash up me bakery. Me hope me never see him again. Me do, me kill his skinny ass wit dis spoon."

A woman with gray dreadlocks streaming down her back and a knit cap on top of her head ran over and threw her arms around the wounded baker. They slipped into pure Patois, tears running down their cheeks. Duke stood back and watched them for a few seconds before turning to Loviccio.

"I don't think we're going to get much more from Mrs. Colony."

Loviccio folded his notepad and stuffed it into his jacket pocket. "Just another exciting day in Brooklyn."

They left the scene in the hands of the uniformed cops and the CSI team and headed back to the squad. Loviccio parked in front of the precinct and looked over at Duke with a puzzled expression on his face. "What's a 'rude boy' and why did she keep calling you Babylon?"

"Many years ago in Jamaica, back when lawlessness and violence ruled the hills, young boys would come down and wreak havoc. Gangs fought each other. Killings were common. The police were given a free hand to bring about law and order. That included beatings and imprisonment without a hearing in many cases." Duke took out a stick of chewing gum and stuffed it into his mouth. "They called these kids 'rude boys' and they were given a choice when captured."

"Ah, let's give the criminals a say in their prosecution."

Duke shook his head. "Only two choices. They could join the Jamaican Army or spend so many years in prison that they'd need a walker and a cane when they came out."

"Join the Army? They gave those kids guns?" Loviccio shook his head. "Something doesn't smell right, Garvey."

"Think about it logically for a moment." Rolling down the window, Duke leaned against the door and counted the reasons on his fingers. "If you put the kid in prison, all you accomplish is to plant the seeds of a criminal career. No one comes out of prison without learning a new trade. Some pick up the skills needed to break into a house. Others become hardened, turning to assault or even worse."

Loviccio nodded in agreement. "Same thing here."

"Second, the Army knows how to fix these rude boys."

"Fix?"

"My mother told me that either path will get you beat. The cane and switch have no eyes. Beat a rude boy or beat a young soldier. In the end, you'll either break the boy's spirit or enhance his ability to deal with pain." Duke smiled. "You learn from the beatings. I certainly did."

"Your moms beat you?" Loviccio pocketed the car keys and reached for the door handle. "Damn, Garvey, I'da bet you was a choirboy."

Duke winked. "I had my moments."

A robbery with one dead in Canarsie had required the balance of the detectives from the squad. Lieutenant Moscowitz, the lone occupant of the 84th Detective Squad, was sitting at The Ghost's desk when Duke and Loviccio walked in. He was holding his head in his hands, balanced on his thumbs.

"Come over here and take a seat." Moscowitz nodded toward two chairs he'd placed by the side of the desk.

"What's up?" Loviccio grabbed one of the chairs and spun it around before dropping into it.

The lieutenant pointed at the other chair. "Garvey?"

Duke sauntered over, giving The Ghost's desk a wide berth. "Ronnie thinks you're taking a chance sitting in that chair. It might still be haunted."

Doing his best to stifle a laugh, Loviccio reached over and punched Duke in the thigh. "Hey, you're the one who's investigating the spirit world."

"You know, I'm having a hard time believing you two only know each other a week." Getting up from the chair, Lieutenant Moscowitz hopped up onto The Ghost's desk and shoved his hands under his thighs. "This is a good thing, though. Jankowsky's sister is having a hard time and Rita's taking a thirty-day-leave to help her out."

Loviccio looked down at the floor. "She's out of rehab again?"

"Yes, and as usual, it only took her a week before she started using. Rita's going upstate to help her mom with the kids and see if she can get her sister clean."

"Again." Slamming his hand on The Ghost's desk, Loviccio turned to Duke. "This will be failed attempt number five. I can't believe her sister's still alive."

"Five shots at rehab?" Duke blew out a breath. "What's the problem, other than the obvious?"

"Money." Sliding off the desk, Moscowitz shrugged. "Her insurance will only pay for two weeks. She needs a couple of months."

"And each time the sister goes, Rita foots the bill for an extra week. Even then, it's a total waste of money." Loviccio got up and walked over to the window. "It's already cost Rita three months pay in the last couple of years."

Duke joined him by the window. "It's family and family comes first."

"Bullshit."

"Really? You wouldn't do the same if you had a brother?"

"Well, first off, I don't have a brother anymore. He died in Iraq. And if he'd gotten his ass in Dutch with drugs, I'da let him overdose and get a view of the long dark before some doctor pulled his drugged ass back from the brink." Loviccio put his hands on Duke's shoulders. "Junkies have to believe that they can die before they begin to live."

Lieutenant Moscowitz took a few steps toward his office, turned and smiled at the two detectives. "Well, you two are going to be a little family, for now. Ronnie, meet your new partner. And since the murder of Major Nussbaum is still an open case and the only detective who was working on it has just retired, you two will add that to your caseload."

"Are you kidding?" Loviccio held his hands out, palms up. "Fuggetabout it. No one's ever gonna solve that murder. Or, for that matter, the other nineteen. Why not give us those cases, too?"

Moscowitz smiled and winked at Loviccio. "You want them? They're yours. I'll have someone from Records bring up the case files and you two can get started on them in the morning."

"Whoa. Wait a minute." Walking over quickly, Loviccio stepped between the lieutenant and his office. "I was kidding. I'm already overloaded. Plus, who's gonna handle Rita's open cases?"

"I've already spread them around. You have the Park Place homicide and this morning's shooting." Moscowitz looked up at the ceiling for a moment. "And the Franciscan brothers murders. That's it. I want you two working on the Nussbaum case for now. If I need you on something else, I'll let you know."

Loviccio stamped his foot. "The Franciscan brothers case has fewer leads than the search for Nussbaum's father. I've been working that shit for over a year and it's going nowhere fast."

"I thought you had a witness."

"She died." Loviccio's voice went up a few notches. "Everything about that case pointed at the father, but his alibi held up. The mother swore she was sleeping and that the neighbor's statement about the argument in the garage was bullshit. The woman just hated the man."

Duke looked at the lieutenant as though he'd been speaking Swahili. "What are you saying, boss? You want us to pick up The

Ghost's dead ends and pretend they go somewhere? I've already looked at his research and it all comes up against blank walls. He took all his notes when he left. Can you get them back?"

Loviccio interrupted. "Does The Ghost really want us to solve the case? I mean, what the hell? If he did, why did he take all his shit with him?"

"Nussbaum didn't take everything." Moscowitz nodded toward the Plexiglas cube on Duke's desk.

"Are you kidding?" Loviccio walked over to the desk and picked up the plastic-wrapped bullet. "This isn't a clue. It's a souvenir. You can buy these online. Bullets encased in plastic. Just name your caliber. Shit, you can probably get different colored plastic."

Taking the cube from Loviccio's hand, the lieutenant held it up close to his eyes. "No, I don't think you can get one like this. All the bullets I've ever seen online are pristine. This one's been fired. I'll bet it really is the bullet that came out of Major Nussbaum's brain. It's a classic. A one of a kind piece of evidence. And I'll bet it can open doors for you two." He nodded. "That's just what this case needs, a fresh pair of eyes." Moscowitz slapped his thigh. "Hey, two fresh pair of eyes. What a bargain!"

"You could put twenty pairs of eyes on this shit and it wouldn't do any good." Dropping dejectedly in his chair, Loviccio spun around and kicked the side of the desk. "Sure, we can get the

DD5s, but without a detective's private notes, you only get part of an unsolved case."

"Not with Frank Nussbaum." Moscowitz took a seat opposite Loviccio and shook his head. "Frank put every word he ever wrote on a notepad into the system. Nothing is missing. The man was meticulous in his record keeping. You don't need his private notes."

"More bullshit." Reaching into his top desk drawer, Loviccio pulled out a notepad with a rubberband wrapped around it to keep it closed. "I have notes on the Franciscan brothers that aren't in the system. Do you really think every detective under your command has the time to type all their notes into a DD5?"

Lieutenant Moscowitz frowned. "Maybe you shouldn't show me that notepad."

"Boss, there are lots of things that we don't and shouldn't show you."

Getting up from his seat, Moscowitz took a step toward his office. "Regardless, the cases are now yours and I want you to work them in the same professional manner as you would handle any homicide in the borough of Brooklyn."

Duke was about to jump in and make the argument to put this case back in the box when the phones rang. Being closest to one, he reached down and answered the call.

"84th Detective Squad. Duke Garvey speaking."

A voice, too soft to be heard by Moscowitz or Loviccio, spoke a few words. Duke grabbed his notepad and pen and wrote down an address. Silence, then a constant ringtone from the receiver in his hands. Duke dropped it slowly into the cradle and laid his notepad and pen carefully on the desk.

He looked back and forth between his boss and his partner, listening to the sound of his breathing for a few moments. When Duke finally managed to speak, his voice was flat, as though he was reading an obituary. "That was Cynthia Carson, widow of the late Keith Carson, an airline pilot. Her maiden name was Cynthia Nussbaum, and Frank is her older brother." Duke took a deep breath. "She wants to meet."

Chapter Fourteen
Clean Clothes, Please

Nussbaum's sister parked the Cadillac in front of Jamison's Bar and opened an umbrella over her head as she got out. Duke saw the car pull up and met her at the door of the bar. Overlooking the Narrows with an unobstructed view of the bridge, it was the watering hole for nearby Brooklyn Community College and filled with noisy students. The restaurant where her father was murdered had stood across the street on the corner. She paused and looked at the vacant lot for a few seconds before hurrying through the open door.

"Mrs. Carson?" Duke held out his hand, raising his voice over the din. "I'm Detective Garvey. You spoke to me on the phone."

"Duke Garvey. Yes, Frank said you were handsome. Said you were much better looking than Ronnie." She paused and took off her sunglasses. "Hmmm, red hair and your features are much more Caucasian than Negro. One of your parents was white?"

Duke paused to let a large group of people barge out the door. With their departure, the volume dropped low enough for him to use his regular voice. "Yes, ma'am. My father."

"Is he a cop?"

Duke shook his head. "No. Just a tourist who split after he impregnated my mother with his seed."

"Ah, the biblical reference. You're a practicing Catholic?"

"No. The occasional Rastafarian, but I don't smoke cannabis and much of what I eat would be shunned by a true believer." Duke nodded toward the booth where Loviccio was waiting. "Ronnie's over there."

Cynthia turned and looked over to where Duke had indicated. "He still looks like an undernourished homeless person. One of these days, he'll learn how to comb what's left of his hair."

"You know each other?"

"Detective, after thirty years, there isn't a cop in Brooklyn who I don't know." She closed the umbrella and stood it by the door. "From Manhattan North to the furthest reaches of Staten Island, Frank Nussbaum, or The Ghost as you've probably learned to call him, was more well-known than the Mayor."

"Wait a minute." Duke shook his head. "How come Loviccio didn't recognize your married name?"

Winking at the young detective, Cynthia smiled. "I've done my best to avoid the NYPD and in particular all the detectives from the 84th Precinct. I guess you don't come from a cop family."

Duke shook his head. "No. I'm the first."

"Well, let's hope you're the last."

Loviccio stood as they walked over. "Good Lord, Cindy, I haven't seen you in ten years. You look great. What happened to Kevin?"

"It was Keith, but no one has ever awarded you points for your memory." Cynthia slid into the booth opposite from where Loviccio had been seated. "I see your wife is still picking out your ties. Is it a clip-on?"

"Nope. Believe it or not, I figured out the Windsor knot one Sunday afternoon while I was watching the Mets." Loviccio put two fingers under his tie and lifted it a few inches.

"You never had enough sense to follow the Yankees." She smiled. "Losers seem to stick to their pack. At a quick count, I see three stains on your jacket and one on your shirt collar. You ate something with tomato sauce, or is it ketchup? And the blue stain on the collar? Did you actually use mouthwash this morning?"

Loviccio frowned. "Can't you ever say anything nice to me?"

"You've lost more weight." Cynthia looked at Duke and raised an eyebrow. "I hope he's not getting you to join one of his moronic diet routines."

Doing his best not to laugh, Duke pulled a stack of menus from the rack at the end of their booth and handed them out. "I know it's getting late, but I've been reading the menu and they have some interesting tapas. We can't drink, but the beer menu has more offerings than I've seen in most neighborhood bars."

"Thanks, but I don't have that much time." Cynthia pushed the menu back to the opposite side of the booth. "I don't like Frank to be alone for very long." She pulled up her sleeve and checked the time on her wristwatch. "He usually takes a nap from five until six-thirty, then I make him dinner."

It was almost five o'clock. Loviccio picked up the menus and shoved them to the far end of the booth. "My partner is wondering about your interest in a broken statue of Christ he's seen."

"Saint Oda's." She sighed. "Did you know that she's the patron saint of the magpie?"

"So I've read." Folding his hands on the table, Duke smiled. "She was born blind, found her sight because of the birds, and dedicated her life to the church."

Cynthia pointed at him. "You've done your research. Ronnie, you could learn from this kid. Pay attention."

Loviccio pursed his lips but stayed silent.

"What's your interest in the broken Jesus?" Pushing his ginger ale off to the side with his pinkie, Duke leaned a bit closer to Mrs. Carson. "Father Xavier showed me your letter."

"He's still alive?" The look of surprise on Cynthia's face was real. It had come on too quickly to be fake. Both detectives knew it, but only Duke relaxed slightly. "He must be ninety, pushing a hundred."

"Eighty-eight, but he could pass for eighty-seven." Duke winked at her. "Spry? Yes, that's the term for an old person who still wears sneakers."

Over the single beer ordered by Loviccio, a ginger ale for Duke, and club soda for Nussbaum's sister, she told the detectives how her late husband, an ardent Catholic, had fostered a love of the church in the formerly Jewish woman. The organ music was the biggest pull, having spent the early part of her life listening to the screeching and off-key a cappella singing she suffered through in the synagogue. Cynthia took special joy in listening to the hymns sung by the church choir. Often, she'd sit in the pew with her eyes closed, swaying back and forth to the melody long after it had ended.

The massive pipe organ that was built into the church honoring Saint Oda could be heard three blocks away and was renowned for its magnificent tonal qualities. It was her favorite Sunday morning destination. Humming to the deep bass notes as she walked inside, Cynthia would cross herself, look down at the marble floor, and smile as the glorious sunshine painted her shoes through stained glass. Regardless of her religious beliefs, music brought her as close to heaven as she needed to be. She said that the sunlight was God's sign to her that she was welcome in His house.

Cynthia twirled the straw in her club soda. "You have to understand. Saint Oda's was a small community-based church, suffering from a nearly empty collection plate. Despite the lack of local funding, the Archdiocese had shoveled money into the aging structure just to maintain a foothold in the neighborhood. Property values constantly seesawed and the Church elders knew the land under the building made the property more valuable than gold. Whether or not they ever intended to fix the broken image was a question that I could never get answered."

"Was the statue always broken?" Duke flipped to a new page in his notepad. "Do you remember when you first saw it?"

"I noticed the crack in Jesus' leg during my first Mass and asked Father Xavier about it. He explained that the black Christ had been carved out of African zebrawood and brought to America in the 1800s by boat. The long sea journey had infused the statue with the damp breath of the ocean. When the piece arrived and dried out, a large crack in the leg appeared. As far as he knew, it had never gotten any wider."

Loviccio finished his beer and waved for a server. "How'd you get involved with fixing it?"

"My late husband was an airline pilot who came from a wealthy family. All I had to do was ask. He told me to offer repair money to the priest, but only after I found a reputable carpenter." Taking a sip of her drink, Cynthia shook her head. "I interviewed six of them, including Nunzio Hernandez, but I decided to leave the decision up to Father Xavier. I didn't know anything about carpentry, but Nunzio had fixed the large bay window in our house when it began to leak, so I gave Father Xavier his name."

Not having any reason to dispute the woman's statements, Duke made some notes, but felt there was something missing. Closing his eyes, he could see the statue's broken leg as clearly as if he'd been standing in front of it. Why he was so sure that he'd seen it before was a splinter that got shoved deeper into his finger with her explanation.

Duke struggled to visualize a connection between Major Nussbaum's murder and a local church with a busted statue. According to Cynthia, her father had only been in the church at Fort Hamilton as part of his official duties. She'd been in several Catholic churches in Brooklyn and only one–Saint Oda's–had a black Jesus Christ over the altar. Added to that, nothing in the investigation had suggested a religious angle to the murders.

They finished their drinks and Duke again suggested ordering something light to eat if she was interested. Checking the time, Cynthia thanked him but declined. It was getting late, and she needed to get back to her brother.

Looking around the bar for a familiar face and seeing none, she opened her purse and took out a small key with a numbered tag. "There's a row of lockers in the Greyhound Station on Livingston Street. At the far end are the largest lockers. This key opens the last one by the water fountain on the bottom row. In there, you'll find six boxes of files. Those are Frank's private notes. Some of them are in his DD5s, but most of them are not."

Duke reached across the table and took the key. "Does Frank know you put them there?"

"No. And I didn't put them there. My neighbor's kid took them out of the trunk of the Cadillac when we got home the other night. Frank wanted me to burn the whole lot. I told him that the kid next door would take care of it. He rakes our leaves and has a burn barrel." Cynthia snapped her purse closed and checked the time again. "The kid took the files to the Greyhound Station on my instructions. I knew that someone at the 84th would take over the case. If for no other reason than pure curiosity." She shook her head slowly. "No one's life should go up in smoke. Those boxes are my brother's life. I want it to go on. I want to know who killed our father."

Loviccio felt a smile coming on and looked down at his lap. The words sounded truthful, but he was having a hard time getting that impression across. "Cindy, we'll pick up where Frank left off. You have my word."

"Bullshit, Ronnie. You're not talking to some skell, Loviccio. I'm a detective's family and you will talk to me with respect." Cynthia leaned across the table and slapped Loviccio's face. "And that's for the snicker, you asshole."

She got up from the booth and turned around to face the two detectives. "Before you start cracking wise and pushing this case off to the side, I want you to think how you would feel if the situation were reversed. Spend a few seconds and think about your father being murdered and how you, a New York City detective, would react if the other detectives in your squad laughed it off. Think how you would feel if they gave up the investigation."

Duke got halfway out of the booth to walk her to the door, but Nussbaum's sister held up her hand.

"I'm a big girl, Garvey. I can find my way out of a bar. I've been doing it for a long time." She zipped her windbreaker and smiled. "See if your slovenly friend there can find some clean clothes before his next tour. He's a disgrace to the gold badge."

Loviccio waited until she'd walked through the door before he cupped his elbow and raised his fist. "*Ah, bah fungool.* Buy me some clean clothes, you bitch."

"Nice." Duke sniffed his left armpit and then leaned toward his partner to sniff again. "You could use some deodorant, Ronnie."

"Oh? You, too?" Loviccio shoved Duke out of the booth. "Let's get over to the Greyhound Station before you start giving me grooming tips, junior." Tossing a pair of twenties on the table, he cursed, "Now I know why I forgot Frank had a sister."

Loviccio parked in a 'Bus Only' spot and lowered the visor with the NYPD placard on the back. Jogging over to the lockers, he matched the numbered key to the last locker on the left, bottom row, and slipped it into the lock.

The same six boxes that were carried down to The Ghost's Cadillac during his retirement parade were piled carefully in the tall locker. Duke grabbed a porter with a handcart and slipped him a twenty. Without breaking a sweat, the detectives moved the boxes into the trunk of their Chrysler.

"It's almost six. I'm supposed to go out to dinner with my wife and our downstairs neighbors." Loviccio started the engine and pulled out of the Greyhound Station. "I'm gonna take the car home. I'll drop you off at the subway."

"Are you going to start working through his files tonight?"

Loviccio snorted as he hit the gas. "Not if I wanna stay married. I'll see you in the morning. Get a good night's sleep. This shit is gonna take days to get through and I want you bright-eyed and smiling when we start."

Rolling down the window, Duke pulled a fresh piece of gum out of his pocket. "My girlfriend's away for one more night. You can bet I'll sleep well." He tinkered with the wrapper for a few seconds and then turned to look at his partner. "What do you think The Ghost is going to say when he finds out where his records have gone?"

"Thank you?"

"Really?"

"Do you think for half a second that he didn't put Cindy up to this?" Loviccio laughed. "That whole business with the uniform and the parade of boxes this morning was just for show. Frank's been waiting for a reason to pass the baton. Well, you gave it to him."

"Hey, don't blame me. I was just being friendly."

Cutting across traffic, Loviccio made a right on DeKalb. "You're going uptown?"

"Yes. Drop me off on the next corner, though. I noticed a Jamaican restaurant on our way over here. I'm going to grab some dinner and then head home to an empty apartment. Juliana isn't coming back until Tuesday night, so I'm dining alone."

Loviccio raised his eyebrows and shook his head in mock pity. "You got a right hand. You got a left. A man is never alone."

Chapter Fifteen
What Is Family?

Duke came out of a light nod with the sound of a door closing. Reaching across his laptop, he lifted the Glock and wiped the sleep out of his eyes with the other hand. The only light in the apartment came from the muted television and the ever-present glow of the city through open windows. Silently, he got up from his chair and moved into the darkest part of the room.

"Go ahead and shoot. Put me out of my misery." Juliana threw her overnight bag on the couch and clicked on the lamp. "I've been driving for nine hours without a break other than for gas and to pee."

"You weren't supposed to be home until tomorrow evening."

She dropped onto the couch with a groan and kicked off her sneakers. "I couldn't take it."

"Your dad?"

"No, the goddamn King of England." Juliana scrunched a pillow behind her head. "Jesus, Garvey, who else could it be besides my dad, the rotting turnip."

Duke laid his Glock on the coffee table and sat down next to her. "He's gotten worse?"

"I've seen junkies with better memories and skin color." Lifting her legs, Juliana moved back far enough that her feet were resting on her boyfriend's thighs. He got the hint and began massaging the foot closest to him. With his take-home dinner from the Jamaican diner in Brooklyn, Duke had opened a bottle of red wine, which was still sitting on the coffee table. She reached over and grabbed it, sucking the lukewarm beverage down her throat faster than a desert nomad at the end of a dusty ride.

"It took him half an hour to get my name right. Then he pissed himself and I couldn't get an orderly to clean him up, so I had to do it." Juliana pointed the nearly empty bottle at Duke. "Do you know how embarrassing it is to have to clean your father's penis?"

"Be thankful you knew your father. Not all of us are that lucky." Switching feet, Duke pulled off her sock and dropped it alongside her leg. "Even my mother has forgotten the man's name." This particular discussion had been repeated several times, more recently as her father's decline had moved onto a steeper slope. Usually, it would quench the fire of her anger.

Juliana bent her knee and removed the sock from the foot Duke had just unkinked. She made a ball out of the pair and tossed it across the room. "I thought she had a photo of him."

"Him? The man who raped my mother? Yes, from thirty-four years ago. I doubt he looks the same. Plus, I have no interest in finding him or knowing who he is. The man saw my mother as an opportunity to relieve his sexual tensions. Maybe his wife wouldn't put out. Perhaps he didn't have one, and this is how the man spent his vacations."

"Well, either way, it's better than spending the day with an eighty-year-old who can't control his bladder, doesn't know who you are, and thinks that Nixon is still President." Juliana drew her legs up to her chest. "I don't know if I can ever go back there again." She shivered and wrapped her arms around legs. "You should offer a blessing that you'll never have to watch your father rot away like mine."

Duke got up from the couch and went into the kitchen for two wineglasses. He came back with them and a fresh bottle from the rack next to the pantry. "You have to go back and see him. You're his only family."

"Bullshit. How can he be family? Because he screwed my mother? Hell, Garvey, he's just as bad as the man who raped your mother. One shot and mom does the rest. You can grow up without a father, but you'll always need your mother." She shook her head. "Fathers just break your heart. You want me to go back to see him again? Justify that shit."

"Because he's family. That's the end of the trail. Without your father you wouldn't be here." He pointed the bottle at her. "That has to count for something."

Closing her eyes, Juliana blew out a short breath. "And you'd still visit someone who couldn't care less if you came or not? You'd drive nine hours in each direction, eat shitty food from truck stops, and sleep in a hotel that's not fit for pimps and whores? Then you'd sit in the room and watch that someone die and occasionally get pissed on if you bent over to see if he was still breathing? And then you'd get up to leave and feel bad because that scratchy, phlegm encrusted voice, complained that you don't stay long enough?" Juliana grabbed the bottle from Duke's hand. "All of that just because of family?"

Duke snatched the bottle back from his girlfriend and nodded quickly. "Yes. That's the way I was raised. Family comes first. Even when that family is small, sick, or spread across the oceans."

"Okay, I'm gonna call more bullshit here."

"What?"

"You're sitting there and spouting off about how important family is, and you just said that your father was of no interest to you. Isn't he half your family? Isn't he the reason for your existence? How is he different than my father?"

Duke placed the wine bottle on the coffee table and picked up the corkscrew. "All that my father did was have sex, once, with my mother. He knocked her up and left. If it wasn't for the Catholic Church, I wouldn't be here right now."

"But he's still your father. He's your family, Duke."

"No. He's not my family. He may be my father, but his only claim to my heritage was to spend one of his vacation evenings with my mother. He didn't raise me, he's had no contact with me, and if he's still alive somewhere, I'm sure my mother isn't the only woman he seduced or for that matter, impregnated." Duke pointed the corkscrew at Juliana. "For all I know, I may have a dozen brothers and sisters in every country of the Caribbean."

Juliana pulled the pillow from behind her back and threw it at him. "You can't have it both ways, Garvey. You can't expect me to stand by my retarded father–"

"He's not retarded, Julie."

"Whatever you want to call it. He's not all there, okay?"

"But he's going to be there for a long time, right? That's what the doctors told you."

"Christ, Duke, he's worse than a child." She got up from the couch and pushed him out of the way. "Hearing you dismiss your father, I can't imagine what would happen if your mother got sick. Would you walk away from her as well?"

Duke grabbed her arm. "My mother is my only true family. I would die for her."

"Would you die for me, Garvey? Am I as important as your mother?" Juliana put her hands on Duke's shoulders. "All these years as partners and now I'm wondering, would you have taken a bullet for me?"

"I did."

"Bullshit. You got out of the car so fast that I didn't have time to catch up to you before you ran into that apartment house." Pushing her boyfriend away, Juliana shook her head. "You violated procedure. If we'd gone in together, you wouldn't have gotten shot and the hostage taker could have been taken alive."

Duke protested, waving the sealed bottle of wine in the air. "The department ruled it a good shoot."

"Only because I lied."

Silence filled the apartment. Even the street noise was muted. Duke put the bottle down on the table and took several steps backward. Standing at the opposite end of the room, Juliana crossed her arms over her chest and glared at him. Her lips were tightly sealed and the look on her face was pure challenge. Fighting to hold back his anger, Duke took a deep breath and stared at her for a few seconds. As cops, they lived for truth. It was never a question of trust between partners. Lives were lost when lies replaced truth.

Duke could feel his chest tighten. "What did you lie about?"

Relaxing slightly, knowing that she was in control of this conversation, Juliana let a smile creep across her face. "I was asked several times why I was so far behind you. Each time, I told the investigators on the shooting board that my door was stuck. Remember the old Crown Vics we used to drive? Remember the dent in the passenger door from where it was hit by the delivery van?"

With a quick nod, Duke closed his eyes and recalled the accident on 14th Street where they were in pursuit and ran a red light. The van that smashed into the side of their blue and white nearly collapsed the door, but the auto shop had resurrected the vehicle even though the door was tight and stuck in the winter. The city had been in the middle of another budget crunch and new cars weren't going to hit the streets for at least another year.

His anger faded. Everyone lied to Internal Affairs.

"I lied to cover your ass, Garvey. So now I'm askin', would you do the same for me? Would you tell a lie for me? Would you go the distance and step in front of a bullet?"

Duke sat down on the couch and put his feet up on the coffee table. Wrapping his hands behind his head, the detective pondered the question for a moment too long.

"That's what I thought." Juliana spun on her heel and marched into the bedroom, slamming the door behind her.

"I'm not the Secret Service and you're not the damn President." Duke whispered the words, not wanting to rekindle the argument in her favor. He nodded twice and closed his eyes. Her sobs were quickly muffled by the sound of the shower. Looking at his watch, he shrugged.

I really don't need this shit tonight.

It was Duke's experience with Juliana that she needed to be alone for a while after seeing her father. She'd been to see him four times since they started living together. Each trip she'd come back in a horrible mood and they were getting worse. Usually, it was fire and brimstone for at least a day, sometimes the rest of the week was a loss. It meant takeout meals, no sex, and intermittent crying jags until Juliana got her father stuffed back into the storage area of her mind.

He took the bottle, a single glass, and the corkscrew out onto the balcony and collapsed into one of the two loungers. Opening the vintage cabernet, he sniffed the cork and left the bottle on the patio table to breathe. Rather than risk further annoyance on her part, Duke went back inside and returned with a second glass. She'd be out there eventually and would drink without a single word to him.

The tension between them had increased with each forced pilgrimage to the nursing home in Pittsburgh. Duke had offered to go the first time, but couldn't get the days off. Seeing how pissed off and cranky she was upon returning, he didn't propose to accompany her again.

It pained him to hear her talk about her father that way. Deep inside, he'd always wished he had a father. When Duke was younger and his mother walked him to school in Negril, most of his friends arrived hand-in-hand with their mothers, so it was acceptable. But when they moved to New Jersey, and she still drove him to school, the young boy was forced to deal with the jeers and catcalls of his classmates who took a bus, walked, or were delivered by their fathers.

He'd never taken to sports, thinking that only a father could appreciate a home run, or a touchdown, or even a winning pace on the track by a son. Father-son days at school were spent at home with his nose glued to a book. It was at his mother's insistence that he took home economics classes and learned to cook. Duke wanted to take wood shop and learn how to use power tools. Instead, his mother bought him recipe books and instructed her son how to use carving knives and a spatula.

The outcome of all this mothering yielded a man who, while virile, trim, and at ease with the opposite sex, could mend his own clothes, make a perfect soufflé, or sear a steak to perfection. Cleaning house, doing the laundry, and shopping for food were as normal to her son as building a desk from Ikea, changing a flat tire, or opening the door for his date.

Duke had the benefit of a mother who wanted him to become the best person possible, regardless of his gender. She knew the world outside of their island was harsh. Men may think they have the physical advantage, but without a woman, man couldn't exist. Putting all the traits of both genders into her son insured he would survive once they left paradise for good.

The police academy solidified Duke Garvey as a man. No one wanted to know about his cooking skills. If his uniform got ripped, it went to the department's tailor for repair. Women there were as tough as the men. Some were tougher. Gender equality was easy once the blue uniform came out of the locker. Everyone looked the same. It was the magic of the bag.

His instructors expected every recruit to perform beyond their abilities. Non-hackers were weeded out with no concern for gender, quotas, or political correctness. The job required strength, intelligence, and common sense. It didn't give a damn what was between a cop's legs.

Duke graduated number three in his class. His mother was proud, but thought he could have at least hit number two.

Dawn was creeping over the horizon when Duke crawled into his side of the bed. He had a few hours to get some sleep before roll call. Juliana was snoring and would probably sleep in as she had the day off. Her empty suitcase was standing by the open door to their shared closet. A moment passed where Duke thought about waking her up and apologizing. But it departed as quickly as it came.

Juliana had sublet her apartment and still had two months to go. She wasn't leaving. The suitcase was just a bluff. At least he hoped so.

Chapter Sixteen
Road Trip

Loviccio and Duke spent Tuesday and Wednesday going through The Ghost's files. Fortunately, Nussbaum was as organized as he was mysterious. The leads he'd followed over thirty years of investigation that lead nowhere were isolated to the two largest cartons. They were in consecutive order with the most recent one in front. It was already seven-years-old.

Nussbaum had come to the conclusion that the shooter was dead. It was the only logical explanation for the sudden end of the killings. Serial killers were either caught and sent to prison or killed in the attempt to continue their spree. It was rare that they would retire or grow tired of taking a life.

To that end, he'd traveled to the far corners of the tri-state area in search of the killer's grave. The Army corporal who was killed filling his gas tank in southern New Jersey at a Turnpike plaza brought Detective Nussbaum to Wildwood, near the tip of the state. Three witnesses at the gas station had reported seeing the same two-tone blue Rambler speed away from the scene. One of them had a partial plate that came back to a former submarine captain who'd washed out because of a drinking problem. The man had sworn to get revenge on the junior officers who'd reported him.

It turned out that the submarine captain was in the filling station half an hour before the corporal and an attendant were gunned down. He burned rubber leaving the area, but only because he was late getting home. The Ghost had found the captain's plot in a local cemetery. He'd been dead a month before his father was killed.

The case of four naval officers who were shot in the same afternoon outside the submarine base in Groton, Connecticut, lured The Ghost to town for a week on his own dime and refusing overtime pay. He interviewed forty-seven people on the base and another fifteen witnesses. Most of them mentioned a loner, living in a mobile home on cinderblocks near the Rhode Island state line. The man, wearing camouflage clothes, had been seen loitering near the sub base for several weeks before the murders and was rumored to still live out there.

Nussbaum drove out to the man's house to interview him only to find him dead and rotting. A needle and syringe hung from the dead man's forearm. According to the local Medical Examiner, he'd been dead several months.

The Ghost had driven almost every road in New York State. In one year, he'd been reimbursed over five-hundred dollars just for tolls. His city-issued Chrysler was on its second engine. The old one was replaced at two-hundred-thousand miles. He'd been to Montauk, the furthest end of Long Island, in search of a woman who'd been arrested twice for shooting at military aircraft leaving from an Air Force base. He discovered that she was just another nutjob who was pissed off at all the noise.

He'd spent so much time at the state capital in Albany that the staff there had painted his name on a parking spot near the front entrance. Documents that required signatures and judicial assistance at the highest level were best handled in person, and Nussbaum had no qualms about driving for hours in pursuit of his goal.

Fortunately, most of the murders had taken place close to New York City, which entailed a minimal expense to investigate. However, the trail that led upstate was costly. The Ghost booked the only suite at a Holiday Inn in Liberty, New York, for ten days. The lead he was following was another dead end, but there was a nearby hot spring and spa where Frank Nussbaum could be found soaking his aching bones at the city's expense.

Detectives Cheng and Tang marched a suspect into interview room three, and then came over to Loviccio's desk. Kelly Tang picked up a folder and read the date. "1983? Are you guys into time travel?"

Loviccio snatched the folder out of her hand and put it back in the storage carton. "Hey, you wanna help? Pull up a chair. Nussbaum's notes are like sloggin' through *War and Peace*. Jesus H. Christ, the guy documented every crap he took, the weather, even the goddamn phase of the moon."

"Are you going to follow up on all the leads? Re-interview all those witnesses?" Peter Cheng kicked a box on the floor. "Ronnie, you don't have enough time left on the job for this task."

"No, but junior does." Loviccio pulled another folder out of the carton and handed it to Duke. "Ah, turn of the century. We're finally into modern times."

Duke took the file and laid it on the desk, off to one side. "Where's the file from upstate New York?"

"The nursing home in Liberty?" Spinning around in his chair, Loviccio reached into the box on the floor and pulled out one of the thinner packets. "Here. It's only a couple of pages. Alice Roman, thirty-nine, died on New Year's Eve."

"Lung cancer, right? Several of the witnesses said that the shooter was a cigarette smoker. Butts were found in the ashtray where he or she had been sitting in the restaurant before the major had been killed." Duke leaned over and read the file his partner had opened. "Flip the page over. It's got her home address."

Loviccio turned the paper over and read it out loud, "810 Sutter Avenue, apartment 6C, Brooklyn."

"Two blocks from Saint Oda's Church." Duke slapped his thigh. "I wonder if she was a parishioner."

Scanning the second and third pages of The Ghost's report, Loviccio found the line marked 'Religious Preference.' It was one of the common elements in all of Nussbaum's files. Why he wanted that data was unknown, but in this case it appeared to be a link that the ancient detective may have missed.

Duke tapped the word on the paper with his finger. "Catholic. Ronnie, I think we should start here."

His partner looked at the two Asian detectives and waved his hands in the air. "Step aside. I think the time travelers are ready to depart."

Reconstructing someone's life after they'd been dead more than thirty years had become a much simpler task in the age of the internet. Old documents had been converted to digital files, faded photos were enhanced and colorized. Searching by keyword had taken the place of the long drive. In less than an hour, Duke and Loviccio had Alice Roman's biography in photographic splendor, complete with footnotes.

Several experts who researched criminal behavior had proposed that murder was genetic, and the two detectives dug into Ms. Roman's past in an attempt to find some criminal history. No records of the woman's relatives could be found. Loviccio suggested that her name was an alias.

The four photos that they were able to find were black and white. A colorized image confirmed that she was Caucasian, probably of Germanic descent. The computer could be adjusted to bring her skin tone from pale to sunburn, which also altered its choice of genetics. It could also be manually adjusted to change the color of her eyes. However, every iteration had one thing in common: the color of Alice's shoulder-length, perfectly straight hair.

"Red. There it is, printed on her driver's license." Duke tapped the screen and nodded several times. "Jah protect. She had red hair." He rubbed his cornrows. "Just as bright as mine. But not as kinky."

Loviccio shrugged. "So? The witnesses said it was everything from dusty blonde to bright red. Just because she has red hair, you think she was the killer?" He slapped the desk. "Come on, Duke. Get off that shit. Lots of people have red hair. Even murderers and cops. Oh shit, Duke. You have red hair. Did you shoot Nussbaum's father?"

Duke grinned. "My hair color came from my father. No one on my mother's side ever had red hair. Maybe he's the killer? Oh, shit. My father is a serial killer." He snorted out a laugh. "I don't know, Ronnie. Could it be that the red hair is just a coincidence or is this a real clue?"

"I don't believe in coincidence, junior. And I don't believe in all that spooky shit you're tryin' to foist on this case." Loviccio closed the screen. "Stop thinkin' like Houdini and get back to the job. This is a homicide investigation, not a freakin' magic show."

Duke pinched the bridge of his nose and blew out a breath. "You're right. What's next?"

"What's next is a ride in the country. Let's see what Liberty, New York, looks like in June." Loviccio reached into his pocket and yanked out the car keys. "I'll even let you drive."

On a good day, it was a boring two-and-a-half hour drive from Brooklyn to Sullivan County. The heat of the city faded as they cruised up Route 17 with the windows down. Duke was tempted to stop for antique shopping as they got closer to the village of Liberty, but his partner wanted to get up and back before dark. His wife had been giving him grief about the overtime and proximity to his retirement.

The Good Faith Nursing home, on the north end of town, had been visited by The Ghost right at the beginning of the new millennium. He'd found the link between Alice Roman and her husband, who'd died in Vietnam, through her military insurance. But the link had been severed when she died. Frank never had the opportunity to interview Mrs. Roman, but knew she harbored ill will towards the military because of her young husband's death.

Nussbaum had read through thousands of reports where civilians had interacted with military personnel, and conflict had ensued. Alice Roman had thrown dishes at the two officers who informed her that her husband had died. She had made verbal threats as they left and continued to hurl household items as the two officers retreated to their car. Police were called when she punctured a tire on their car with a steak knife and attempted to stab the men as they changed the flat.

She held additional credibility as a suspect. Coming from Brooklyn and thus having familiarity with the military base, Alice Roman was no stranger to the location where the murders took place. However, nothing beyond that could be found to tie her to the slaughter. The technology didn't exist to produce the photos and documents the two detectives had gathered in just a few minutes. That morning, back when Nussbaum investigated Mrs. Roman, all he carried were thoughts in his head and the words he'd written in hundreds of notepads. The Ghost had no pictures to show the military widow and not enough evidence to pursue her further.

Duke parked in the semi-circle in front of the whitewashed building and handed Loviccio the keys. "I'm okay being the chauffer in one direction, but I'll let you have the wheel on the way back."

"You managed to stay at exactly the speed limit." Loviccio yawned. "Three hours and ten minutes? You weren't going for any land speed records."

"I didn't want to get a ticket on my first road trip as a detective."

Loviccio raised his eyebrows. "Right."

An orderly pushing a wheelchair stopped and pointed at their car. "You can't park there."

Loviccio pulled his gold badge from his coat pocket and held it up for the man to see. "VIP parking pass."

The nursing home had been dragged into the information age kicking and screaming. All of their records, other than the last ten years, were still on paper and stored in a basement room with no air conditioning. The facility's director assigned a woman from the housekeeping staff to assist the detectives in their search, but she disappeared shortly after unlocking the room.

"What are we looking for?"

Loviccio took a carton of files and propped open the door. "Patient records for late 1987 and employment records for the same time. I want to know who had contact with Alice Roman. If we're really lucky, someone is still alive and can remember the woman. Perhaps in her dying days, Mrs. Roman had a change of heart and confessed."

"Oh, so now you think she's the murderer?" Duke's sarcasm flowed without restraint.

"Right now, no one else has that honor. She's our only lead. We follow it and see if we can make a case. If we can, our job is done. If not, we go on to the next suspect. It's a long, boring process of elimination. But the reward is great."

"The reward?"

"Yeah, the paycheck that appears in your bank account every seven days. You were hoping for a certificate of merit or a handshake from the Mayor?" Loviccio laughed. "The job is all about closing cases. That's what you're paid to do. Work the case, do your job, and if you live long enough, enjoy your retirement."

"Full joy."

"What?"

"In Jamaica, we don't say 'enjoy' because it sounds too much like 'end joy.' So instead, we say 'full joy.' Take the full enjoyment." Duke smiled. "And I plan on living long enough that the last check I write will bounce."

Loviccio shook his head. "Well full joy your time in this dungeon and let's find what we're looking for and get the hell out of here."

It took over an hour, but Duke hit the patient files at the same time Loviccio located the personnel records for the year in question. Duke whipped Mrs. Roman's file from a box and laid it open in front of them. The daily logs began a bit less than four months prior to her death and covered the woman's last months in thirty-minute increments. They split the pile of records to go through them faster, but the task still took over an hour to complete.

Loviccio found the nurse's name in his stack and stood, holding the paper in his hand. "Nine pages, eighteen days, and all the nighttime entries are signed by the same nurse." He handed one of the sheets to his partner and whispered the name, "C. Carson."

Together, they shuffled through the personnel files for the year in question and found Cynthia Carson's payroll reports. The Ghost's sister had worked at the Good Faith Nursing Home for three weeks beginning in December 1986 and was terminated on New Year's Day, 1987. The reason for her dismissal was listed as, "Patient died."

Chapter Seventeen
Searching For Ghosts

The drive back to Brooklyn was under two hours. Twice, Loviccio hit the emergency lights when a New York State Trooper pulled out from concealment and gave chase. They parked the Chrysler in front of the precinct with the gas gauge sitting on empty and smoke coming from under the hood. For most of the ride, Duke had been on his phone trying to locate Nussbaum's sister. The only number they had was disconnected.

"Frank must have known his sister was working at that nursing home."

Duke nodded. "You, who doesn't believe in coincidences, how do you explain that?"

"I can't. That's why we need to find her."

Leaving the car unlocked in front of the 84th Precinct, the two detectives ran up the stairs to the squad and dropped their notepads on Duke's desk. Loviccio opened his department laptop and logged in to the NYPD's database. Three listings for Nussbaum came up in a search. Two of them were Frank's, and neither had a home phone number.

"Call H.R. and see if they have a number." Loviccio trotted over to The Ghost's desk and started pulling out drawers. "Maybe he has phone numbers taped inside."

Duke placed the call to Human Resources and wasted five minutes convincing the civilian on the other end of the line that he was really a detective with the 84th squad. It required the authorization of someone higher up the food chain to give out a cop's private telephone number. The officer who took over the call wanted Duke to submit a form in triplicate for the information. Duke told him to stuff the form up his ass.

Loviccio grabbed the phone on Nussbaum's desk and laced into the officer in a combination of street slang and Italian vulgarity. The officer at the other end told Loviccio, in Italian, to kiss *his* ass, and hung up the phone.

"Son of a bitch." Hitting the redial key, Loviccio stood with the receiver in his hand and stared at the ceiling. Realizing that honey was going to work better than vinegar, he lightened his tone and asked politely to speak to whoever was in charge. Continuing the pleasant dialog with the officer who was next to pickup the line, he waited patiently for the answer.

"I'm sorry, detective, but Frank Nussbaum doesn't have a number on file with the department. We do have one for his sister." The officer read the number. It was the one that had been disconnected.

Duke leaned over and whispered, "What about his address?"

Loviccio nodded and asked where The Ghost lived. For his patience and even tone, he got the information and thanked the officer before hanging up and continuing his Sicilian profanity.

"Jersey? The Ghost lives in Jersey?" Lieutenant Moscowitz had strolled over to see what the noise was about. "I thought he lived on Staten Island."

"The New Jersey address is his sister's house. I guess he's living with her. She said that she takes care of him. Must be round the clock." Loviccio held up a piece of paper he'd found taped to the inside of one of the drawers. "There's an address written here on Victory Boulevard near the golf course. I think that's Nussbaum's father's house. He must have used that address for a while before moving in with his sister."

"We need to check them both." Moscowitz turned toward Cheng and Tang. "You two head over to the address in Staten Island."

Loviccio handed Duke the car keys. "Your moms lives in Jersey. You can drive. I've had too many problems with Jersey cops."

Cynthia Carson's house was the smallest on the block of cookie cutter houses. From the massive oak trees and crumbling driveway, it obviously outdated the rest of the neighborhood by at least twenty years. The three-story suburban family boxes on either side of her looked down on the roof of her ranch house. It was the only house on the street with a one-car garage. Of course, the Cadillac in the driveway was a tiny nod to wealth, but it was a dozen model years older than the BMW on one side and the Porsche on the other.

A large Jewish star adorned the gate through the white picket fence that bordered the property. A much smaller plaque with a pistol and the words, "We Don't Call 911" was screwed to the front door. Duke looked for a button to push and, not finding one, rapped the door with his knuckles.

They could hear a television set through the door. The six o'clock news was starting with the familiar opening theme song for one of the local channels. Loviccio tried to look inside through a slit in the curtains but was unsuccessful. Duke waited a few seconds and then knocked again.

The door opened just wide enough for the barrel of a shotgun to fit through. Nussbaum shouted at the two detectives, "It's loaded and I've already shot someone today."

"Today, Frank?" Loviccio leaned into the crack and held his gold badge at eye level. "They let you shoot people on Thursday in Jersey for sport?"

The Ghost pulled the weapon into the house and opened the door. "What do you want, Ronnie?"

"We need to talk to your sister."

"She's not here."

"Bullshit." Loviccio took a step into the house. "Her car is here. What, is she out roller-skating? Is it time for her skydiving lesson? Maybe she'll drop down on the front lawn. We'll wait."

Cynthia's voice came from inside the house. "Let them in, Frank."

Without another word, the Ghost led the two detectives into his living room and muted the television. He stood the shotgun in the corner behind a hanging spider plant and plopped down into a huge corduroy beanbag chair. Duke did his best to make eye contact, but Nussbaum was more absorbed with the silent newscast and wouldn't look at him long enough.

Cynthia came into the room wearing pale blue sweats with a hoodie. She was barefoot, and the lights reflected off her gold glitter toenail polish.

"I didn't expect to see the two of you so soon." She sat in an armchair that had survived at least one century, maybe two, and folded her legs underneath.

"We've been on the road most of the day." Loviccio leaned forward on the couch they'd taken over. "Been up to Liberty, New York. Quaint little village in Sullivan County right off the highway. Plenty of opportunity for antiquing, but I wasn't in the mood."

"You went to the nursing home." Brushing an errant lock of hair from her forehead, the younger of the two Nussbaums shook her head. "You two schlepped all the way up to the Good Faith instead of just making a phone call?"

Duke pulled out his notepad and laid it on his knee. "Your number is disconnected."

Cynthia got up from her chair and walked out of the room. She returned with her cellphone and looked at Duke. "Call it."

Taking his phone from a jacket pocket, Duke punched in the number. The same recording he'd heard earlier about the line not being in service played loud enough for all to hear. Ending the call, he showed her the phone with number still on the screen.

"You reversed the last two digits." Cynthia laughed. "I guess the job is hiring dyslexics these days."

Loviccio stared at the floor and shook his head a couple of times. "Okay, forgetting about the phone call, tell us about your short stint as a nurse at the Good Faith Nursing Home."

"There's not much to tell. Knowing that I had just completed nursing school, Father Xavier asked me to go there to see about a dying parishioner."

"Do you remember her name?" Loviccio leaned closer.

"Alice Roman. She was a young woman, dying of lung cancer." Cynthia closed her eyes in thought. "I had seen her at Saint Oda's a couple of times. She always sat in the last row of pews. I never spoke to her until I saw her that first day at the Good Faith."

Duke corrected the phone number on his notepad and pointed his pen at Frank's sister. "Did you spend much time talking to her in the nursing home?"

"She was only coherent for short periods. I got there about four months after she'd been admitted. The doctors kept her pretty well doped up most of the time. Lung cancer is a rough way to go,

- 212 -

especially near the end when a patient spends every second trying to suck in enough air to stay alive."

Cynthia stood and walked over to The Ghost. "You have to remember. This was just a few months after our parents died. I was more than happy to get the hell out of the city and go someplace to calm myself. You saw what it did to Frank."

"We understand, but we'd like to get you two some closure, to put this case to rest." Duke closed his notepad and looked over at his partner. "Just one last question and then we'll be out of your way."

She raised her eyebrows. "What is it?"

"Did Alice Roman ever say anything to you about her past? Did she ever mention anything she might have regretted?"

Nussbaum's sister put her hands on her brother's shoulders and closed her eyes. "I've forgotten many things in my life, but the last words of Alice Roman will forever stick in my memory." Opening her eyes, Cynthia took a deep breath and spoke softly, pacing her words. "She said that there wasn't enough time to do all that had to be done to balance the scales. I asked her what scales she was trying to balance, and she replied that they were the scales of life and death."

Duke held his breath for a few seconds and then asked, "Did she say how she was going to balance them?"

"Yes." Cynthia looked at the two detectives and whispered, "She said many more would have to die."

The newscast had gone over to commercial, and The Ghost finally gave his attention to his visitors. "Hello, Ronnie. What are you doing here?"

"Evening, Frank. We're working your case." Loviccio smiled. "Me and the new guy."

Nussbaum squinted at Duke. "Ah, the pastry kid."

Duke held out his hand. "Duke Garvey."

"He won't shake it." Cynthia walked around in front of The Ghost. "He's afraid of disease."

Dropping his hand to his lap, Duke sat back in the couch. "We're looking into Alice Roman as a possible suspect in your father's murder."

"Alice Roman?" Nussbaum looked over at his sister. "Do you know her?"

"I did, Frank. A long time ago." With a pat on his shoulder, The Ghost's sister and caregiver nodded toward the door. "It's late and I need to fix him dinner."

The detectives stood and walked out of the living room. Loviccio stopped and said goodbye to The Ghost, but the newscast had resumed and the man's attention was once again locked on the screen. They let themselves out, but heard the deadbolt click as they walked away from the front door.

Chapter Eighteen
Mother Knows

The Lincoln Tunnel was backed up due to an accident and the two detectives sat in the traffic, trying to find a reason not to suspect Alice Roman as their serial killer. Loviccio wanted to accept the woman just to close the case. The facts were clear: her husband had been killed in Vietnam, she'd expressed anger at the military, and lastly she'd told a young Cynthia Nussbaum on her dying bed that she'd killed many and needed to complete the task.

"Without a real-time interview with the woman, all we have is hearsay." Duke rolled his window up and flipped on the air conditioner. "We don't know what Alice's state of mind was when she made the dying declaration. They pump cancer patients full of opiates near the end. She could have been hallucinating."

Loviccio hit the horn to awaken the driver in front of them. "We need to follow Alice Roman backwards from the nursing home and find out where she was and who she interacted with in her short life. Someone has got to be alive who knew her and can fill in the blanks."

"What about the priest?"

"Exactly." Swerving into the other lane, Loviccio pulled alongside the inattentive driver and flipped him his middle finger. "I knew we shoulda taken the bridge."

"Do you want to go see him now?"

Loviccio looked at the time on the dashboard clock. "Screw that shit. It's almost seven o'clock. My wife is going to kill me and overtime isn't happening. Nah, tomorrow's another day. There'll be bodies and criminals galore. Go home and get some rest. Throw a hump on that girlfriend of yours and you'll see much more clearly when the sun comes up in the morning."

Juliana's suitcase was still sitting in front of the closet when Duke walked into the apartment. He'd stopped at the florist on the corner and bought a dozen roses, hoping to repair the damage done last night. The bed was made, and the apartment was clean. Several large, filled trash bags were sitting in the kitchen.

The table was set with their everyday dishes along with the wineglasses they'd used last night. The oven was empty and nothing that looked as though it could be dinner was in the refrigerator. Duke figured that she was out picking up their meal and would arrive home momentarily.

He hung his sport jacket in the closet and changed out of his long pants and dress shirt into a pair of gym shorts and a t-shirt. Thinking it might be too casual for the situation, he switched the gym shorts for jeans and the t-shirt for a polo.

Duke was deciding on footwear when Juliana stomped into the apartment and dropped four large paper sacks from the supermarket on the counter.

"Something special for dinner?" He walked over and gave her a kiss on the cheek.

"It's for tomorrow night. My friend Barbara from the two-seven is coming over for dinner." Juliana began unpacking the bags. "It's her birthday, and she broke up with her boyfriend over the weekend. It's the least I can do."

"I see there are only two chairs." Duke put on a look of faux disappointment. "I'm not invited?"

"You were until your mother called."

"My mother called you?"

She nodded. "Yeah, apparently, she's been trying to reach you all day, but your line was busy each time. She called around five and said she must see you."

"She said 'must' not 'like?'"

"Yep. Used the word twice. It sounded important." Juliana noticed the roses sitting in the sink. "Oh, good. I was going to get flowers for the table."

Duke opened his mouth to tell her that they were an offering of peace, but her cheerful demeanor and bustling around the kitchen told him to close it and keep his comments to himself. He walked out on the balcony, sliding the door shut behind him to call his mother. It would be only his second call home to his mother since the promotion early last week.

Mother Garvey answered on the first ring. "Boy, you lose me number?"

"No, mother. I've been busy. We're working a major homicide case."

"You work nighttime?"

"No."

"You go to work before de rooster crow?"

"No, mother. Roll call is nine o'clock." Duke turned and mouthed the word 'wine' to Juliana. She nodded and tiptoed over to the wine rack, keeping eye contact with Duke the entire time.

"So, you got time in de mornin' an time in de evenin' an no time to be callin' you mother?"

Jamaican guilt rivaled the Jewish version for its pure logic. Duke nodded slowly. "You're right, as usual. My apologies."

"Apologies are for sinners. You a sinner, Duke? You done someting bad?"

Duke let out a long breath. "No. Apology retracted. Detective work is not the same as being a street cop, mother. We have set hours, but when a case must be solved, we work overtime to get it done."

A familiar sucking sound, followed by an exhale and a cough, told Duke that his mother was medicating prior to her bedtime. He waited while she took a second and third toke off her pipe before she continued her admonishment.

"What kind of food do de detective eat, Duke? Me sure it noting a true Rasta man would put in his mouth. Jah protect." She took another toke. "Me raise you natural. Don't say city make you eat food not fit for de goat."

"Mother, I'm eating well. My girlfriend is almost as good a cook as me."

"You still livin' wit dat lady cop?"

"Juliana."

"Julie what? Speak up, Duke. Don't be mumblin'."

"Juliana Tolkowski. We were partners when I was in the patrol division." Duke sighed. She did this on purpose every time he mentioned a girlfriend. "She wants to meet you."

"To arrest me?"

He shook his head and groaned. "No, mother. I told her about the ganja. She doesn't care as long as you don't smoke it when we're there."

"You bring her for dinner tomorrow night?"

"Not tomorrow. She's making dinner for her girlfriend."

"Me thought you say she your girlfriend. She a lesbian?"

Duke chuckled. "Jesus, mother. No, she's not a lesbian. It's a fellow cop. She's making her friend a birthday dinner."

"You know me birthday soon come."

"Eight months is not soon."

"Soon enough. Soon you not forget."

"Have I ever forgotten your birthday, mother?" Juliana came out onto the balcony with two wineglasses, a bottle of cold white wine from the refrigerator and the corkscrew. "Mother, it's been a long day and we're about to open a bottle of wine."

"Cool wata would be more refreshin'. Ya, mon."

"We'll each have a large glass of water when we're done. Promise."

"Promise? Make no promise, Duke. Tell no lies. Be truthful. Rastafari."

"Okay. No promises, but is it okay if we toast to your health?" Duke smiled. "Long life is never a promise."

"Ya, mon. And when you not too busy bein' de detective, me want to hear about how you burned you fingers."

Duke's heart skipped several beats. Burned his fingers? Nussbaum's bullet in the Plexiglas box? How did she know about that? "Mother, what are you talking about? What do you know?"

Mother Garvey laughed and took another long hit off the pipe, squeezing out her words as she struggled to hold it in. "Come have dinner. We talk then."

The line went dead.

Chapter Nineteen
Calling In A Favor

Loviccio was at his desk on Friday morning when Duke walked into the squad carrying a large bag of oranges. His neighbors had just returned from their six-month hiatus in Florida and had brought back a dozen bags of fruit, as they had been doing for several years. He dropped the bag on his desk and untied the knot that kept it closed.

"Here, fresh from the sunshine state." Duke put an orange on his partner's desk. "What's going on?"

"Zipper stopped by last night during the evening shift and left word that he may have some information on the Park Place murder." Loviccio picked up the orange and smelled it. "He's going to be at the Starbucks on Kings Highway and Flatbush at eleven. Wants to talk to you."

"Just me?"

"Yeah. Told Vargas that the 'Oreo' should come alone."

Duke shook his head. "There's a level of distrust amongst the young blacks of this city that I spent years fighting to overcome when I was a beat cop. Juliana, my former partner, is white and the black girls had no problem with her. It's all about respect. One of these days, skin color will be as unimportant as the color of your eyes."

"One of these days, criminals will wear signs identifying them." Loviccio rubbed his nearly bald scalp. "And one of these days, my hair will grow back. Don't sweat it, junior. I'll be nearby. You're not going in there alone."

Moe Jackson strolled over and nudged the bag of fruit. "New diet?"

Duke put his hands on his waist. "You think I need one?"

"As long as you eat normal food and don't go grazin' with the urban farmer, you won't have a weight problem." Jackson leaned closer to Duke. "You start shittin' radishes and bean sprouts, you've only got Ronnie to blame."

"Kiss my ass, you hairy beanpole." Loviccio yanked the switchblade from his pocket and snapped it open. Moe stepped back and put his hands in the air. "Relax, Jackson. This tiny blade wouldn't do more than scratch the surface of that bag of bones you call a body." He cut the orange in unequal quarters and stuffed the largest section into his mouth.

"Isn't that Jankowsky's knife?" Jackson grabbed two oranges out of the bag and stepped out of Loviccio's reach.

"Yeah. She left it with me. Didn't want to have any sharp objects around her sister." Wiping the blade clean on his pants, Loviccio pressed it closed and dropped the weapon into his top desk drawer.

Moe tossed one of the oranges to his partner just as Lieutenant Moscowitz came out of his office with a pink call sheet in his hand. "Two shot on our side of the Williamsburg Bridge. Looks like it went down in front of Peter Luger's Steakhouse."

"Robbery?" Jackson put his orange down on Duke's desk and checked the time. "It's nine-thirty in the morning. They don't open until noon."

"No. Looks like road rage gone bad." Moscowitz handed him the paper. "Three sector cars from Midtown chased them across the bridge. Shots were fired from the two vehicles they were chasing. They'll fill you in when you get there." He looked expectantly at Duke. "You two solve Nussbaum's murder?"

Loviccio nodded with a clown's smile on his face. "Yeah, that and the Jimmy Hoffa case. You want the fives?"

"Ronnie, you might think this is a fool's errand, but I got a phone call at eleven o'clock last night from the Chief of Ds." Walking over to Duke's desk, the lieutenant picked up Jackson's orange and flipped it in the air. He spun on his heel and caught it behind his back with one hand. "He's taken a personal interest in the case. Apparently, he, as well as several others with brass stars up their asses, owe Nussbaum favors."

"Favors?" Loviccio pushed his chair back from the desk. "Why didn't I see this shit coming?"

"Because you never look ahead. Jesus, Ronnie, all the years I've been boss here and you're the only detective I've ever met who can't see five seconds into the future." Hopping up onto Duke's desk, the lieutenant shoved the bag of oranges out of his way and pointed at Loviccio. "More than forty years on the job and you didn't think there would be people who owed him? Frank Nussbaum has more cops in his back pocket than the MTA has trains."

Duke grabbed the bag of oranges that was about to fall off his desk. "We may have a lead."

Turning toward him, Moscowitz raised his eyebrows. "I'm listening."

"Nussbaum's sister worked at a nursing home upstate where a woman, who had expressed hatred for the military, died of lung cancer." Reaching into his coat pocket, Duke pulled out his notepad. "Alice Roman went to the same church as Nussbaum's sister when the sister was a practicing Catholic. When the woman took ill, the priest there sent Nussbaum's sister, who was Cynthia Carson at the time, to look after one of his parishioners. Thus the connection."

"The connection?" Lieutenant Moscowitz shrugged. "To what?"

Loviccio raised his eyebrows and shrugged. "To something, but we don't know what just yet." He slapped his thigh. "Look, boss, it's the first lead on this case in more than thirty years. You want us to follow it or should we sit here and juggle oranges all day?"

"Follow it. Get some real answers." Moscowitz shoved his hands in his pockets and walked back to his office. "But just for today. Nussbaum's old man isn't the only corpse with an unknown killer. The bodies are backing up and I don't need two detectives sitting at desks when there are witnesses to be questioned."

Duke called after him, "What about the Chief?"

Stopping at the doorway, the lieutenant looked back at Duke and smiled. "I gave him your phone number."

Loviccio laughed.

"Yours, too, Ronnie." Moscowitz chuckled as he walked into his office and kicked the door closed.

Jackson and Albertini grabbed two citrus apiece and a portable radio from the rack as they headed out to the shooting call. Moe stopped in the hallway, leaned back in and held his cellphone to his ear.

"Ring, ring. Chief Benson calling. Is Ronnie there?"

Loviccio grabbed a chunk of peel and threw it at him. "I hope your oranges are rotten inside."

The two partners spent the next hour and a half writing DD5s and reviewing the files in Nussbaum's cartons that pertained to his trip to Liberty, New York. While Loviccio worked up a history on Cynthia Carson, her late husband, and her short career as a nurse, Duke dug through the internet looking for anything about Alice Roman that might be archived there. The data from their previous searches was a good start, but any additional information would require some serious investigation beyond the first page of search results.

He started with the murder that took place just prior to Nussbaum's father losing his life. A captain, leaving on a three-day pass, was shot at a fast-food restaurant on the Garden State Parkway in New Jersey. He was ten miles from Fort Dix and had stopped with his girlfriend to get burgers and fries.

The captain was shot at point-blank range by a killer in camos. His friend took a bullet in the face and lived long enough to describe the shooter as a female. She was certain because she was one of the witnesses that didn't see an Adam's apple and the killer's feet looked too small for a man. Of note, however, was the cigarette that drooped from the shooter's mouth and the tobacco stains on her teeth when she smiled before pulling the trigger.

Tang and Cheng rolled into the squad as the two detectives were wrapping up. Neither of them wanted fruit but were interested in where The Ghost's case was headed. Duke told them nowhere. Loviccio claimed they were onto something big.

It was time to head over to the diner and talk with Zipper. If nothing else, maybe they could close that case today. It wouldn't be The Ghost's, but it would be enough to keep the Chief of Detectives out of their hair.

Zipper was waiting at a table in the back, close to the restrooms, when Duke walked in the door. He'd seen the detective hike up the block alone and was smiling when Duke sat down across from him.

"I seen the dude."

"Which dude are you referring to?"

"The dude what came out of Marsden's building on Monday morning."

Duke folded his hands on the table. "I thought you said you were having sex with your girlfriend that morning."

"No, man. I was on the way to see her when the dude come out of the building."

"Okay. You saw him again?"

Zipper nodded. "Yeah. Last night. I was workin' and I seen him around seven. Maybe seven-thirty. He was standin' outside the bodega, talkin' on the phone. Man was pissed off somethin' fierce. Shoutin' and dancin' around like ants got a hold of his nuts."

The temptation was for Duke to take notes, to document every word Zipper was saying. But something told him to sit and let the man talk. He'd write it down later, but for now, Zipper's mouth was in overdrive.

"So, I goes outside with some trash, and he's got the phone on speaker." Zipper smiled and the collection of gold teeth blinded Duke.

"And?"

"And, I hears the voice on the other end of the line call him by name."

Duke yanked his notepad out of his pocket and flipped it open. Memory wasn't going to cut it. "Go on."

"It's gonna cost ya, Oreo." Zipper sat back in the booth and folded his hands behind his head. "Information at this level is pricy, my man."

"How much?"

"Five hundred." Smiling, Zipper leaned forward and whispered. "If'n your asshole partner was here, it'd be a grand. I'm cuttin' the brotha a favor."

Slowly, Duke pulled his wallet out of his back pocket and took out a fifty. "If your information leads to an arrest, there'll be another one. For five hundred dollars, you'd better be ready to walk the suspect into the squad, type out his confession, and drive him to Rikers."

"Damn, give a brotha a break. Fifty dollars? What the hell?"

Duke slid the bill back into his wallet.

"Whoa, just wait a minute, jamf." Zipper reached over and snatched the fifty out of Duke's hand. "I may be broke, but I ain't crazy." He stuffed the bill into his shirt pocket and leaned over closer to Duke. "Barry Mulholland is what the dude on the phone called the guy."

"Mulholland? You're certain?"

"Yeah, man. I ain't deaf." Reaching for a napkin, Zipper wiped his hands and dropped the spent sheet into his water glass. He stood and was about to leave when Duke grabbed his arm.

"Jamf?"

Zipper smiled. "Jive ass mother–"

Duke cut him off. "I got it."

"Damn, Oreo, don't you know your *Dirty Harry*?"

"That's your inspiration?"

"Do ya feel lucky, punk?" Zipper made a gun out of his fingers and pointed it at Duke. "Now go find faggoty-ass Barry so I can get that other Hamilton." Spinning away from their table, Zipper grabbed a donut from a patron at a nearby booth and jogged out the door.

Reaching into his jacket pocket, Duke pulled out the portable radio and keyed the mic button. "Did you get all that?"

Loviccio's voice came through loud enough to turn heads. "Jamf? That's some funny shit, Duke."

Chapter Twenty
Rich Folk With Attitudes

Over a hundred Barry Mulhollands came up in a database search from Motor Vehicles. Duke saved the results as a spreadsheet and then sorted them by height. Both witnesses had put their suspect at over six feet, which eliminated all but twenty-four men. Seven were deceased, dropping the group to seventeen. Loviccio looked at the list on Duke's computer screen and shook his head.

"More than half of these are under thirty. Zipper said the guy was much older."

"Okay. I'll cut them and the last guy on the list. He just reached seventy-five." Duke deleted the lines and turned around to look at his partner. "That leaves three."

Loviccio read the addresses. "One on the Upper East side, one lives in Roslyn, Long Island, and the last one is here in Brooklyn. Whaddya say we start with him?"

Barry Mulholland lived on the corner of Baltic and Clinton Street in Cobble Hill, some of the most expensive real estate in Brooklyn. They'd rung the doorbell several times with no answer and were sitting in their unmarked car, trying to guess what it would cost to live there.

The townhouse to Mulholland's right had a For Sale sign with a realtor's phone number in a window. Duke called the number and got a recorded message that asked for the listing number. He got out of the car, hiked up the steps to read the number off the sign, and was walking back to the car with the answer when a silver Mercedes convertible with the top down pulled up behind their Chrysler.

Duke shoved his phone in his pocket and strolled casually toward the sports car at the same time that Loviccio got out and nudged the door closed with his butt. He reached the tall, olive-skinned man first.

"Barry Mulholland?"

The man looked at Loviccio and frowned. "If you're a realtor, the answer is no. I'm not selling."

Loviccio produced his badge as Duke came up alongside him. "I'm Detective Loviccio from the 84th Detective Squad and this is my partner, Detective Garvey."

Duke leaned over and looked inside the open window of the Mercedes. "This is the new GTC Roadster?" He whistled out a long breath. "A hundred and fifty thousand dollars is the base price."

A puzzled look crossed Loviccio's face. "I don't want to know how you have that information at your fingertips, partner."

"I test drove one a couple of months ago." Duke sniffed the interior and smiled.

Mr. Mulholland cleared his throat. "Are you detectives investigating something, or is one of you going to make me an offer on my car?"

Stepping back, Duke noticed the wedding ring on the man's finger. "Your wife drive one of these, too?"

"No. My wife doesn't drive."

"You own a gun, Mr. Mulholland?" Hopping up onto the sidewalk, Loviccio moved closer to their suspect and raised his eyebrows."

"Why do you ask?" Mulholland's face was stone. His voice was as even as a carpenter's level.

Loviccio smiled and shook his head. "See, I would think a rich guy like you would understand how this works. We're the investigators, so we get to ask the questions. Your job is to supply the answers."

"Jamf." Duke grinned.

"Yes, we own a licensed pistol. It's loaded and in my nightstand." An indignant tone took over Mulholland's voice. "Before you ask any more questions, gentlemen, I should inform you that I'm a criminal defense attorney and unless you have a warrant, we're done talking."

"Something bothering you, Mr. Mulholland?" Releasing the last button on his sport jacket, Loviccio leaned against the Mercedes. "We're just having a friendly conversation out here on the street and admiring your car."

- 232 -

Duke nodded. "I'm still undecided between this and the new Porsche. Perhaps you could take a ride to the squad and fill me in on how it drives." He took several steps back from the vehicle and took a picture with his cellphone. The shot was wide enough to capture Barry Mulholland's aggravated face.

"Perhaps you can get your cheap fabric off my car before you scratch the finish and I have to file a complaint with the civilian review board." Mulholland took a step closer to Loviccio and then thought better of it. "I'm going inside now, gentlemen. If you have any further questions, please come back with a warrant."

Barry Mulholland pulled his key fob from his pocket and set the alarm in the expensive sports car. He walked up the steps, two at a time, and vanished behind the heavy wooden door to his townhouse.

Loviccio leaned back and folded his arms across his chest. "So, whaddya think?"

"I think he's uncouth, ill-mannered, and not enough of a suspect to convince a judge to issue a warrant."

"Uncouth?" Loviccio squinted at his partner. "Who taught you to talk like that?" Checking the time, he shrugged. "It's gonna take an hour to get to Roslyn or an hour to get to the Upper East Side."

"I dated a girl in Roslyn. There's a great Russian deli next door to the movie theater. You drive and I'll buy lunch." Duke turned and headed back to their car.

"Yo, Garvey." Loviccio stood on the sidewalk, swinging the keys in his hand. "There's an all-you-can-eat vegetarian buffet on East 72nd and the river. I'll buy and you drive. That way I won't get agita."

Lunch was both inexpensive and not what Duke was expecting. He ate two portions of meatballs in gravy that he swore were pure beef. Finding out that nothing on the buffet came from a land-living creature, he made a point of tasting as many of the entrees as his hunger would allow.

Shrimp, scallops, and several fish preparations were offered. Loviccio explained that true vegetarians would shun them, but the owners of the restaurant were aiming for a wider clientele. The place had a full bar and an extensive selection of craft beers. Four jumbo televisions were showing live sports from around the world. One smaller one had the stock market ticker running across the screen, with a muted analyst mouthing words in the background.

Duke added the restaurant to his list of favorites on his phone. Juliana had been complaining about his rich cooking of late. Perhaps this would be to her liking.

"You want to get a warrant and go back to the rich asshole's townhouse?"

Wiping his lips, Duke shook his head. "Only if the other two Barry Mulhollands don't pan out. This one seems too clean to be our suspect."

Loviccio nodded. "You've got good instincts for a rookie."

Finished with lunch, Loviccio paid and they drove the ten blocks to their next suspect. Parking across the street from the second Barry Mulholland's address on East 81st Street, the two detectives crossed to the doorman's stand. Together, they held out their badges and introduced themselves. Duke took the lead.

"We're looking for Barry Mulholland. Apartment 1218. Is he home?"

The doorman nodded. "Of course. Mr. Mulholland is a writer. He rarely goes out except for doctor's appointments. He's got a fellow living with him who acts as caregiver, shopper, and does all the housekeeping."

Loviccio shook his head. "Whaddya mean, 'He rarely goes out?' Why not?"

"He's a double amputee who never got over the loss of his legs. Climbing accident in northern New Hampshire. Got caught in a rockslide and the only way they could get him out was to cut his legs off right there on the side of the mountain. He wrote two books about mountain climbing before the accident. Now, he only writes romance novels. Some best sellers, written under a fake name, a woman's name."

Duke looked at his partner and shrugged. "Well, at least I found a new place to eat."

The tidal wave of commuters that poured into Manhattan that Friday morning had reversed course and cars were rushing from the city faster than lemmings over a cliff. Despite spending the day in the busiest city in the world, their occupants needed to get out and back to the city streets in time for the nightlife. Home to change and then back to party. This ebb and flow of automobiles was a living thing. Sometimes its pulse was fast, others seemed as though time stood still. Rush hour rarely meant speed.

Loviccio joined the long lines of traffic slipping into the Midtown Tunnel and rolled up the windows. In the eighteen minutes it took to crawl back to sunlight, both detectives double-checked their weapons. Barry Mulholland of Roslyn, Long Island, was their third and last suspect. They both wanted him to be the killer. Getting there at this time of day added stress to the drive. Duke was glad that his partner was driving.

They radioed central dispatch of their destination and asked for local backup just as the exit ramp off the Long Island Expressway came into view. The detectives were met several blocks from the Mulholland residence by three marked cars from the city of Roslyn, including a K-9 unit. A sergeant got out of one of the black and whites to bring the two detectives up to speed on the sole occupant of the residence.

"He has a concealed-carry firearm permit and several weapons in the house, according to our records. One of them is a thirty-eight caliber Beretta." The sergeant flipped to the second page. "Two arrests for disorderly conduct, but one case was thrown out when the complainant decided it wasn't worth the effort to pursue. The other got him a suspended sentence and a slap on the wrist."

A fourth police cruiser pulled up to the scene, and an officer got out with the search warrant for the Beretta. Duke had spelled it out to the assistant DA on their drive out to Roslyn.

The sergeant flipped to the last page of Barry Mulholland's life history. "Both of the arrests were at after-hours clubs that cater to the whips and chains crowd."

Loviccio smiled. "Third time's the charm."

The trick was to bring Mr. Mulholland to justice without seriously damaging him, which would work against the state in court, or killing him, which always left some unanswered questions. The officers on the scene decided to let Duke and Loviccio knock on the front door under the pretense of investigating an automobile accident. He was their suspect, despite the jurisdictional issues.

The pair were twenty-feet away from the house when a shot was fired from a second-floor window. The bullet went wide, missing Duke by several yards, and the two detectives took cover behind a large oak tree.

"Why is he shooting at us?"

Loviccio shrugged. "He doesn't like Jamaicans?"

"I haven't spoken a word. How would he know?"

"Maybe it's your hair. Have you ever thought about a hat?"

Duke peeked out around the tree in time to see a curtain flutter out the open window. Turning, he saw the Roslyn cops advance on the house from the sides. The sergeant shouted to them to stay where they were. Duke looked at his partner. "Nice fat tree. Let's follow the sergeant's advice."

Two of the marked cars rolled up in front of the house. An officer who jumped out of the unit closest to the house took cover behind the car and held up a megaphone, calling out to Barry Mulholland. He gave him the usual warning about the house being surrounded and that they would take him out of there one way or another. For the cop's efforts, Mr. Mulholland threw another shot out the window.

The next twenty seconds were choreographed tighter than a Broadway show. A cop stood up from behind one of the cars and fired a teargas round through the open window. From opposite sides of the house, uniformed officers in battle gear rushed the front door, blasting it open with a battering ram.

The K-9 officer released his dog, which bounded silently into the house. Moments later, screams could be heard, and the cops stormed inside. No additional shots were fired, and it wasn't a full minute before they led Barry Mulholland from the house in handcuffs. Duke took a picture of the prisoner with his cellphone so that Zipper could verify they'd captured the correct person.

An officer came out of the house with the .38 semi-automatic Beretta in an evidence bag. He handed it to Loviccio. "Looks as though at least four shots have been fired, assuming he started with one in the pipe."

"Two in Vincent Marsden and two in the dirt." Loviccio sighed. "At least he shoots better than the Mets hit fastballs."

Chapter Twenty-One
Dreams

The excitement of closing his first case as a detective still held Duke in its grip. He started typing the DD5 without asking his senior partner if it was okay. For his part, Loviccio was more than happy to get out of Brooklyn early on a Friday afternoon. It was the last few days of June and the air conditioning in the squad was still not functioning at full capacity. Both detectives had the weekend off.

Kelly Tang was making a keyboard dance at her desk on the other side of the squad, and Moe Jackson was banging the keys with two fingers right behind her. To an outsider, it sounded as though the secretarial orchestra at a major corporation was performing their last symphony before the weekend.

Finishing first, Duke sent his entry to the printer. He generated three copies. One, he placed on his partner's desk. A second copy went into the file he'd started in a deep desk drawer with hanging folders. The last copy he signed and was about to drop on the lieutenant's desk when the phone rang.

Detective Jackson tapped the flashing light and answered the call. He listened for a few moments and then told the caller to hang on. Turning toward Duke, he waved the phone in the air. "It's for you. A female caller and she's pissed."

Duke punched up the call on the phone in the lieutenant's office and took a seat in front of his boss's desk. "Detective Garvey."

"You were in my sector and didn't bother to call?"

"Julie, we were having lunch and then we had an interview to conduct."

"Ever since you got that gold badge, you seem to think I'm less important." Juliana coughed. "Three weeks as a detective and you're already looking down on the uniformed cops in your precinct."

"Who told you that?" Duke sat up straighter and kicked the door closed.

"Word gets around. Remember, I have friends who work in the six-two and the rest of the Brooklyn precincts."

"And you're having them spy on me?"

"No, but they've seen you on the street with that slob, Loviccio, and you're bossing uniformed cops around like they're minions under your control."

Duke held the phone away from his face and stared at it as though it were a bag of dog crap. "This is all about your father, isn't it?"

"Screw you, Garvey. Do you think every time I get upset it relates back to my dad? Are you that narrow-minded?" Juliana coughed again and Duke waited until she cleared her throat. "I knew when you got that promotion that it would swell your head."

"Come on, Julie. You know that's bullshit." Duke jammed the phone between his shoulder and left ear. "Nothing's changed except you. If I didn't know you better, I'd figure this was your way of breaking up with me."

"Breaking up with *you*?" Juliana laughed. "Garvey, I'm the best woman you ever slept with. You said so. Remember? Or was that just bullshit to get into my pants?"

"After three months together, you still think it's all about sex?" Looking up at the ceiling, Duke shook his head. "All those 'I love yous' and the tender touch…that was me trying to get laid? Wow, Julie, you really need to get your head out of your ass."

Juliana's coughing got worse, and Duke sat and listened to her hack for the better part of two minutes. Finally, realizing that it was almost six o'clock and his shift had been over for an hour, he interrupted her diatribe for the last time.

"You sound like you're about to cough up a lung. Why don't you find something to drink? Go and sit on the balcony and meditate for a while. I'll be home in an hour and we can figure all this out calmly."

"You'll be home in an hour to an empty house, Garvey."

Duke closed his eyes and pinched the bridge of his nose. "You're moving back with your roommate? What about the sublease agreement?"

"What do you care?"

"You're right." He nodded. "What the hell do I care? I thought we had something, but obviously I was wrong. You weren't kidding when you said that our relationship was an hourglass that was running out of sand."

"And now it's empty."

"You took all your stuff?"

Juliana's voice picked up a sarcastic edge. "Even the bottle of your favorite sex lotion. Go buy another one online for a hundred bucks."

Duke hoped his next question came with the right answer. "What about the new ceramic tea kettle?"

"I've got it and don't even think about asking for it back. You gave it to me as a gift, and I don't care that it's a priceless antique."

"It's a good thing you don't know my bank account password."

The sound of gulping came over the line. Juliana swallowed within a few decibels of a burp. "You're the one who screwed this up, Garvey. You've got no one to blame for our breakup but yourself. Do me a favor and lose my number."

"As you wish." With a sigh, Duke ended the call.

He sat there for a few minutes, cursing Juliana, her sick father, and Nussbaum's sister, who still had more to tell but was going to need some additional prodding. He'd been hoping that some part of his life would be stabilized. Having a girlfriend was the first step. The move from the street to the detective squad seemed under control. However, life had taught him that control was more of an albatross around his neck than an eagle carrying his dreams into the clouds.

Setting the problem of Juliana aside, Duke got up from the lieutenant's desk, careful to make sure everything was as his boss had left it. Walking down the stairs to the main lobby, he called his mother and asked if she was free for dinner.

"Ya, mon. Come an eat. Mother feed you good."

"Seven-thirty?"

"De food be ready de moment you walk in de door." She ended the call.

Duke paused in the lobby and walked over to Sergeant Williams. "Sarge, you're married, right?"

"Yeah, Duke. Why do you ask?"

"You understand your wife?"

"Whaddya mean?" Sergeant Williams leaned over the counter and pointed at Duke. "If you're askin' if I can respond properly to my wife's desires and commands, the answer is no. I've been fakin' it for twenty-seven years. Best advice I can give you is do the opposite of what you think is right. You're bound to hit the target once in a while."

"Was it the same way when you were dating?"

Williams twisted his mouth to one side. "Nah. Back then, I'd take her out to look at the stars in Central Park. We'd share a bottle of wine. I always made sure she had more than me." He laughed. "After a while, I not only couldn't understand what she was talkin' about, but neither could she."

Duke shook his head. "I tried that."

"And?"

"She can out-drink me."

It was late, and Duke was too hungry to ride the rails and deal with a bus. He summoned a rideshare car and sat back with his feet on the seat for the one-hour drive to his mother's house in the wooded hills of suburbia.

In the first year and a half after they'd moved from Jamaica to New York City, Duke's mother worked as a cook in an authentic Jamaican jerk shack on 128th Street. Next door to the tiny restaurant was a combination soda fountain and candy store that also sold lottery tickets. Mother Garvey saved ten dollars out of every paycheck for a swing at her dream.

When she won, after nearly a thousand dollars invested in Quick Pick tickets, Duke's mother shared a forty-four-million dollar Grand prize with two other ticket holders–a pair of female lawyers from Westchester. After taxes and accountant's fees, she cleared nine-million dollars. The front page of the *Daily News* with her and the other two women who had won was framed and hanging in her bathroom. Mother Garvey blew it a kiss every time she flushed the toilet.

One million dollars of her winnings went into a house with a kitchen large enough to butcher a steer and serve a nine-course dinner to royalty. Duke was certain his mother was going to enlarge the pantry so she could sleep in it. A total of five million dollars was used to build a new wing on the hospital in Negril where Duke was born. Most of it was for advanced medical equipment and construction costs, but a company in Dallas that outfitted helicopter ambulances agreed to sell one to Duke's mother at cost and ship it to Jamaica at their expense.

The house came with a three-car garage and circular driveway. Nothing besides trashcans were in the garage, and the only cars that had ever used the driveway made deliveries or picked up his mother if she needed to go somewhere. She'd never learned to drive in Jamaica and had no need to waste time gaining the skill in America.

To occupy her days, Duke's mother had purchased a demolition company and renamed it Rasta Blasta. She hired only Jamaican workers and set about the city, looking for old buildings that needed to be razed so that they could build new ones. It was her own way of reincarnating the earth. The woman took pleasure in blowing things up and insisted on taking sole responsibility for pushing the button that set off the series of charges.

Her greatest success to date was the demolition business. Opened during a lull in the construction industry, it had thrived from day one. The single team of four employees she'd listed on the company payroll had grown to five full-time teams of half a dozen highly trained demolition experts on each. The company's first year profit covered their offices, warehouse, and vehicles, leaving his mother with a six-figure income on top of her investments.

Duke had ridden around the city in a taxi with his mother many times to see the vacant lots once the debris had been cleared. She said it was urban rebirth and someday a new building would grow there. Featured several times on local television, the Jamaican mother of one took every opportunity to talk about her son, the cop, and how proud she was to be able to bring hope and joy to her fellow ex-pats. In Duke's eyes, she was an angel with dreadlocks and a sugar cane switch to keep her cherubs in line.

Mother Garvey was standing in the open front door with an uncapped bottle of Red Stripe beer as Duke stepped out of the rideshare car.

"Dat tie don't match de shirt." She handed him the beer and flipped the tie with one finger. "You get dress in de dark?"

Duke put the tie back inside his sport jacket. "I thought we had a deal."

"What deal?"

"I wouldn't give you cooking advice and you'd mind your comments about my wardrobe."

"Me say dat?" She cocked her head to one side.

"Not in so many words, but yes." Duke tilted the bottle and drained half the Jamaican beer with one gulp. He grimaced and wiped his mouth with his handkerchief. "It's warm."

"Me jus get home. De icebox lazy." She grabbed his hand. "Come. Tell me bout de new job."

Duke let his fingers wrap around her bony digits as she led him into the house and out to the back patio. A traditional steel drum cooker was pumping smoke from the vent in its lid. He inhaled and suburban New Jersey became the lush, tropical hills of Negril and he was ten years old.

"We gone eat outside. Me get de new bug zap an been keepin' count. Maybe kill all de mosquitoes in New Jersey. Ya, mon." Duke's mother ushered her son into a lounge chair and handed him a cloth napkin. "Me get de rice an peas from de kitchen. Make festival an callaloo, too."

"Mother, you know I don't eat callaloo. It's lawn clippings with hot sauce."

"Mon, you eat callaloo or you don get chicken." His mother smiled and poked Duke's cheek. "Cold beer in de cooler." She spun around and scurried into the kitchen through an open pair of French doors.

Duke was anxious to grill his mother about her knowledge of the hot Plexiglas cube, but time had taught him that food came first. Despite what most observers would think was a hastily prepared meal, considering the brief interval between Duke's phone call to his mother and his arrival at her house, Mother Garvey had been cooking since shortly after one o'clock that afternoon.

Of course, it was Friday, and she was basically stocking up for the weekend. The Yankees were playing, and she didn't know against which other team, nor did she care, but it was a religious experience that his mother shared with a dozen of her neighbors. She cooked the food, they brought the beer and whiskey, and together the group watched sports in her sixteen-seat home theater, sharing a bong.

Pacing himself, Duke ate two thighs and a drumstick before sitting back in his seat and rubbing his stomach.

"That was better than usual. Organic chicken?"

"No, mon. Same as always, an same as always, you be tryin' to bullshit you mother." She scooped the last of her rice and peas together with some chicken bits and coco bread, stuffing the load into her mouth. Pointing at Duke with her now empty fork, Mother Garvey winked. "But me love you for sayin'."

Duke leaned over and kissed her forehead.

"So. You burn de fingers?"

"Why do you ask?"

She smacked his arm with the fork. "Me know. Me you mother, Duke. Me know when de pain come. Me know when sadness push away gladness. You think Jah don't tell me when me boy hurt?"

Duke snorted out a short breath of disbelief. "I don't believe you. Someone on the squad told you what happened."

Another smack with the fork. "Boy, no one tell me noting. You hurt. Me feel it. Maybe not strong as you, but me know dat someting give you pain. All mother know dat. All mother know when dem children suffer. It deep pain in de heart. Jah protect. Rastafari."

He did his best not to argue, but she was asking for belief without logical proof. Duke took another piece of chicken from the platter between them and dipped it into the small bowl of jerk sauce. He was about to bite into it when his mother reached over and pulled his arm down.

Looking hard into his eyes, Duke's mother brought her voice down to a whisper. "Me have a dream. Dark dream. Dread. Me see de ghost wit evil green eyes." She shivered so violently that Duke dropped the chicken. Leaning close to her son, Mother Garvey's words were laced with more fear than he'd ever seen. "Me see death."

Chapter Twenty-Two
Comin' Back

Duke could hear himself breathing. He saw his mother sitting next to him and her mouth was moving, but no words were coming out. At least he didn't hear any of them. Her words, still ringing in his ears, had shaken all the scientific faith he'd relied on to make sense of the world. Duke stared at his mother without speaking long enough that she finally realized he'd slipped away.

"Do you hear me words, Duke?" She reached over and shook his elbow. "Mi tellin' you tings an you lookin' at de clouds."

Duke landed. "Tell me what you saw in your dream."

"Mi tell you already. But you not listen."

"Tell me again, mother. My mind was elsewhere." Duke sat up on the lounger and swung around to face her. "Please. I'm listening now."

"Tree nights now. Same dream. Mi see de man's face wit glow in de dark green eyes. Him scared. Him know death soon come. Mi can taste de fear." Mother Garvey grabbed Duke's hands. "Dem eyes be growin'. Gettin' big like de full moon. Closer an closer an den me wake."

"Tell me what else you remember from his face."

"Not much face, mon. Jus de eyes. Big an green like de light bulb in back of de balloon." His mother used her fingers to open her eyes as wide as possible. But she looked away from her son as she did it.

Duke saw her jaw tense just before she turned her face. "What about his nose? Did you see his nose, mother?"

She hesitated, folding her hands in her lap. Mother Garvey's head drooped, and she pulled in several deep breaths before reaching out and taking her son's hands in her own. "Ya, mon. Mi see de nose. Mi see de lips an de whole face of de man about to die. But de eyes so bright, it hard for me to see more."

Reaching into his shirt pocket, Duke pulled out his cellphone and found the picture of Major Nussbaum. "Was this the face you saw? Look hard, mother. Focus."

Leaning forward, his mother took the phone and stared at the image. Her breathing became rapid and shallow. Duke thought she was about to hyperventilate and grabbed the phone back from her.

"It was him, wasn't it, mother?"

"Ya, mon," she whispered. "How do you know?"

Duke laid the phone on the lounger and closed his eyes. "Because I saw him, too."

"Jah protect!" Falling back onto the seat, Mother Garvey wailed, holding her clasped hands in the air. "It de comin' back." Her head fell against her chest, bouncing and shaking as she sobbed.

"What's coming back?" Duke lifted her chin. "And how are you seeing the Major's face?"

"Who de Major?"

"A murder victim. The father of a detective who's spent his life trying to solve the homicide." Blowing out breaths as fast as he sucked them in, Duke shook his mother's shoulders. "How is this possible?"

Mother Garvey composed herself and stood, murmuring as she walked back and forth across her patio.

"Rasta man believe life never end. Die an soon, comin' back. Maybe woman comin' back as man. Maybe as woman again. De shell rot away but de spirit never die. De spirit find de new shell. Find de baby still in de womb an combine wit it to make new life. Rastafari."

"Reincarnation?" Duke shook his head vigorously. "As a Rasta, you believe in reincarnation?"

"As a Rasta man, you believe, too."

"Mother, I hate to use the word, but that's bullshit."

His mother walked over and slapped Duke's face. "Mi raise you better dan dat. You wan speak like rude boy, go back Negril an get gun. Be rude boy, but not me son."

"Are you finished?" Duke rubbed his cheek. "That might have worked twenty years ago, but it's an empty threat now. Your little boy is now a man, a police detective, and someone who deals in facts. Reincarnation is not a fact, it's a religious theory, a part of your Jamaican heritage that you've accepted with the same blind faith that you believe there is an all-mighty named Jah."

Closing her eyes, Mother Garvey mumbled a soft prayer, holding her son's hands. When she was finished, she looked at Duke with tears running down her cheeks. "Comin' back is as real as you standin' in front of me. But dat not de issue here. No, mon." She squeezed his hands tighter. "When me see dem green eyes, dat dead man's face, dat a dream. Jah showin' me someting." Pausing, she took a deep breath and let it out slowly before finishing her thought. "But when you see, it a memory."

"How is it a memory? I never shot anyone with green eyes." Taking several steps back from his mother, Duke searched for a reason for this sudden madness. "Are you stoned? Did you smoke too much, mother?"

"How me smoke too much?" She laughed. "That not possible."

He walked back over to his lounger and sat down. "We're on the verge of solving a cold case that's more than thirty years old. We've got a suspect with opportunity and motive. And I have no idea what crazy ideas you're trying to force into my head." Duke folded his arms across his chest. "What are you saying, mother?"

"Mi sayin' you been there when de man shot. Maybe witness."

Duke grinned. "Nice try. Not witness. You're saying I, in some kind of weird previous life, shot the man with the green eyes. That's it, right? That's what you're trying to tell me?"

Mother Garvey was silent for nearly a minute. She opened and closed her eyes several times and Duke could hear what sounded like a prayer as she mumbled in Patois. Reaching down, his mother pulled a cold Red Stripe from the cooler between them and twisted off the top. Without taking a breath, she chugged the brew and carefully placed the empty bottle on the patio.

"Mon, when me little girl, me father tell story of great farmer. Him say, farmer turn desert into cornfield, grow dem crops wit no wata, no rain. Him say, people call farmer de true servant of Jah. Rasta mon, dig de Earth and make someting new. But farmer tell people it not him, it de Earth. Him say de Earth be comin' back. Life never die. It always be comin' back."

"That's crops and good farming techniques." Duke shrugged. "It's not the same with human beings."

Mother Garvey picked up the empty beer bottle and poked him in the stomach. "No, mon. It de same ting. You made two pieces. One half flesh, de odder half spirit. Flesh rot, spirit go on forever."

Duke held his hands up. "Okay, fine. I'll buy that part. But to say that I was a killer? Where do you get that?"

"You see de eyes?"

"Yes."

She squinted at him. "You see more den dat?"

Duke grabbed a beer and twisted it open. "You tell me."

"Me got noting to tell."

"Really?"

"Ya, mon." His mother cocked her head to one side. "Truthful."

Taking a long pull from the beer, Duke sat the bottle on the ground and opened the top button on his shirt. He told his mother about the encounter with The Ghost, the cracked leg of Jesus, and then pulled the Plexiglas cube with the fatal bullet out of his pocket.

"I picked it up, and it was on fire. The tips of my fingers looked like I'd grabbed a hot potato and held it too long." Duke handed it to her. "Nothing now, right? Same as it was when Detective Jankowsky held it, five seconds after me. I'm running out of explanations, mother."

Throughout his entire recitation, Mother Garvey had stared at him with the empty bottle going back and forth from her left hand to her right. When he was done, she dropped the bottle into the cooler and reached for him.

"You come from two worlds. One pure, the other soiled. The Rasta in your blood fight wit de dirt on de white man's soul. Some dat dirt rub off on me when him rape me. At de moment him push life into me body, de spirit of one gone be comin' back. Dat spirit meet de two worlds an know dat one be trouble de odder be joy. It make de choice an little David Garvey born wit de smile stead de frown."

"And the spirit? Where was it before?" Duke knew the answer before she spoke it, but wanted to hear it from his mother's mouth.

"Dat spirit comin' back from de dark place. Dat spirit be in de soiled body before it find you." She chuckled. "Dat spirit find out der is mother who not gonna let it go dark place dis time."

Duke jumped up from the lounger and looked down at his mother. "You're saying I was a serial killer in a previous life and one of my victims was Frank Nussbaum's father?"

"No, mon. Me sayin' he was de last victim of de soul dat now find good instead of evil when you born. Old soul live wit Satan. New one live wit Jah. Evil turn to good because de baby reject de old ways come before."

Chapter Twenty-Three
Once A Killer

Duke spent most of the one-hour ride back to his apartment trying to convince himself that his mother was wrong. In thirty-three years, his mother had never lied to him about anything. She'd never shaded the truth, cut it in half, or kept something hidden from her son. She'd also never been wrong about anything. It was as though the woman was incapable of telling a lie or making a mistake.

According to his mother, she'd only slipped once, but the error had produced positive results. She often thanked Jah for David Garvey, despite the horror that created his life. It wasn't her fault or her weakness that led to rape. The tourist was drunk, she was high, the crowd was dancing closer and closer. It was sex in the heat of the moment, willing or not.

If she was right and reincarnation really happened, then Duke wondered if she was correct that he was indeed the murderer. Taking it step-by-step from that point, he further considered what the legal ramifications would be and even if it could be proven in a court of law.

The rideshare car was two blocks from his apartment when the worst of the situation hit.

What if the job finds out? The thought slammed into his head. What would his partner say? Would the Chief of Ds ask for his badge? Would the DA seek to indict him? He got out of the car and walked away without closing the door. The driver called after him, but Duke was too deep in the roiling ocean of thought to hear his shouts.

He couldn't tell anyone on the job. That would be the kiss of death and reincarnation or not, he wasn't going to get another shot at a gold badge. The department would put him in front of a team of headshrinkers that would recommend pulling his badge and weapon. He wouldn't even be fit for desk duty. Even the Sanitation department would hesitate before giving him a job.

Duke punched the elevator button several times, begging it to get to the lobby. Despite his initial reservations, Duke realized that he had to tell someone. This was too big to keep to himself without going nuts.

As much as it pained him, he knew there was only person he could trust. Stepping into the elevator, Duke brought up Juliana in his Contacts and tapped her telephone number.

It took ten minutes of begging, apologizing, and promises, but an hour later, his former partner, girlfriend, and lover was sitting on his balcony with a glass of white wine in her hand. Duke gave her chapter and verse, covering everything from the first glowing encounter with Nussbaum to his mother's proclamation.

Juliana gulped her wine and put the empty glass down on the table as if it were a hand grenade with a loose pin. "Tell me you don't believe her."

"I wish I could." Duke refilled her glass. "My mother's never lied to me. She's a Rastafarian. I don't know if you understand what that means to the true believer. My mother believes that an untruth out of her mouth will bring instant death. Jah will toss a lightning bolt out of the sky."

"My mother tossed me out of the house when I was thirteen. That was after trying to sell me to the gypsies." Juliana drained her second glass and reached for the bottle. "You can't tell this to anyone."

"No kidding."

"I'm serious. They have padded rooms for people who tell stories like that and swear they're true."

Duke held up his glass and waited for her to fill it. "I'm not going to tell anyone yet, but here's the question."

"What?"

"Can I be held liable for the actions of a previous life?"

Juliana shook her head and stared at him in amazement. "Are you kidding? Jesus, Garvey, only you would ask a question as dumb as that. You're worried about the legal aspect of reincarnation? That's the dumbest shit I've ever heard."

"Why is it dumb?"

"Well, first of all, nobody besides the Hare Krishna people believe that shit for real. You plan on getting an orange robe and finger bells?"

Duke curled his lips. "Of course not."

"Everyone I know. Everyone you know, except for your crazy mother, believes that death is the end. When you die, your life is over and all your sins go with it. When my brother was killed, he had four grand outstanding on his credit card. It was wiped clean. Too bad the mortgage was in my sister-in-law's name. She coulda owned the house free and clear." Juliana filled his glass and put the bottle on the floor between them. "Even if we were to assume that reincarnation was possible, the law cuts you free from previous transgressions."

"I never heard that." Duke paused while an ambulance screamed by below them. "So, legally, even if I was Alice Roman in a previous life, I couldn't be prosecuted for her crimes in this one."

"No, but the department shrink would be looking to carve out pieces of your brain and send them off for research." Juliana closed her eyes for a moment. "All this time we've known each other and you had this crazy shit bouncing around in your head. How did I not see this?"

"It's never been an issue before." Duke brought the glass up to his lips and stopped. "What your saying is, legal or not, the job wouldn't keep me around for very long."

"They'd drop you like a bad habit. Haul your ass right into the rubber room. If you have half a brain still working in that thick skull of yours, say nothing. You told me that Alice Roman is the most likely suspect for the killings. Write it up that way and close the damn case. Your partner will be happy. The job will be satisfied. And you'll get a couple of attaboys added to your jacket."

Duke's cellphone vibrated in his pocket, and he pulled it out to check the call. It was a number he didn't recognize, although it was local. He let it go to voicemail and waited a few seconds for a message. None was recorded, but it gave him the time to mull over her solution.

"I can do that." He nodded, sure of his decision. "Yes, close the case. That's what the job requires. Make The Ghost happy, put a tick mark in the win column for the squad."

"There you go." Juliana punched him lightly in the shoulder.

"But what about me?"

"What about you? You've covered your ass. You want a commendation from the Chief of Ds? What's the problem, Garvey?"

Duke took a sip of wine and put the glass down on the table. "How about this scenario? Let's say that just for argument's sake you accept that reincarnation is possible. In your previous life, you were Adolph Hitler. How do you feel about that, Julie? Got some Jewish friends you'd like to tell about it?" He reached out and grabbed her hands. "I'm a cop. How do I live knowing that I was once a serial killer?"

"Fine. I'll buy into your reincarnation bullshit for the sake of getting some sense into your head. That was a past life." Juliana frowned. "Maybe I was Mother Teresa in my last life. This one is certainly a step down. What does it get me either way? Maybe you were Jesus?"

"I'm being serious. If my mother is correct, then it's possible I could become a serial killer as well."

Juliana shook her head. "Man, you're really taking this to extremes. You're afraid of turning into a serial killer? I don't think so. You're already thirty-three years old. Don't most serial killers start in their teens?" She winked at him. "Come on, Garvey, this is all bullshit anyhow. No one knows what they were before, that's if there even is a before. You're making yourself nuts over some religious crap that you didn't believe yesterday."

"Look, this might sound like bullshit to you, but it's a huge part of my mother's religion. I don't follow all the Rastafarian ways, and I've never given much thought to reincarnation, but I have to consider the source." Duke finished his glass of wine and stood. "I need to go for a walk. Wanna come?"

She looked up at him and grinned. Getting up from her chair, Juliana took his hand. "Do you really think I came over here to walk? Let's go into the bedroom and have a good old-fashioned exorcism. Maybe that will turn your head around."

It was just after midnight when Juliana tugged the door to Duke's apartment closed and headed toward the elevator. She'd left a Post-it note on the bathroom mirror to call her later that evening after her tour. Duke had the day off and rolled over, fluffing his pillow in a futile effort to get some sleep. Reaching over, he felt the hollow in her side of the mattress and yanked the covers off the bed with a sigh. Five minutes later he was in the shower and ten after that, he was on the street. It was 1:30 in the morning.

Several years before he moved to the townhouse and once the city had completed the neighborhood renovations, he'd mapped out a twelve mile, round-trip route on the FDR Drive that ran alongside the East River. The city had constructed a tree-lined path with a crushed cinder running lane for the serious joggers. Duke ran the trail in the evenings when he was working day shift and at dawn when he was assigned to nights.

He was surprised by the heavy foot traffic in the middle of the night. One group of runners wearing identical orange tank tops was large enough to clear the entire pathway. Duke chuckled as the tiny lights in their sneakers blinked as they passed him, scattering random dots of red on the ground.

At the park, across from his favorite Spanish restaurant, Duke dropped down onto a bench with his arms stretched out on the back. Behind him, the insomniac city was far enough away that the occasional siren or backup alarm didn't interfere with his thinking.

If I was a beat cop, we'd go out drinking and blame this all on the beer. I guess detectives don't do that. Christ, what would Loviccio say? Duke snorted. *Probably blame it on my diet.*

Bending over, Duke retied the laces on his sneakers. *How can my mother really think I was a serial killer? If anyone in her past was a criminal, it was the jerkoff that raped her. My father? Huh. What a joke. Maybe that's whose green eyes we're seeing.*

A young jogger stumbled in front of him, and Duke got up to help him. The man regained his balance and sped away without looking back.

And this whole reincarnation crap. Where the hell did that come from? She never spoke about coming back from the dead before. Christ, all that pot she's smoking has truly rotted her brain. Maybe it's the demolition work? She's out there, sucking in all the dust and crap from those old buildings. Who knows what kind of weird pollutants are blown into the air each time? Look what happened with all those people who breathed in dust from the Trade Center Towers. She needs to see a doctor.

Duke did a few stretches and checked his watch. It was 1:52 and a light breeze was coming off the East River. A buddy of his from a Midtown South precinct had arranged a softball game for nine. He pushed off the concrete bench and headed for home, no closer to a resolution than he'd been an hour ago. However, Duke was absolutely certain of one thing: Alice Roman wasn't going to cost him his gold badge...dead or reincarnated.

Chapter Twenty-Four
Deathbed Confessions

The softball game got underway twenty minutes late. So many cops showed up to play that they were able to break the group in half and take over a nearby field. Duke, who played second base, was warming up when a cop ran out to him, holding Duke's cellphone in his hand.

"I heard it ringing in your gym bag. This is the third call."

The name on the screen was Ronnie, his partner. Duke dropped his mitt on the grass and answered the call.

"We need a catcher if you're not doing anything."

"A what? Never mind. Where are you?"

"Central Park, second base."

"Screw that shit. Get over to the squad."

Duke held the phone at arm's length and scrunched his face. He tapped the speaker button on. "I'm off this weekend."

"Not anymore. I'm logging you in right now. Nussbaum's sister called, and she's coming down here. She'll be here before noon. Apparently, something's bothering her and she didn't want to talk about it where The Ghost could hear."

"What about the priest? We still need to talk to him."

"We'll see what Cindy has to say first and then decide if he can add anything to it. But I need you here. She doesn't seem comfortable with me."

"No kidding." Sighing, Duke picked up his mitt. "I'll be there in an hour."

"The taxis are on strike?"

Duke pursed his lips. "Fine. Half an hour, but I'm wearing cleats."

"I don't care if you're wearing a dress." Loviccio ended the call.

Thirty-five minutes later, Duke clomped into the 84th Detective Squad and tossed his baseball glove onto his desk. Loviccio was on the phone and motioned to his partner to join in the call.

Father Xavier was on the other end of the line. Loviccio had called him about stopping by later that afternoon.

"Sure, I'll be here, but I don't know what else I can tell you."

"We're trying to collect some additional background information on Alice Roman." Loviccio spun his notepad around so that Duke could read his notes on the conversation so far.

"As best as I can remember, she was a conflicted woman. She often came for confession several times a month. Something was troubling her that she never managed to reveal." The priest paused for a moment. "I spent some time thinking about the two women after our last conversation. My memory isn't what it was, but sometimes details pop into my thoughts when I'm alone."

"Did she have any friends?" Tapping a pen on the side of his head, Loviccio looked over at Duke and shrugged.

"No. As I recall, she was always alone. Never came to Mass with anyone and rarely talked to any of the other parishioners."

Loviccio laid the pen on his desk. "Why'd you send Mrs. Carson up to see after her then?"

"It was the Christian thing to do."

Duke joined in. "Hello, Father. It's Detective Garvey."

"Good morning, son."

"Did Mrs. Carson ask you to send her, or was it your choice alone?"

The priest paused before answering. "I honestly don't remember. Cynthia had just finished nursing school and I guess I was just concerned."

"You're sure about that, Father?" Duke hopped up on his desk.

"It was a long time ago. But I can't imagine any reason for her to volunteer. Like I said, Alice didn't have any friends that I knew of. I must have thought it would be a good idea."

Loviccio folded his notepad closed. "Thanks, Father. If we need anything more, we'll be in touch." He hung up the phone and looked at Duke. "Well, if nothing else, he verifies Cindy's story."

"You don't believe her?"

"Not completely, but we'll know for sure in less than an hour." Loviccio looked down at Duke's shoes. "What happened to your cleats, and where'd you get a sport jacket if you were playing softball?"

"I stopped at the apartment and changed."

"And you got here in half an hour? What'd you do, find a taxi with wings? And what's with the glove?"

Duke shook his head. "No. Rideshare. For what the city's paying us, I figured I can splurge. And the glove?" He shrugged. "It helps me remember that I'm supposed to be somewhere else besides here right now."

Cynthia Carson walked into the squad an hour later. She was wearing large dark sunglasses and the same floppy hat that Duke had seen when she drove away in the Cadillac. Sitting down next to his desk and removing the hat and glasses, it was obvious from the streaks in her mascara that she had been crying.

Duke reached into his top desk drawer and took out a box of tissues. He handed it to her and looked over at his partner. "I'm going to take Mrs. Carson into interview room one where we can have some privacy."

"I'm going to make a pot of tea." Loviccio turned to Cynthia. "You want anything?"

"Just a bottle of water." She sniffed. "And I'll take these tissues with me."

With his partner and Nussbaum's sister seated comfortably in the interview room, Loviccio went into the attached observation area and rolled up the blinds over the one-way window. He tapped the speaker button so he could hear what they were saying. Pulling a metal folding chair over, the senior detective adjusted the volume and sat down.

The first couple of minutes were spent with Duke calming the distraught woman. Between sobs and blowing her nose, she revealed little other than something was deeply bothering her. Finally, Duke pulled the box of tissues out of the way and took the woman's hands.

"Whatever it is, you've got to tell someone. Keeping a secret bottled up inside you is the start of ulcers, losing sleep, and eventually, you'll go crazy as you try to remember who you've told and who's still in the dark."

Cynthia composed herself and sat up straighter in her chair. "I've only told Father Xavier, and that was a long time ago."

Looking at the one-way mirror, Duke knew his partner was watching and listening on the other side. He was certain that Loviccio was cursing the priest and, at that moment, understood why his mother had left the Catholic Church in favor of Rastafarian ways. Did the priest just lie to them on the phone or was his memory at fault?

"What did you tell Father Xavier that's troubling you now?" Duke squeezed her hands lightly. "Whatever it was, you need to tell me and get it off your chest."

"You've got to promise me you won't tell Frank." She stared hard into the young detective's eyes. "It'd kill him."

Duke shook his head. "We don't want that."

"I'm not kidding." Sitting back hard in the metal chair, Nussbaum's sister pleaded, "What I'm going to tell you goes no further than this room or I'm getting up and walking out right now."

"You've got my word."

She pointed toward the one-way mirror. "What about Ronnie? Is he sitting on the other side of that window?"

"No. You heard him. He went out to make a pot of tea and, hopefully, one of coffee. It's Saturday, and no one makes a fresh pot. As lazy as he is, he probably went down to Starbucks on the corner." Duke unfolded his notepad and clicked his pen. "It's just you and me."

"Okay." She sniffed and said it again. "Okay. When she was in church, something about Alice Roman bothered me. She was too quiet, too much a loner. Always sat in the last pew, away from everyone else. I've seen the type before. They shun human contact, but eventually, they break down and start looking for friends. No one can live alone forever. No one can hide from the outside world."

"No argument there." Duke smiled. "Man and woman are gregarious creatures."

On the other side of the glass, Loviccio frowned. "Gregarious? Where the hell do you learn this shit, Garvey?"

Cynthia continued, much more relaxed than before. "The Saint Oda's community was a small, tight group of neighbors. Not many strangers went to our church, at least not on a regular basis. So when Alice stopped coming to Mass, I asked Father Xavier to find out why. I was concerned that something had happened, but I didn't know her address. He sent some kid over to her house and was told by a neighbor that Alice had taken ill and was in a nursing home upstate. Knowing that she had no friends, I volunteered to go check on her."

"Why?"

"Mostly because I was new to the nursing profession and wanted to try out my skills. But also because she was a woman with secrets that were eating her alive. I could see it in the way she kept losing weight and how she was nervous all the time. Once in a while, we would eat lunch in the same diner around the corner from the church after Mass. Always in separate booths or opposite ends of the counter. She never acknowledged me. Never came over to sit closer."

Nussbaum's sister shook her head. "Plus, the woman was chain-smoking unfiltered Camels. I couldn't stand to be near her anyway, but I hoped that if she sat down next to me, I could talk her into giving them up."

"Not even to nod her head or say hello?"

Cynthia shook her head. "Who does that other than someone with a weight on their shoulders? When Father Xavier told the congregation that Alice Roman was ill, possibly dying, I saw it as a chance to find out what was bothering her and jumped at the chance to nurse someone."

"So you relocated to Liberty and got a job at the Good Faith Nursing Home." Loviccio nodded. "Downright charitable."

Ignoring his remark, Cynthia continued. "I was assigned to her care the day I got there. I walked into Alice's room with a cup of hot coffee from a Starbucks on Route 17. It was way better than the swill they brewed in the nursing home's kitchen and I was certain it would show her I was a friend."

Duke scribbled some notes and laid the pen on the table. "Did it work?"

She smiled. "Yeah. Almost immediately. It was like she'd been waiting for someone to unload on for years."

Picking up his pen, Duke looked at the woman expectantly. "Go on, please."

"Well, you know she lost her husband in Vietnam, right?"

Duke nodded.

"He volunteered against her wishes and she was pissed about it. When she got the news about his death, she originally blamed him, but quickly morphed her hatred toward the military. For the few short weeks I knew her before the cancer took her down, all she did was bitch about the Army and how all the officers should fight and send the soldiers home."

"A common complaint." Flipping to a clean page, Duke cocked his head. "Did she say if she ever did anything about her anger?"

Cynthia paused, and Duke could see the tears well in the corner of her eyes. She wiped them away with one of the used tissues in her hand and looked down at the floor for several moments. Slowly, she brought her face up and looked at him.

"She said she'd killed a bunch of soldiers to get back at the military for taking away her husband."

Duke leaned closer to her. "Did she give you any details? Dates? Places?" He was hoping for a miracle.

"No. This was all during the last few days before she died. Sometimes she could talk for hours. But others, when the drugs kicked in, she could only speak for a few minutes at a time before nodding off."

"How do you know she had anything to do with your father?" Placing his hand on her shoulder, Duke lowered his voice. "I understand how hard this must be for you."

The tears flowed, and Nussbaum's sister did nothing to stop them. "When she said she'd shot the soldiers, something inside me knew that one of them was my father. I knew she lived in Brooklyn not far from Saint Oda's and ate at the same diner my father went to with his girlfriend."

"You knew about the girlfriend?"

"Everyone did. It was common knowledge. My mother did her best to ignore it, to put up with my father's infidelity. She figured it was the Army way. Frank was the only one who denied the woman's existence. When she was murdered, along with my father, my mother saw it as closure. Her suicide was the last act of a scorned woman."

"Why didn't you say anything all these years? Why let your brother spend his life looking for the killer that you thought you'd found?" Shoving his chair back from the table, Duke leaned closer to Nussbaum's sister. "Why make Frank suffer?"

Cynthia Carson got up from the table and walked over to the one-way mirror. She turned and looked at Duke, then spun around and pointed at the glass. "Because my father molested me until I was twelve years old. When he was murdered, I felt redeemed. He got what he deserved. As far as I was concerned, my brother could spend the rest of his life trying to solve the crime. I wasn't going to help him convict the woman who put that scumbag in the ground."

Chapter Twenty-Five
Up On The Roof

Loviccio was gone from the squad when Duke walked Cynthia downstairs to her car. He hoped his partner wasn't headed to Saint Oda's to lean on Father Xavier. As far as the junior detective could tell, they had all the evidence they needed to close this case. Upsetting a Catholic priest wouldn't help. The statement The Ghost's sister had given would satisfy the District Attorney and please their boss. Keeping the information from Frank Nussbaum would be a different story.

Vargas and Collins were arguing over a call in last night's Mets loss when Duke returned to the squad. Collins looked over at him and said that Loviccio was up on the roof. Fearing that his partner was about to jump, Duke turned and ran up the four flights of stairs to find him.

Momentarily blinded by the midday sun, he didn't see Loviccio at first and spun around wildly, looking for what he thought was his distraught partner on the verge of suicide. Why the senior detective would want to kill himself never entered Duke's mind, but he couldn't come up with a better reason for the man to be on the roof.

"Over here." Loviccio called to the junior detective, waving as he sat on a rusted lawn chair.

Shielding his eyes, Duke saw him and the ring of ratty web chairs. "What are you doing?"

Loviccio shrugged. "Working on my tan. Come on over. There's plenty of seating available. Reserved this morning for the detectives of the 84th Squad."

Duke walked over and took what appeared to be the sturdiest and cleanest of the chairs. "Too bad there's no beverage service up here."

"You'd be surprised, junior." Loviccio reached under his chair and tugged the remaining four cans of a six-pack. He ripped one from the plastic ring and handed it to Duke. "You've just closed twenty homicides, twenty cold cases, with one statement. That calls for a celebration." He yanked another beer free and popped it open.

"I didn't do it alone."

"Bullshit. If not for you, Cindy would never have crossed my radar. You connected with her, junior. You got her to give it up." Drinking half the beer in a single gulp, Loviccio slammed the can on the arm of his chair. "Do you have any idea how long I worked on that case with The Ghost?"

"Ten years, according to the DD5s."

"Ten goddamn years on that same case and we got nothing." He slammed the can again. "Not a single goddamn lead that went anywhere. Do you know how frustrating that was?"

Duke nodded. "Lot of wasted effort."

Loviccio finished the beer and crushed the can, tossing it over the edge of the building into the alley below. "And now, with the solution in hand, we have to keep a huge chunk of it to ourselves." He opened another beer and chugged it.

"There's no reason to let Frank know about his sister's involvement." Duke shook his head. "If he didn't figure it out all those years, I'm sure he hasn't a clue."

"Maybe she'll tell him." Loviccio looked at Duke expectantly. "Maybe her conscience will get to her. What's the difference? You think Frank is gonna toss his sister out? Hell, no. She owns the damn house. Plus, what good would it do to get him pissed off at the only person who's stood by him through thirty years of an obsession most of us could never understand?" He leaned forward and frowned. "Knowing The Ghost, I wouldn't be surprised if he already knew and just wasn't going to say anything until you and I figured it out. Maybe that's why she swore you to secrecy."

"I doubt it. She was pretty emphatic that Nussbaum must never know. I got the feeling from her that he was in the dark on this one." Looking around behind himself, and satisfied that they were alone, Duke pulled the ring and opened the can of beer. He took a couple of sips and spit out the lukewarm beverage. "Yuck. You could have at least gotten cold beer to celebrate."

"Hey, be thankful there's enough for both of us. Usually, I'm not that generous."

Duke looked up at the clouds and grinned. "Is this one of the benefits of the gold badge?"

"Yeah, that and the ulcers." Putting his half-finished can of beer on the tarpaper, Loviccio got up from the chair and walked over to the short wall that formed the perimeter of the roof. "You'll get a promotion for this. Three short weeks as a detective and you're about to make second grade. Twenty homicides. Shit, Garvey, some detectives go a whole career and don't solve that many cases and you did it in one day. This is truly a miracle that will never be repeated. I can see the front page of the *Daily News* right now: Detective Duke Garvey sets a new world record for most cold cases solved in a single day. Hell, the Mayor will have her picture taken with you, junior, right there on the steps of goddamn city hall."

"Hey, we worked as a team." Duke pointed his can of beer at his partner. "And we just got lucky that Mrs. Carson knew the killer. You told me that most cases are solved with a lucky break. Okay, we got ours."

Loviccio laughed, spitting out a few drops of beer. "You're not going to last very long as a detective if you start waiting for Lady Luck. Nah, detective work is a grind. You follow leads that go nowhere. You question witnesses who know nothing. And when you finally drag a suspect into the interview room, the first thing they do is lawyer up. Game over."

"We still have to tie Alice Roman to the other murders."

"Nah. No one other than The Ghost still has any interest in those cases after all those years. One or two family members of the soldiers she killed were still asking questions, but that was at least five years ago." Loviccio clapped his hands. "This one's over, junior. Case closed. Dick Tracy would be proud."

"And you feel comfortable laying all the blame for these murders on Alice Roman?"

Loviccio smiled. "Comfort in this job is not something that comes easily. Yeah, I'm okay with puttin' it all on her shoulders. She hated the military. She lived alone, and from what little we've been able to construct from her past, she did a lot of travel by herself."

"A traveling saleswoman with a beef against the Army? Gee, can't be too many of them around."

"I'll bet there's a few, but none of them have ever confessed to killing soldiers."

Nodding, Duke took a sip and forced the warm beer down his parched throat. What few clouds that had slipped over the two detectives were fading quickly, letting in the summer sun to bake the roof. Nussbaum's eyes, the Major's eyes, the bullet speeding away from the barrel of the gun, the images of death were burnt into his memory. Even with his eyes closed against the glare, Duke could see them. He took a deep breath and stared at Loviccio's face.

The urge to tell him about his mother's pronouncement was strong. Duke tossed an opening sentence back and forth in his mind, not sure what words would be the correct ones to make his partner believe he wasn't crazy.

"Let me ask you a really weird question."

"Remember, I'm a married man and I'm armed." Loviccio stumbled back to his chair and collapsed into it with a sigh.

Duke pursed his lips and considered his words carefully. "Legally, what happens if someone commits a crime in a previous life and–"

"A previous life?" Loviccio closed his eyes and laughed. "Oh shit, The Ghost has gotten to you. Goddamn, Garvey. A previous life?" The laughing got the best of him and Loviccio doubled over, then fell out of the lawn chair.

"Forget it." Duke shook his head. It was a stupid idea.

Loviccio got back in the chair, still chuckling. "No. Tell me more. A previous life." He wiped tears from his eyes and pointed at Duke. "Detective Garvey, we shall now investigate crimes from previous lives. The NYPD will go nuts trying to figure out the back pay. And let's call what's her name from the *Daily News*. She can start a ghost of the week column."

With his partner now laughing so hard that his face was bright red, Duke spilled the last of his beer on the tarpaper and folded his arms across his chest. "Just forget it, Ronnie. You're drunk."

Loviccio nodded. "Halfway, but getting there."

Detective Collins came out onto the roof and tossed Loviccio a tin of breath mints. "The boss is in his office. He's looking for you two."

"How'd he find out so fast?" Popping open the mints, Loviccio put three of them in his mouth before handing the tin to his partner. "I'll bet he's fightin' with his wife again."

Lieutenant Moscowitz met the two detectives in the hallway. He was filling a coffee cup and put it down next to the pot to applaud them. "In all my years on the job, I've never had such good news."

"Thanks, boss." Duke stepped in front of Loviccio and shook the lieutenant's hand.

"Ronnie, you must be relieved." Moscowitz moved around Duke and put his hands on Loviccio's shoulders. "All those years, all that legwork, and finally it's over."

"Junior did it." He smiled. "A lucky break was all it took."

"I'm putting you both in for a commendation." Returning to his coffee cup, Moscowitz added three sugars and held the beverage in the air. "Here's to the best two detectives the NYPD has ever seen."

Duke was fairly certain his partner had left the last can of beer on the roof. He heard him thank the lieutenant, but then the pop of a beer can tab came from inside Loviccio's sport jacket. Moscowitz looked down at the floor, shook his head twice, and then walked back into the squad without another word.

Chapter Twenty-Six
Heavenly Advice

The moment the lieutenant walked into his office, Duke grabbed the can out of Loviccio's hand and dropped it into a wastebasket. He led his partner downstairs and out of the precinct. Even with the light breeze, the temperature was stuck in the mid-nineties. Duke bought four bottles of water from a hotdog vendor and directed Loviccio across the street to their bench in the park.

"Look, I've got to tell you something and I need you to focus." Duke unscrewed a bottle and put it into his partner's hand. "Drink this."

"It's not beer." Loviccio held the bottle eye-level and squinted. "Water?"

"Yes." Duke nudged Loviccio's hand. "Drink it. I'd like to believe you're partially sober."

"I'm fine."

"You drank most of a six-pack by yourself. You're several blocks from fine and heading in the wrong direction."

"If you say so." Loviccio tilted the bottle into his mouth and drank until it dribbled down the front of his sport jacket.

Duke sat down next to him and opened a second bottle for himself. He finished it, with much better accuracy than this partner, and put the empty next to him on the bench.

"Against my better judgment and my girlfriend's advice, I'm going to tell you something that you may have a hard time believing."

"You're from another planet?" Cracking up, Loviccio slapped his thigh. "I knew it. I knew from all those fancy words you use, Garvey. Goddamn, which planet, junior?"

Duke managed a smile. "Jamaica, Ronnie. It's a very special planet in the blue waters of the Caribbean Sea. Someday, you should go there. Nice beaches, friendly people, your diet would fit in like you're a yardie."

"A yardie?"

"A local. You'd be playing in a familiar yard."

"I'm the wrong color."

"You'll tan." Duke laughed. "Jesus, Ronnie. Nobody cares about your skin color in Jamaica. That's an American thing."

"You'll come with me?" Loviccio was slurring his words and having trouble sitting upright.

Duke put his arm around his partner's shoulder. "Yes, Ronnie. You and I will go to Negril and sit naked on the beach. We'll drink white Jamaican rum and fish for snapper."

"They got beer? I don't like rum."

"Delicious beer and it's always served ice cold." Duke pulled his phone out of his pocket and checked the time. "It's almost three. We should log out and get you home."

Loviccio tilted away from Duke and collapsed onto the bench. Moments later, he was snoring.

A quick search of Loviccio's pockets yielded his partner's wallet and driver's license. Duke summoned a rideshare with his phone and gave the driver an additional twenty dollars to make sure his partner made it into his house. Just before he closed the car door, Duke pulled Loviccio's Glock from his holster, ejected the round in the chamber and clicked on the safety.

With the car pulling a u-turn, Duke opened the app again and called for a second car to take him over to Saint Oda's Catholic Church. He had questions that he doubted Father Xavier could answer, but it was the only place he could think of to start.

The priest was in the confessional, so Duke took a seat in a nearby pew. He pulled a copy of the Bible from the rack on the seats in front him and opened it to a random page. The words were the same as he remembered from his childhood when his mother had dragged him to Sunday Mass. The young boy had sat reading from the holy book, not understanding much, but he liked the rhythm of the sentences.

Mother Garvey had vacillated between the Catholic Church and the teachings of the Rastafarians for much of his early years. It wasn't unusual for the boy and his mother to attend early Mass and then spend the afternoon with one of his uncles, learning about the natural life, the reason for dreadlocks, the importance of ganja, and how it all related to Jah. Duke made the decision to ignore both religions in private and to be a good Rastafarian boy for his mother's benefit.

A woman came out of her side of the confessional, paused to gaze at Jesus, and genuflected. When she was gone, the priest stuck his head out of the tiny hutch and waved at Duke. He stood and walked over to where the detective was seated and smiled at the young detective.

"I didn't expect to see you again." Father Xavier looked at the statue of Christ. "Still trying to solve the mystery of the broken leg?"

"That and all the other ones the City of New York throws at me." Duke got up from the pew and stood in the center aisle. "If you've got a few minutes, I have some questions I'd like to ask."

The priest checked his wristwatch. "Sure. Let's go downstairs to my office."

Duke shook his head. "If it's okay with you, Father, I'd like to have a witness." He nodded over his shoulder at the statue. "We can sit up front and talk, if you don't mind."

They took seats in the first row of pews, facing each other. Duke reached for his notepad and then thought the better of it. He folded his hands in his lap and looked at the priest.

"What's the Church's stand on reincarnation?"

"We teach that the body and soul are one. When the body dies, the soul goes to Heaven. Some day there will be a resurrection, but it doesn't happen daily and certainly not on an individual basis." Father Xavier quoted the Bible's chapter and the appropriate verse and then asked Duke the basis for his question.

Duke hesitated. "If I tell you something, it's the same as speaking to a lawyer. You're bound by a canon of ethics not to reveal our conversation, right?"

"Yes, if you want to call it a confession."

"Fine. Let's use that term. Hypothetically."

"As you wish, my son."

Taking a deep breath, Duke lowered his voice. "When I first walked in here and saw the cracked leg of Jesus, I knew I'd seen it before."

Father Xavier shrugged. "Everyone has moments of déjà vu."

"No, Father, this was much stronger than that. I was absolutely certain that I'd seen that crack in the black Christ's leg and it was in this church." Duke looked around and nodded. "No question about it. And it wasn't like I'd seen it just once. The statue was familiar to me, as if I'd seen it all the time. I was concerned that no one had repaired it. It truly bothered me."

Shaking his head slowly, the priest reached for Duke's hands. "It's a powerful image—Christ on the cross. We look at it and marvel at the Son of God. How much He sacrificed. How much He suffered." Squeezing Duke's fingers, Father Xavier smiled. "There are three black images of the Lord in all the churches in New York.

Two are in Harlem and this one at Saint Oda's. When you first saw it, the moment was so intense that it formed a false memory in your mind. You thought you had seen it before, but in fact, it was your first time. Even though you say you don't believe, the image of Christ was so strong that it fooled you into thinking this one was the statue you saw somewhere else."

"I don't know, Father..."

"Trust me, son. I've been here for most of my life and I've never seen you before."

Duke looked up at the statue, squinting to see if there was some detail he remembered beyond just the memory of the broken leg. Sliding his sunglasses off the top of his head, he stood and tried to see something that just wasn't there. He slipped the glasses into his jacket pocket and shielded his eyes with his hand. Nothing changed.

Leaning closer to the priest, Duke opened his eyes as wide as possible. "Look at my face, Father, and try to imagine me as a woman."

Father Xavier slid back a few inches. "Are you thinking about a sex change?"

Duke laughed. "Not in this lifetime. Seriously, try to see my face as a woman."

"You're not kidding?"

"No. Dead serious." Duke moved closer to the priest.

Taking his glasses out of a pocket, Father Xavier wiped them clean on his sleeve and put them on. Reaching over, he took Duke's chin in his hand and turned the detective's face left and right. Finally, he got as close as possible–Duke could smell the priest's mouthwash–and stared into his eyes.

"You need a good night's sleep." The priest sat back and stowed his spectacles. "Bloodshot and tired would be my diagnosis. But you'd make a very attractive woman."

Duke dropped his hands into his lap. "Thanks, Father. That's all I've got."

The priest adjusted his collar and stood. "There's a conflict raging inside you. I don't know how the broken statue of Jesus is tied into it, but you're not going to find peace until that conflict is resolved." He looked around the church. "This is a good place to work on that problem, and I'm always available if you need to talk some more."

"Thanks again." Duke stood to leave, but paused, with his head cocked to the side. "You ever question your faith, Father Xavier?"

"Daily." The priest winked at him. "And then I get out of bed."

Duke tried calling Juliana just before he went downstairs to catch the subway. The call went directly to voicemail, and he hung up without leaving a message. Holding his Metrocard in his hand, the detective took a step off to the side to let the other travelers pass. The faster he resolved the last of his girlfriend's issues the better. Reaching for his phone, Duke was about to summon a rideshare car, when the uptown train pulled into the station.

He sprinted for the turnstile, but dropped the card and had to stop and pick it up. By the time he swiped it, the doors were closing and the next train was fifteen minutes away. Duke muttered a curse and walked over to take a seat on a nearby bench. A quarter of an hour was plenty of time to ponder his fate.

Alice Roman had been dead for more than thirty years. Her spirit had come back to haunt him. Duke was sure of it. Reincarnation was his mother's belief, not his. Ghosts, on the other hand, were all over the place. Frank Nussbaum was the perfect example.

Juliana was right. No one was going to believe that he was the reincarnation of a serial killer. It wasn't logical that a killer would come back as a cop. Duke stared at his reflection in a window on a stopped train that wasn't going anywhere near his apartment. He shrugged. It wasn't even logical to believe that someone would come back again. Why would they? Did anyone really deserve a second chance? Duke shook his head. Now, he was certain his mother was stoned when she claimed he had a previous life. Next, she'd tell him he was going to come back as a dog. He covered his mouth with his hand and laughed.

To discuss this with anyone else on the job would be career suicide. They'd bust him so low that the only beat he'd walk would require a broom and a dustpan. If Alice Roman were still alive, it would be a whole different story. But she was dead, nothing but dust by now. Putting this entire thing on her was not only convenient, but it was the logical choice. She killed all those people, not him. This whole previous life shit was just that–a bucket of steam that was evaporating right before his eyes.

The correct train pulled into the station and Duke took a seat away from the few passengers already onboard. Distance from other people comforted him when heavy thinking was required. It was worse when he was in uniform. Civilians didn't understand the concept of off-duty. Most of the time, he'd change into street clothes for the ride home. On those few occasions when Duke was hurried, he felt more like a target than a friend when he took the subway. The only thought on his mind was to get the hell off the train as soon as it stopped at his station.

He'd lived thirty-three years as someone who not only solved problems, but also eliminated any chance they'd ever reappear. The Ghost wasn't his dilemma to begin with, but with a single piece of pastry that had changed. Without hesitation, the great-great-great-grandson of a Jamaican hero who never shirked a challenge gave the Major's murder the full-court press. It wasn't just luck. Duke Garvey shook his head. It was genetics. He was going to be one hell of a detective because somewhere in his past, a great man had stood up and fought for what he believed was right.

Duke got off the train and walked up to street level with a happy bounce to his step. He would put this foolishness behind him and accept the accolades he was due. Stepping out into the late afternoon sunshine, Duke crossed over 34th Street and headed left towards his building.

Mother Garvey was sitting on the stoop.

Chapter Twenty-Seven
Memories and Fingerprints

Duke's mother got up from the stoop in front of his apartment with a cellphone glued to her ear and orders in Patois streaming from her mouth. She held up a finger to let him know she'd be a moment longer, but then pulled him down to kiss his cheek. Shaking his keys, Duke pointed at the door and mouthed the words, "Come inside."

Mother Garvey tapped the mute button and shook her head. "No service in de lift, mon." She resumed the call, but walked up to the top step and sat down.

Duke hadn't noticed the small cardboard box covered with red "Warning - Explosives" labels that was wedged into a corner by the door. His gaze shot over to his mother who just nodded her head and wiggled her finger once more. Two joggers stopped at the bottom step and stretched. He told them to move away, pointing at the box, and pulled his badge out of his pocket.

With the call finished, his mother got up and kicked the box over to Duke. "Fresh jerk pork an two bottles of de sauce you like."

"You couldn't find another box?" He bent down and touched the box as though a rattle had come from inside. The smell confirmed his mother's claim, and he grabbed it with one hand, tucking it under his arm. "This is a nice surprise. I wish you'd called first, I was at the squad and could have been tied up all day."

"Dey make you work de weekend?"

Duke nodded. "Rotating schedule. I was off, but my partner called me in. We just closed twenty homicide cases. I think it's a department record." He smiled. "I might get a promotion."

"Ya, mon? Make you de chief?"

"Detective second grade."

"Me remember when you in de second grade. Get into a fight wit boy tree years older den you over de girl."

"Did I win?"

"No, mon." She laughed. "You lose de tooth an have de black eye for de weekend. Mash it up so bad, me almost take you to de clinic."

Duke held the door open for his mother. "Are you staying for dinner?"

She shook her head. "No, mon. Me got a date uptown. Just wanted to bring you de pork an dis ting." Mother Garvey reached into her shoulder bag, dug around for a few moments, and pulled out the Plexiglas case with Nussbaum's bullet. "You leave dis at me house de odder night. Me tink it evidence, so bring it to you. Done wan no bullet souvenir." With a huff, she dropped it into Duke's hand.

It was cold. He expected the boxed bullet to be red hot, hoping that it would respond to his touch with his mother present. Detective Jankowsky hadn't believed him. Perhaps his mother would. But the cube was unresponsive. He juggled it from hand to hand and then stuffed it into his pocket with a sigh.

"It was evidence but now, you're right, it's just a souvenir." Duke leaned over and kissed his mother's forehead. "A date? Uptown? Full joy!"

Mother Garvey called for a rideshare and one pulled up seconds later. Just before she got into the car, she turned and looked at Duke with her mouth wrinkled to one side. "You keep talkin' bout de girlfriend. When me get to see her? Me not gettin' younger. Soon come de grandchildren? Ya, mon."

Duke blew her a kiss and slipped into the safety of his apartment building.

He'd hoped to find Juliana waiting for him, but only the rhythmic ticking of his grandfather clock welcomed him home. Duke put the box of jerk pork on the counter in the kitchen and went into the bedroom to change. A shower would have done him a world of good, but his stomach took command. He stripped down to his socks and slipped on a pair of gym shorts and his favorite reggae t-shirt.

Back in the kitchen, Duke dumped the warm pork onto a cutting board and sliced it into strips as wide as his thumb. From his collection of pots and pans, he dragged out the heavy cast-iron skillet and started it heating on the stove. A whole stick of butter went into the hot pan before he laid out the strips of pork on the melted butter.

While the meat sizzled, Duke cracked three eggs into a bowl and whipped them along with some chopped scallions. He dumped the mixture on top of the pork and let the eggs cook until they were almost solid. With the skill of a master chef, Duke flipped the entire concoction in the air, catching it with the pan to finish cooking.

He'd named it Green Eggs and Jerk, an homage to one of his favorite authors, and had been cooking it for breakfast since he was ten years old. The grandfather clock chimed seven o'clock in the evening. The meal was only twelve hours late.

Sitting at the kitchen table an hour later, with the food cold and congealed, Duke tossed the Plexiglas case back and forth. In an effort to convince himself that charging the late Alice Roman with twenty murders was the right choice, he'd been re-reading Cynthia's statement.

What made little sense was why Alice stopped killing. If she knew she was dying, wouldn't she ramp up her efforts and try to kill as many soldiers as possible? From what he'd read, serial killers didn't have a quota.

And Alice never admitted to a specific murder. She never said that she was the one who shot Major Nussbaum. *It was just*

Cynthia's intuition, right? Was she blaming Alice to finally get even with her father? Whew, that's some conscience cleansing. Duke looked out the window and muttered, "Is Loviccio making this too easy?"

He put the bullet on the table next to his plate and took another bite of the cold eggs. The Ghost had said this was the clue to solving these crimes. *Why didn't he solve them, then?* Duke tried to balance the little box on one corner. *A bullet. A bullet. A...*

His mind froze mid-thought and he asked himself out loud. "All the reports said the shooter wore gloves. What if she wasn't wearing them when she loaded the pistol?" Duke held the Plexiglas container in the air and talked to it. "She fired four rounds in the restaurant. Where are the spent casings? Where are your brothers that stayed behind? Two unfired bullets have to be somewhere." He slammed his hand on the table so hard that his fork jumped out of the plate and landed on the floor. "Fingerprints. We need fingerprints."

Duke gave five seconds thought to calling his partner, but decided Loviccio was probably fast asleep. Slipping sweatpants over his gym shorts and switching the Bob Marley t-shirt for one with the NYPD logo, he tied his sneakers and ran down the five flights of stairs. A taxi had just discharged its passengers at the building next door. Duke jumped into the front seat and held his gold badge up to the driver's face.

"Eleven Front Street, Brooklyn, and drive it like you stole it."

Twenty-one minutes later, they skidded to a halt in front of the Property Clerk's Office on Front Street in Brooklyn. Duke gave the driver a fifty and ran up the steps.

The sergeant on duty was unfazed by Duke's appearance and equally uninterested in his exuberance. Forms needed to be filled out, authorizations were required, and it was Saturday night. Something in the man's lack of enthusiasm told Duke that results were going to come at a snail's pace. He laid the forms on the counter and called Loviccio.

It took an hour, but disheveled and in a sour mood, his partner stormed into the Property Clerk's Office and threw his weight around. The sergeant, not more than a year younger than Loviccio, put up a good fight, but not enough to win. Duke had been ushered out of the room for several minutes while the two men verbally battled. When he came back, his partner was holding the door to the evidence locker open and waving him in.

They spent another hour and a half searching through dusty boxes and spider webs for the physical evidence from the Major's case. Duke found the box with the .357 magnum first. The pistol was in a sealed evidence bag with a handwritten label that said, "No Prints."

Loviccio shouted, "Got it!" and dropped a second cardboard box on the floor between them. Lifting the lid and tossing it to the side, he shuffled through the contents and then removed an evidence bag filled with shell casings and bullets from the bottom. Another label was on the side facing away from Duke, and he hoped it read something different.

"Removed by Detective Frank Nussbaum." Loviccio smiled. "Frank always liked to sign his work."

They signed out the two evidence bags and drove over to the Ballistics Lab. The King had pulled weekend duty and was eating a hot dog when the two detectives rushed in.

"Well, the Duke of Earl and Mister Smelly Pants. The hell you doin' here so late at night?"

Loviccio moved the King's hot dog out of the way and put the bags on the table in front of him. "Fingerprints, my man. We need you to examine these shell casings for fingerprints."

The King pushed the bags off to one side and picked up the last piece of his meal. "Gonna cost ya."

Reaching into his back pocket, Loviccio took out his wallet and gave Duke a ten-dollar bill. "Three hot dogs with mustard, ketchup, and hot onions. Go out the back door and take a left. There's a vendor on the corner who works around the clock. Get me a Diet Coke."

By the time Duke returned, The King had mounted all four of the spent casings in a microscope and shot digital images of the fingerprints. He ate two of the hot dogs and checked the unfired rounds.

"Same prints. Your shooter must have loaded the weapon without gloves. You're in luck for a change, Stinky."

"You're eating that shit and you talk about *my* odors?" Loviccio bagged the casings and bullets. "Thanks, man."

The King mumbled something unintelligible with his mouth full of food, waving as the two detectives rushed out the door.

Duke grabbed his partner in the hallway. "Now we have to find Alice Roman's fingerprints. I saw in Nussbaum's files where she was arrested for stabbing one of the soldiers that told her that her husband had died. There should be a fingerprint card for that arrest."

Scratching the back of his neck, Loviccio closed his eyes for a moment. "She was booked for assault and then the charges were dropped."

"Doesn't matter. If she was booked, then she was still fingerprinted." Duke smiled. "You've got to love the system."

"Yeah, but that was more than thirty years ago. You think a fingerprint card from that far back is going to be easy to find?"

Duke shrugged. "That's why they pay us the big bucks, partner."

Over the years, the NYPD had gone to great lengths to convert all their paper files to digital. Quite a bit of the paperwork since the beginning of the new millennium was already digitized and loaded onto a bank of massive servers. However, going back to the previous century required manual searching. The two detectives dug through fingerprint cards for more than two hours before finding the faded, dog-eared one with Alice Roman's name on the top.

Duke brought up the images The King had generated on his cellphone and compared them to the tattered card. "It's a match. No question about it. Alice Roman loaded the weapon that killed Major Nussbaum and the three others." He shoved his phone closer to his partner. "Holy shit, Ronnie. We really did solve the case."

"Happy now?"

Duke gave him half a smile and turned away. Happy wasn't close to what he was feeling. *No, Ronnie, Alice Roman didn't kill them. It was me in my previous life.* He shivered and pushed the thought to the back of his mind. It wouldn't stay there for very long. The closer they got to the truth, the more it pained him. The depth of that pain into his soul was now an unsolvable problem for the junior detective. How was he going to live with the knowledge that he or she was responsible for all those deaths? How could he go on as a New York City cop?

Other than his mother, who he could trust with his life, only one other person had the details of his involvement in these killings. Fortunately, Duke knew that Juliana would stay silent as long as he didn't mention it again. Loviccio wasn't someone he felt comfortable with any longer. The senior detective had been willing to close the case on the flimsiest of evidence. Even though he was right, the path to that conclusion was as shaky as a rope bridge in a windstorm.

But Frank Nussbaum deserved the truth. The Ghost had dedicated his life to solving just one crime and had never reached that goal. Sure, they could tell him that Alice Roman was definitely the killer, but in Duke's mind, that was only half the story. His was the hand that fired the bullet in the little plastic box. It was not a fact he could hide from for very long.

Chapter Twenty-Eight
Putting A Ghost To Rest

Loviccio had offered to drive Duke home, but the younger detective declined. He needed the time alone to do battle with his problems. Discussing the case with The Ghost was the first contestant into the ring. Half an hour on the subway and Duke still hadn't been able to find a reason to tell Nussbaum the whole story. Every plan he formulated ended with the same result: he'd be seen as crazy and The Ghost wouldn't give a damn or wouldn't believe him.

His second quandary was dealing with a partner who relished shortcuts and reached conclusions with facts as porous as Swiss cheese. The entire eleven years he was a beat cop, Duke had gone out of his way to do the job by the book. Just because he now had a gold badge, he wasn't going to do slipshod work.

To date, he'd never had a bad bust. He knew when the kid he'd seen selling drugs was lying about having more concealed in his shoes and waited until the narcotics were in plain sight before arresting him. When a woman came out of a fancy hotel, fixing her makeup and looking as though she'd just danced the Macarena, Duke gave the woman enough time to score her next trick before busting her for solicitation. The bodega owner who was robbed three times would have gotten away with the insurance claims had Duke not sat and watched the tiny grocery and seen the man smash his windows before dialing 9-1-1 the fourth time.

Duke's arrests went to court and then to jail because he understood the system and the importance of doing his job how the NYPD required it to be done. The law was inflexible and so was Officer Garvey.

It was how he'd been raised. Do everything right the first time and you don't have to fix your screw-up on a second pass. Know what's behind a door before you open it and let trouble loose. And his mother's favorite: never make the same mistake twice. Find a new one and get it out of the way.

Loviccio was on the opposite side of all these concepts, and Duke wasn't sure it made sense to partner with him much longer.

Newspapers were being delivered when Duke reached street level from the subway. He stopped at the newsstand on the corner and read the headlines of the three major New York papers. The pending garbage strike was front-page news on two of them. The *Daily News* led with the Mets win. Duke pulled a dollar from his wallet and bought a copy.

Outside of the job, no one knew that twenty homicides had been solved in one night. The paper was filled with the usual: politics, local news, the weather, sports, and the funnies. Duke yanked the classified section out of the paper and put it into the trash. He read the local section while he was waiting for the elevator and was about to check the weather forecast when the doors opened at his floor.

Juliana was seated on the floor outside his door. Her suitcase was behind her and she was talking on the phone. Duke folded the newspaper under his armpit and sat down next to her.

Ending the call, she dropped the phone in her lap and smirked. "You knew I'd be back, didn't you?"

He nodded. "I've been told that I'm irresistible."

She punched his shoulder. "You can be a real asshole sometimes, Garvey."

"It's not intentional." Duke turned slowly and stared into her eyes. "I wish I could blame it on the job, but I've always had a stubborn side."

"And I've got to come to terms with my father." Nodding several times, Juliana pulled her knees up to her chest. "It's not easy watching someone you love fade away. I hope you never have to go through it."

Duke stood and reached down to her. "Come on. It's late and I've been working on this shit all day. What do you say we open a bottle of wine and watch the sun come up?"

They missed the sunrise and most of the morning. When Duke rolled out of bed just before eleven, the apartment smelled from bacon and toast. He slipped back into the sweatpants Juliana had dragged off his body hours ago and padded into the kitchen.

"What the hell's got you snoring so badly?" She flipped the eggs and frowned. "I thought the subway had been rerouted through your apartment."

Duke shrugged. "Maybe all the dust in the file room."

"Breakfast is ready. Let's eat, get in a run, and then you need a serious shower." Winking at him, Juliana turned off the stove and portioned the eggs onto a pair of waiting plates.

He took the seat closest to the window and tilted the chair back on two legs. "I tried to tell my partner about the previous life shit."

"Are you crazy? I thought we talked this out. You can't tell anyone on the job. It'll be the end of your career. I doubt even Animal Control would hire you if they found out."

"Don't worry. He was drunk and made a joke out of it." Duke rocked the chair forward. "Did you make coffee?"

Juliana shook her head. "No. You're out. You want tea? I brought back the ceramic kettle you like so much."

He grinned. "Sure."

She filled the teakettle and put it on the stove. "Did you tell anyone else?"

"No, but I had an in-depth discussion about reincarnation with a priest."

"That must have been fun."

He nodded. "More for him than me. I came away knowing less than I did before I started."

"That's it?"

"Well, I laid it out in detail for my mother."

"And?"

"She swears I'm the reincarnation of Alice Roman." Duke laced his fingers together and smiled. "But she says it's okay, that I've got my good and bad sides under control and I won't turn out to be a serial killer."

Juliana laughed. "Now I feel safe."

The teakettle whistled, and she walked over to the stove to turn it off. Pouring the water into Duke's favorite cup, she dunked a tea bag into it several times and added two teaspoons of sugar. "Here, just the way you like it." She placed the cup on the table in front of him and stood there, waiting for her boyfriend's approval.

"Are you waiting for a tip?"

She shrugged. "A kind word would go further."

"I thought my apology three hours ago was enough."

"As a prelude to begging for sex?" Juliana shook her head. "Not so much."

"Okay, then I'm sorry."

"For what?"

Duke furrowed his brow. "I don't know, but you're standing there like if I don't apologize for something, you won't let me drink my tea. So, for whatever it is that I need to apologize for, once again, I'm sorry."

"You need to trust me, Garvey. Here's the perfect example. If I tell you that speaking about this reincarnation shit is a bad idea, you need to listen." Juliana walked around to the other end of the table and sat down. "Trust is the foundation of any relationship. Lose the trust and the relationship ends."

"You know I trust you." He sipped the tea. "I always have. Remember, we were partners for years. The job requires trust between partners."

"Yeah, but that's in a sector car. When the uniform comes off and we're just two people walkin' the street, trust is what keeps us going."

"Fair enough." Reaching across the table, Duke took Juliana's hands in his. "I want you to trust me enough that you'll unpack your bag and throw it away."

"You're serious?"

"As a mad woman with a gun in her hand."

"You'll come with me next month to visit my father?"

Duke pushed the chair back from the table and shook his head. "Let's not get carried away."

It was two-thirty in the afternoon when Juliana suggested a run, and within the hour, they were jogging north on the river path. The temperature was once again going to spike in the mid-nineties, but a steady breeze was blowing inland. They headed south again as they hit the pier, and she took off in a sprint. Duke did his best to catch up to her, but she crossed under the FDR Drive and was waiting for him on the corner.

He was about to cross the street when an NYPD cruiser came screaming around the turn in the highway. It was followed seconds later by another and Duke jumped back onto the sidewalk, waiting for a moment to safely cross. The sound of sirens was close and both cops instinctively ran towards them.

Rounding the next block, Duke's street, a mass of sector cars, flashing lights, and uniformed cops with their guns drawn was surrounding the entrance to his apartment building. Standing at the top of the stoop, in full dress uniform, was Frank Nussbaum. Alongside him, and dressed in a pink terrycloth robe and matching slippers, was his sister. The scene became even more surreal when Duke realized The Ghost was holding a large pistol aimed at Cynthia's head.

Duke's off-duty weapon was hanging in the bedroom closet. But Juliana had strapped a small, semi-automatic to her ankle out of habit. She drew it as they approached. Spotting a friendly face from the two-seven, Juliana quickly introduced Duke, mentioning that he was unarmed. The cop walked back to her cruiser and returned with the shotgun from the trunk.

A sergeant from the local precinct had taken command of the scene and jogged over as soon as he spotted Duke.

"Detective Garvey?"

"Yes." Duke patted his sweats. "Sorry, I don't have my badge."

"You know Frank Nussbaum?"

"Yes. We're both with the 84th Detective Squad."

"Well, your fellow detective is threatening to kill his sister, and he's been calling for you for the last twenty minutes. The guy at the newsstand on the corner saw him get out of a taxi and drag his sister up the stoop. He was banging on the door and pushing buzzers, but no one would let him in."

Duke looked at the shotgun in his hands and gave it back to the cop. "Let me talk to him. Do you have a vest?"

Properly garbed, Duke walked across the street toward The Ghost with his hands in front, palms up. He stopped on the sidewalk and looked around at the show of force that filled 34th Street.

"Was this part of your plan, Frank?" Duke pointed at the three cops in battle dress standing to his right. "Who are you going to shoot first? Your sister? Me?"

"I have no gripe with you, David. I'm only here so you can tell me the truth."

Cynthia's face was pale. Sweat and tears had formed trails down her cheeks. Duke could see her lips quivering, but she appeared to be too afraid to speak.

"Then let's end this. What do you want to know?" Duke took a few steps toward a nearby light pole.

Nussbaum moved closer to his sister and dug the pistol into the soft flesh behind her ear. She winced and tilted her head slightly, but The Ghost pushed the weapon deeper. "I've heard a bunch of lies from my sister. Now, I want to hear the truth from you."

Nodding, Duke took another step toward The Ghost and his captive. "Put the gun down and I'll tell you anything you want to know."

"You have much experience with an armed suspect holding a weapon to a civilian's head, Garvey?" He grinned. "It rarely works out well for both parties."

Duke pushed the memory of the nineteen-year-old kidnapper from his mind. "Then let's make this an exception to the rule. We don't know each other, but I've heard a lot about you. Let me tell you something that you might not know about me."

"I'm listening."

Duke leaned against the light pole and took a couple of deep breaths. He was slightly winded from their race, but the current situation didn't allow him to relax after exercise, as was his routine. What little training he'd been given for hostage situations wasn't enough to defuse an ex-cop with a gun at his sister's head. However, what he knew without a doubt was that lying to Frank Nussbaum would be deadly for Cynthia.

"I was raised as a Rastafarian. One of the most sacred of our beliefs is the truth. To lie about something is a sin. Jah looks down on sinners with disdain. They are made to suffer for their lies." Duke pointed at the sky. "I believe in my heart that if you were to ask me a question, and I were to be less than truthful, Jah would strike me dead. I will not lie to you, nor would I spout bullshit to anyone else. You have to trust my faith, Frank."

Nussbaum laughed. "You must smoke a lot of marijuana if you think I'm buying into that."

"You gave me the bullet, your only piece of evidence. Why did you do that, Frank? Isn't that a sign of trust?"

Blowing out a soft breath, The Ghost sighed. "I saw something in you, Garvey. Something in your eyes that told me you could pry away the layers of time and uncover the secrets that had been kept from me for thirty years. You were a fresh face, unencumbered by the doubts of your fellow detectives." Smiling, he tapped his sister's ear with the gun. "I told my sister that you would find the killer, and you did. I'm proud of you, Garvey."

"And I'm proud to have solved your father's murder, Frank. But this is not how I would have expected you to celebrate."

"Celebrate what?" Nussbaum's face hardened, and he shoved the weapon back into his sister's hair. "One case ended, but another one begins. My sister's allegations about my father have to be investigated. There is no closure yet, detective."

"What good would it do to smear your father's name, Frank? He's gone thirty years and you two are his only survivors. Do you really think he'd want you to end your life like this?"

Nussbaum laughed. "My life ended three decades ago, Garvey. Why do you think everyone calls me The Ghost?"

Duke nodded. The man had a point there. "It was your choice, Frank. You could have put this to bed a long time ago. I read it in your notes. You knew the killer was dead and that all your efforts were going to be in vain, but you soldiered on despite what the others thought of you, I admired you for believing that a solution was achievable."

"Bullshit." Stroking his sister's shoulder with the butt of the gun, Nussbaum frowned at Duke. "If you're trying to appeal to some sense of honor in the job, the sanctity of the blue wall, and all that other crap, I'm not buying it anymore, Garvey. What I learned from our dear Cynthia here is that even those closest to you will shove a knife in your back with their lies if it suits their purpose."

"Okay, then buy into this. If you're here on a suicide mission, then go ahead and blow your brains out, but let Cynthia go."

"My sister? The woman who deprived me of the chance to arrest my father's killer?" The laughing took on an evil tone, and he grabbed her closer. "No, detective, she's the reason we're all here today. Do you think the taste of revenge grows sweeter with time?" Nussbaum cocked the hammer. "Let's find out."

The shot came from over Duke's right shoulder. He was certain he heard the bullet whiz past his ear. Nussbaum's head snapped back as the round smashed into his forehead, but not before The Ghost's finger squeezed the trigger.

If Cynthia Carson had been six inches taller, the bullet would have gone in one ear and out the other. It grazed her skull, tearing out some gray hairs that she wouldn't miss, and left the woman deaf in one ear, but otherwise unharmed. She fell to one side, grabbing the railing to break her fall. Frank tumbled forward, dropping the weapon just before his face smashed into the sidewalk. Her brother had finally become the ghost he'd spent his life imitating. Duke was sure the man would haunt his building for the rest of time.

Juliana had fired the shot that killed Frank Nussbaum. She was only ten feet behind Duke and made the split second decision that saved Cynthia's life. He walked over to the blue and white where she was seated and knelt down, holding her hands.

"It was a good shoot. No one will question your actions. You had no other choice."

"I never killed someone before." Juliana's hands trembled slightly, but her voice was strong. "The way his head snapped back. Did you see that?" She blew out a breath. "Holy shit, Garvey, I always joked about the little pistol on my ankle. I figured it would be good enough to bluff someone if I didn't have my Glock. But, wow, that shit nearly blew his head off."

Duke looked over the roof of the cruiser as they loaded the body bag into the Medical Examiner's van. "I'm going to the hospital with his sister. You're going to need to sit down with the watch commander and give a statement for the shooting board."

"I know her. She was one of our instructors at the academy, and we've stayed in touch." Juliana's shoulders relaxed. "Go ahead. I'll be fine."

"Are you sure?" Duke took her hands. "I know what you're going through. I know where your head is at right now. I've been there, Julie. If you need to talk to someone, start with me. Please."

Juliana squeezed his hands. "I know."

He stood, leaned over, and gave her a kiss on the lips. "Hey, at least I waited for you this time."

An emergency room nurse cleaned up the blood and put a Band-Aid on Cynthia's scalp wound. The nurse had shaved the area in the event the damage was worse than first suspected and was relieved to find nothing more than a shallow half-inch wide furrow. While Duke held her hands, a doctor tested her hearing and said it would come back by the following morning, but she would have some residual hearing loss. He suggested devices if it became a problem.

"Devices?" Cynthia had a frightened look on her face.

"Hearing aids." The doctor shrugged. "But I don't think you'll need them."

Alone, as the nurse and doctor moved on to the next patient, Duke took a seat next to Cynthia's bed on her good side with his notepad in his lap.

"You told him?"

"He knew." Cynthia pulled her legs up to her chest. "I made dinner for him that he wouldn't eat and I was so frustrated that I left and went for a drive. When I came home, he was sitting on the porch. I could see the anger in his face from the far end of the driveway. He was slapping his palm with his old nightstick. He grabbed the car keys out of my hand and refused to give them back."

"That was three days ago." Narrowing his eyes, Duke shook his head. "What took so long?"

She nodded. "He's been percolating, seething, marching around the house like an animal. He wouldn't talk to me. Wouldn't eat a meal in the same room as me."

"Why didn't you call?"

"I was afraid to do anything to provoke him." Rubbing her bad ear, Cynthia's tears sparkled as they dripped down her cheeks. "I finally got down on my knees in front of him and told him everything. He seemed to handle it okay until I got to the part about dad molesting me. I told him about the bathtub and the breakfasts we shared in my bed when mom overslept."

"Jesus. He didn't know?" Duke closed the notepad. Not everything had to go into a DD5.

Cynthia wiped her face. "If he did, he didn't say anything about it and I guess that got me angry."

"How angry?"

She rubbed her hands together. "I started screaming at him that Dad was an evil bastard who deserved to die. He screwed around with more women than you can imagine. Oh, everyone looked away except me. I knew he was unfaithful. The bitch who was shot with him? He'd been having sex with her teenage daughter until the mother caught them. She threatened to tell my mom if Major Henry Nussbaum wouldn't toss the daughter and take her on instead."

"Did Frank know all this about his father?"

"If he did, he never let on."

A nurse stepped into the room to give Cynthia a pain pill and an antibiotic. "There's a minor risk of infection, and I'm certain you'll have a nasty headache in the morning. Change the bandage after you shower. We're just waiting for the discharge papers and you can go home." She stopped at the doorway and turned to Duke. "I remember you. Officer Garvey?"

Duke stood and smiled. "It's Detective Garvey now."

"Even better." She winked and left the room.

With his tongue jammed in his cheek, Duke hid his embarrassment, slowly turning back toward Cynthia. "Why did he bring you to my place?"

"He wanted to hear it from you. He wanted to get confirmation that his sister had kept this from him all those years."

"At gunpoint?"

"Come on, Duke, the man was a cop for nearly forty years. It was how he got things done. If you stick a gun in someone's ear you'll get results much faster than with words."

Duke took a deep breath. "Was he coming to kill me?"

"I don't think so. I think all along it was his plan to shoot me in front of you as some sort of weird object lesson. Then, I think he was going to blow his own brains out as a final up-yours to the job."

"You know he'll get an Inspector's Funeral."

She nodded. "He deserves it."

"No argument from me."

Cynthia sat up in the bed and swung her legs over the side. "I'm going to get dressed now."

"There's a female officer waiting outside. She'll drive you home." Duke stuffed the notepad in his back pocket. "Are you going to be okay? If you want, she'll stay with you as long as necessary."

"I'll be fine." She let a half-hearted smile force its way across her face. "I'll miss him, Duke, but at least he's gone to wherever he's going with the knowledge that the case was closed."

Chapter Twenty-Nine
Convince Me I'm Wrong

Duke hadn't expected to see his partner when he stepped out of the blue and white. Loviccio was stretched out on the stoop in front of Duke's building, eating from a foil bag.

"Falafel from the best joint in the city." Loviccio wiped his mouth on the back of his sleeve. "I'da got you one, but I didn't think you ate this shit."

"Frank's dead."

He nodded. "I heard. Officer Tolkowski put one between his eyes. Nice shot."

"I didn't think I'd see you until Monday." Duke grinned. "How's your head?"

"In much better shape than Frank's." Wrapping the balance of his snack in a napkin, Loviccio tossed it into a trashcan by the curb. "Was he coming for you or your previous life?"

That got Duke's attention. "I wasn't sure you were listening. You made quite a few jokes."

"I was listening. A couple of beers aren't going to dull my detective skills." Loviccio got up and dusted off the seat of his pants. "Let's go inside. I need to piss."

While his partner relieved himself, Duke boiled water for tea. Juliana had left a note on the kitchen table that she was with her friend, the watch commander, and would hopefully be back in time for dinner. He recalled the simplicity of *his* recent interaction with the shooting board and gazed wistfully at the grandfather clock. It was always a long, drawn out procedure when a cop had to justify their actions to a peer group. Police officers needed to be held to a higher standard, but sometimes those judging saw themselves as deities and went too far.

Hearing the toilet flush and the sound of running water, Duke let out a sigh. At least Loviccio had sanitary skills when it came to his bodily functions. How the man could be such a slob and yet so OCD about his little chunk of real estate in the squad was a mystery Duke knew he'd never solve.

His partner backed out of the small powder room, zipping his fly. On the way across the living room, Loviccio stopped at the coffee table and rummaged through the magazine pile, snatching a copy of *Runner's World.*

"You're serious about this running shit." Loviccio flipped through a couple of pages of the magazine and then dropped it back onto the pile.

"You have to stay in shape for this job, Ronnie." Duke pointed at the way his partner walked, hunched over and nearly stumbling. "What are you going to do when you retire? Lie around and rot or spend the rest of your life exploring the world?"

"My wife wants to explore the storage locker and our attic. She says there's enough mystery up there to keep me busy for years." Grabbing his pants, Loviccio hitched them up.

"No one lives forever, but exercise will keep you going longer than beer." Duke filled a pair of glasses with water and placed them on the table.

Nodding, his partner walked into the kitchen, pulled a chair from under their table, and spun it around. He dropped down onto the seat and rested his arms across the back of the chair. "Precisely why I'm here."

"Oh?"

"Do you really believe you were Alice Roman in a previous life?"

The kettle answered first, whistling loud enough to wake the dead. Duke slipped a tea bag into each of two cups and added the boiling water. "You want milk? Lemon?"

"Whiskey?"

"Sorry. Only wine."

"Then why the hell did you make tea?" Loviccio laughed. "Just sugar, junior."

Duke placed a bowl with sugar cubes on the table, taking one for his cup. "I don't know if I believe it or not. I'd really like someone to convince me that it's bullshit, but that's not what I'm hearing."

Reaching across the table, the senior detective moved the glass of water out of the way and held Duke's wrist. "It's bullshit. Trust me."

"You're an expert?"

"No, but I'm a detective with the NYPD." Loviccio sat back in his chair. "My job is to look at the facts and make logical decisions based on science, not voodoo."

"It's not voodoo, it's something that millions of people believe." Duke sipped his tea. "Science has never disproved reincarnation."

His partner laughed and shook his head. "Science hasn't found Jimmy Hoffa's body either. So what's your point? We rely on science to prove things, not tell us that they're wrong."

"Okay, Mister Science, explain what I saw in Frank's eyes? Tell me how the bullet got hot one second and cool the next? Where's the logic in all that?" Pushing his teacup out of the way, Duke leaned across the table. "I knew the second I saw that crack in Christ's leg that I'd been there before. You want to call it déjà vu? Go ahead. But what the hell does that mean anyhow?"

"It means you *thought* you'd been there before, but in reality, it was your first time in the church. Maybe you saw a black Jesus in another church and the memory of it was what confused you." Loviccio dumped two sugar cubes into his cup and then added a third, stirring the tea with his finger until they disappeared.

"And it just so happens that was the church that Alice Roman attended. How do you account for that?"

Loviccio shrugged and tasted his tea. "This is some strong shit. What the hell is it, Duke?"

"Assam black. We buy it at an Indian bodega on 44th Street." Leaning back in his chair, Duke gulped his tea and put the nearly empty cup down hard on the table. "You didn't answer my question."

The senior detective shrugged again and reached for the sugar. "Jesus shoulda drunk this stuff. It'd heal everything that was broken." He added one more cube to the cup and tasted it with just the tip of his tongue.

In the brief silence that fell over the kitchen, Duke finished his cup and made a second one. Loviccio's wife called and his partner went out on the balcony to argue with her in private. Duke sent a text to his girlfriend to check on her status. It was marked delivered, but no reply came back to him.

Loviccio stomped back in, sweating and panting. "One of these days." He slammed his phone on the kitchen table and sat down backwards. "Don't ever get married, junior. Even if you shoot her, you'll still end up in prison."

"Look, I'll accept your theory about the broken statue, but how do you explain the bullet?"

"It was only hot when you touched it, right?"

Duke nodded. "And only that one time. What's your point?"

"You imagined it."

"And the burns on the tips of my fingers? I imagined those as well?" Duke held out his hand, but the temporary damage had healed completely and the fingertips of one hand were identical to the others.

"Rita said the box was cold, and that was seconds after you'd said it was burning your fingers." Loviccio folded his hands on the table. "Science says it's not possible. I agree. You might have thought it was hot, but there's no evidence to support your claim, detective. You are the only one who claims to have seen burn marks. Is it possible that you imagined them?"

Duke got up from his seat and walked over to the sink. Turning, he pointed at Loviccio with his empty teacup. "I know what I saw in The Ghost's eyes."

"You saw exactly what you wanted to see, junior." Getting up from his chair, Loviccio walked over to his partner. "You wanted to believe he was really a ghost and in your mind, he was. You made up your mind to see things that weren't there. People do it all the time, even cops."

"Bullshit." Duke pushed him away. "I know what I saw, Ronnie. It was as real as you standing in front of me with that dirty shirt and stained shorts."

Loviccio walked back to the table and sat down. He spun the teacup around several times and eventually stopped with the handle facing him. "Let's assume for a moment that you're correct."

"In what regard?"

"In what regard? Jesus, Garvey, you've got to stop talking like an English teacher." Pushing the cup off to the side, Loviccio folded his hands together on the table. "As weird as it sounds, I'm gonna buy into the theory that you are indeed the reincarnation of Alice Roman. For the sake of argument, yes, you were a serial killer in your previous life."

Duke sat down across from him. "Go on."

"I'm going to arrest you for the twenty homicides that Alice Roman committed. We're going to present the case to the District Attorney who will then have me placed in a padded room where they feed me nothing but mushy bananas." Grabbing Duke's hands, Loviccio's voice went up an octave. "Do you get where I'm going with this, Garvey?"

"You think everyone will assume you're crazy." Duke smiled. "And they'll lock me in an adjoining room."

Loviccio clapped his hands. "Congratulations, detective, you solved another one."

"You know, I'm beginning to think you *should* be locked in a padded cell."

"Sorry, junior, but there are members of the NYPD that came to that conclusion years ago."

With a sigh, Duke sat back in his chair and folded his arms over his chest. "I'm not crazy."

"I didn't say you were."

"But you're thinking it."

"Well..." Loviccio reached for his teacup and held it up in front of his partner. "If I drop this cup on the floor, what do you think will happen?"

Duke snorted. "It'll break, you'll get tea all over my kitchen floor, and I'll have to clean it up."

"What if I told you that the cup won't break?"

"I'd say you're wrong."

Loviccio put the teacup down on the table. "Why?"

"Because Julie dropped one several weeks ago, and it smashed into a million pieces. Thankfully, it was empty." Duke slid his cup away from the edge of the table with his index finger.

"So, you have prior experience with cups and your tile floor."

"Yes. Where are you going with this?"

"Prior experience, junior." A look of satisfaction came over Loviccio's face. "No one has any real prior experience with reincarnation. You don't know anyone and neither do I. If someone, anyone, had been reincarnated don't you think they would have told the world? Don't you think the scientific community would have investigated their claim?" He pushed back from the table. "Reincarnation is not science. It's never been proven or tested. If you really were Alice Roman in a previous life, you'd be able to prove it, junior. We're detectives. We live for proof, not supposition or religious mumbo-jumbo."

Duke was about to retort when the door opened and Juliana walked in.

"Ronald Loviccio, who let you into Manhattan?"

"You know each other?" Duke looked back and forth between them.

"Detective Loviccio was temporarily assigned to my precinct around eight years ago. We had a homicide involving two drug dealers from Brooklyn. A task force was put together because the two dead men were getting their drugs from a pier in midtown. I had arrested one of them on an unrelated charge but had developed a rapport with someone close to the source." She shrugged. "It was my one shot at undercover work and then back onto the street."

"I recommended you for a promotion." Loviccio got up from his seat. "But I guess it didn't work out."

Juliana laughed. "Your recommendation almost got me assigned to Staten Island. Jesus, Ronnie, you can't imagine how many toes you've stepped on." She pointed at the teacups. "Don't drop them, they break real easy."

"Have you told her?" Loviccio nodded toward Juliana.

Duke nodded. "Yes, and she agrees with you."

"That you're crazy?" Walking over to the table, Juliana took a seat between the two men. "I told him that Internal Affairs would jam a flashlight so far up his ass looking for answers that his lips would glow with his mouth closed."

"Internal Affairs would just be the beginning." Counting on his fingers, Loviccio laid out Duke's future. "First, they'd send you out to Lefrak City to spend the day with the department's shrink. Then, the DA would open a review of every case you ever touched. Defendants would claim you were possessed when you testified. I can see dozens of cases being overturned because of the reincarnation of Alice Roman."

Juliana reached over and took Duke's hands. "Listen to him, Garvey, this is your career you're talking about. You just became a detective. How tough do you think it would be for them to bust you back to patrolman?"

"She's got a point there, junior."

Duke got up from the chair and walked over to the window. Without looking back at them, he defended the only reason that was left to him.

"You two experts are forgetting a very salient point."

Loviccio leaned over and whispered to Juliana, "What's 'salient'?"

"Important," she replied and looked at Duke. "Go ahead. What's more important than your job?"

"My conscience." Turning, Duke stared at his two companions as though they were foreigners and he was giving them directions. "You're both so concerned about the job and how it will react to me that you've lost sight of how it affects me directly."

"Directly?" Juliana looked at Loviccio. "Were we being less than direct?"

Loviccio shrugged. "Not that I can tell."

Duke shook his head. "Listen to me. I know this sounds like madness, but I'm the one who has to live with it. I don't believe in reincarnation. At least, I didn't until a couple of days ago. But there are some things in this world that just can't be explained with science or logic. You both see this as some religious thing that you don't understand. To my mother and all the true Rastafarians in the world, this is as common as eating breakfast or drinking a beer."

"Ah, that explains it." Loviccio winked at Juliana. "They're drunk all the time. No wonder it makes sense."

"God dammit, Ronnie, I'm trying to make you understand that not everyone believes in the same end to life as you and Julie." Walking back over to the table, Duke leaned on his knuckles. "In your religion, you die and rot away. End of the trail. But to a Rastafarian, life starts again, in a new body. We believe in a life force that goes on forever, moving from one mortal shell to another when the time comes."

Juliana slapped the table. "Okay, how come you're a detective and not a serial killer?"

"I don't know. Maybe it's because of my mother bringing me up the right way." Duke shrugged. "Who knows what kind of sad childhood Alice Roman suffered through? If she turned out to be a killer, perhaps it was because of her parents. What if her father was a murderer?"

"What if you stop coming up with these unfounded suppositions?" Juliana got up from the table and took the two teacups over to the sink. "All I'm hearing is you trying to talk this into your head as reality. You're forcing yourself to accept facts not in evidence. Think about how this would play out in a courtroom. I can hear opposing counsel screaming objections. We've all spent enough time in a witness box, watching logical people present an argument." Juliana shook her head. "There's no logic in your words, just passion. You can believe what you want, Garvey, but don't try to get us to play along."

"I'm not asking you to believe, just don't make me ignore my faith." Duke was about to continue his argument, but his phone rang over on the counter.

Juliana picked up the cellphone and walked it over to him. "Cynthia's calling. You'd best answer before she calls Alice Roman."

Chapter Thirty
Belief And Acceptance

Cynthia Carson was three blocks away in a diner on 37th Street. She begged Duke to come alone, hearing the voices of Juliana and Loviccio arguing in the background. He agreed, but asked Juliana to order a couple of pizzas, figuring that he wouldn't be long and it was best to keep his guests fed while he was gone.

"What are you going to tell her?" Juliana got up and stood between Duke and the door. "Keep in mind who she is while you're talking to her. Frank had just as many friends as he had enemies in the department. What you say to her might end up in the wrong person's ears if you're not careful."

"This coming from the cop who killed her brother this morning." Duke shook his head. "Don't worry about me. And save me a slice, okay?"

Duke jogged the three blocks to the diner, wiping the sweat from his forehead as he rolled in through the revolving door. Cynthia Carson was seated at the last booth in the back by the restrooms. She was dressed completely in black.

"I was sure you'd mourn your brother, but I'd have bet even money that you wouldn't start so soon."

"I'm not mourning, Duke. This was all I had to wear that was clean. Frank trashed my clothes."

"You look good in black, then." Duke smiled. "You'll need those clothes for his funeral."

She nodded. "Yeah, I've been to a dozen Inspector's Funerals over the years. I'm not looking forward to this one. Christ, the phone hasn't stopped ringing. The Mayor called twice, and I refused to talk to her. I half expect her to drive down from Gracie Mansion and bang on my door."

Duke waved to a server and ordered coffee for himself. "You want anything?"

"No. Just to talk. I'm fine with water."

The server refilled her glass and went off to get Duke his coffee. Pulling a napkin from the holder at the end of the booth, Duke wiped several drops of water from the table and balled it up. "So, what do you want to talk about?"

Cynthia opened her purse and took out a small piece of paper. She unfolded it and laid it on the table in front of Duke. The note had a single sentence scrawled across the paper in Frank Nussbaum's handwriting. Duke lifted it with his thumb and forefinger as though it were evidence.

Five words filled the paper: "Ask Him About The Eyes." Each word had the first letter capitalized for importance. Duke read it out loud and then asked, "Frank wrote this?"

She nodded. "He stuffed it into my blouse pocket just before we got out of the taxi in front of your building. What's he talking about?"

Duke flipped the paper over several times. "Well, first it shows that he didn't really intend to kill you. Why would he have given you the note?"

"I hadn't thought of that." With a sigh and deep breath, she relaxed a bit.

Folding the note and stuffing it into his pocket, Duke lowered his voice to almost a whisper and leaned in closer to the late Frank Nussbaum's sister. "I have to tell you something that you might find hard to believe. But I want you to know that I've come to believe it as gospel. I've only told this to three other people. Two of them are cops, the third is my mother."

"Your mother?"

"Yes. The woman who raised me to believe certain things that folks outside Jamaica might find unusual and difficult to accept." Duke looked around the diner to make sure no one was eavesdropping.

Cynthia took a long drink of water. "I'm a very accepting person, Garvey. After what I've gone through, I doubt you could tip my boat."

"Good." Duke paused while the server placed his coffee on the table. When he walked away, Duke pushed the cup off to the side and reached for Cynthia's hands. "Do you believe in reincarnation?"

"The Buddhist thing about coming back from the dead?"

He nodded.

"Not really. I've read some articles about it, and when the Dalai Lama came to New York several years ago, I went to hear him speak." She shrugged. "Not the most believable presentation, but he did have a very soothing voice. I started meditating after hearing his lecture, though."

Duke pulled the coffee closer and added two sugars and a splash of cream from the container on the table. "I'm a Rastafarian and in our religion, we look at reincarnation as the natural chain of events. You die and your body, your shell, is left behind while your life force finds a new one."

"What happens if the body already has a...what did you call it?"

"A life force. It's what you probably call the soul."

"Every person is born with a soul. How does your life force fit in?" Cynthia took another long drink of water and held the nearly empty glass in midair so the server could see it.

"We believe that at the moment of conception, the nearest life force joins with the newly formed embryo to give it life." Pulling a fresh packet of sugar from the tray, Duke tore it open but didn't turn it over to spill out its contents. "The paper is your body. The sugar inside is your life force. You can put the sugar into as many different packets as you want. They can be any color, any size, and any shape. As long as you don't dump it into a cup of coffee, the sugar will last forever."

Cynthia smiled. "What happens to your life force if you fall into a cup of coffee? Do you dissolve? Does the force melt away?"

Duke shook his head. "Well, most Rastafarians don't drink coffee, so as far as I know, it hasn't been a problem."

"You drink coffee."

"Yes, and wine and the occasional cocktail. I'm what you might call a reformed Rasta man." He laughed. "Even the Amish have cellphones these days."

Leaning back from the table, Cynthia narrowed her gaze at Duke. "Why are you telling me all this? What's it got to do with Frank?"

Duke took a long breath and blew it out slowly. "I believe, at least I think I believe, that I am the reincarnation of Alice Roman."

The first laugh from her mouth was short, a sputter, but the next ones grew louder and more animated. Cynthia finally reached a peak where she was crying, laughing, and spitting the water she'd tried to drink at the same time.

"You know, if I didn't hate my brother so much, I'd probably kick you in the balls under the table." She composed herself and swallowed the last of the water in her glass. "Why would you say such a ludicrous thing?"

"I wouldn't say it if I didn't believe it."

She laughed harder. "Come on, Garvey. Reincarnation? You were Alice Roman? First of all, everything I've heard about reincarnation is that you come back as the same sex you were before."

"That's not true."

"The whole thing's not true, Garvey." Cynthia slammed the empty glass on the table. "When you're dead, you're dead. Do you think Frank Nussbaum is wandering around in a new body right now?"

Duke pursed his lips. "Yes."

"God, I hope it's a crippled one. I want him to suffer like I did when I was little. Maybe he'll get raped by a parent." The venom was spilling from her mouth. Her anger stunned Duke. "Garvey, I thought this would end one day. I can see that it's far from over. Please tell me that you don't intend to make the NYPD aware of your belief."

"Don't worry. I've already heard that side of the argument from two people who know." Tossing the unused sugar packet into his cup, Duke pushed it to the end of the table. "But it still leaves me with the problem of being the former Alice Roman."

Cynthia got up from her side of the booth and came around to sit next to Duke. She put her arm around his shoulder and pulled him close.

"You're not the former Alice Roman. You're David Garvey, a detective with the NYPD. If you were truly my father's killer, don't you think my woman's intuition would have figured it out?"

"My mother did."

"Really?" She released him and moved a few inches away. "Your mother believed you were once a serial killer in a previous life?"

Duke shrugged. "Well, I don't think she was convinced I was the serial killer, but she made a valid argument for reincarnation."

"Fine. Let's go with that." Cynthia took his hand. "Let's agree that reincarnation exists. Maybe I was a famous opera singer in a previous life. I like that one. It explains why I sing in the shower. But let's stop with specifics. Yes, you lived before, but not as a serial killer, not as Alice Roman. Who ever you were, it was a good person. Maybe even another cop. Can you live with that, Detective Garvey?"

"Half a belief is better than none at all." He reached for her hand. "Agreed."

Loviccio had done some serious damage to an onion and green peppers pizza. Juliana ate one slice of the plain and left the rest for Duke. They were sitting on the balcony when he walked in.

"I thought you were going home to your wife?"

His partner shook his head. "She's cooking dinner."

"And you're here eating pizza?"

He nodded. "Yeah, like I said, she's cooking dinner. Maybe the dog will eat it, but when I left the house she was looking for a bottle of arsenic."

Juliana poured Duke a glass of wine. "All is well?"

"Yes. We came to an agreement of sorts."

"Good." She leaned closer to Loviccio and sniffed. "You need a shower. Go on home. If you don't show up for roll call tomorrow, I'm sure Detective Garvey will be able to solve the case without you."

Juliana lured her boyfriend into the bedroom after the two of them literally pushed Loviccio out of the apartment. The day had been overtaken by weirdness, and she needed grounding in the form of sex. However, Duke's mind was far away from the pillows and off in search of answers that he knew he'd never find.

It took her over an hour to get him aroused. It took him less than ten minutes to finish. Not Duke's usual performance, but Juliana let him pass. He promised a second round later, and she took his hand and asked with a wicked grin. "When you've been reincarnated?"

They returned to the balcony after sunset with a fresh bottle of white wine and the cold pizza.

"You're still not convinced." Juliana folded a slice of pizza and bit off the end.

"Would you be?"

She shook her head. "I don't have to be. Remember, you're the one who thinks he's been here before." Juliana put the slice down on the table. "The only thing I want you to be convinced about is that if you screw up your career, you screw up our relationship at the same time."

"You'd leave me if the job let me go?"

"Honey, I'd run so fast that even my dust will have settled before you know I'm gone." Laughing, she picked up the slice of pie and winked at him. "Even if you *do* get a job with the Sanitation Department after they take away your gold badge and gun."

Chapter Thirty-One
Officially, It Never Happened

Duke called his mother's cellphone after roll call on Monday morning. She was in the middle of another conversation and told him she'd ring him back when she was done. Loviccio was out at the range. He needed to shoot his six-month re-qualification and wouldn't return to the squad until noon. An early morning drug bust still had the night shift detectives at the scene, and from the tone of his voice, Lieutenant Moscowitz had lost another battle with his wife.

A robbery at a jewelry store in Crown Heights was the first call of the morning for the day shift. Moscowitz kicked open the door to his office and pointed at Peter Cheng. "When your partner gets out of the crapper, 862 Eastern Parkway, Klein's Jewels of Distinction. Robbery and assault." He scanned the room. "Take Garvey and Jackson. Jesus Christ, two detectives qualifying on the same freaking day?"

Owing to a scheduling error, Detective Albertini was also out at the range. Duke could hear the lieutenant screaming at someone over the phone as they hurried out of the squad. It was not a good day to be the boss.

Streetside, he got into the passenger seat of Jackson's unmarked car and immediately understood why Albertini's biceps were so huge. Flying around the corner on two wheels, Duke did all he could to hang on.

"Do you have a pilot's license?" Duke grabbed the handstrap and pulled himself against the door.

Moe turned down a one-way street the wrong way and leaned on the horn and siren at the same time. "This is a shortcut."

"To the Emergency Room?"

Jackson laughed as he slammed on the brakes, nearly hitting a pedestrian. "I didn't take you for a pussy, Duke."

"Pussies have nine lives. I only have one." Duke let the last few words drift off into a whisper.

Mr. and Mrs. Klein, eighty-one and sixty-seven, respectively, were seated at opposite ends of the bench inside a city ambulance. Both were holding bloody bandages against the sides of their heads. Mrs. Klein also had an ice pack on her right eye. A uniformed officer walked over and flipped open her notepad.

"Three assailants. All young Hispanics, according to the wife."

Kelly Tang looked at the woman. "How do you know they were Hispanics, Mrs. Klein?"

"Duh, because they spoke Spanish." She raised her eyebrows. "And one of them called the other Carlos."

Duke looked away and unsuccessfully fought a snicker.

Mr. Klein shushed his wife. "Detectives, we don't know what they were. It all happened so fast. I don't think either of us could identify them again."

"Oh, I could." Mrs. Klein nodded her head several times and pointed at her husband. "I saw them plain as day, Harry."

"Velma, you have no idea what you saw. They clonked you on the head and the tall one with the beard punched you in the face."

Kelly smiled. "So, you saw a tall Hispanic with a beard?"

Harry Klein pursed his lips. "Did I say that?"

Grinning, Detective Cheng held out his hand to Mr. Klein. "Why don't you come with me? We can sit in our air-conditioned Chrysler that's just come from the car wash and you can tell me exactly what you saw. Okay?"

Separating the two Kleins, Kelly continued the interview with the wife seated in the back of the ambulance while Duke and Jackson organized the canvass. The owner of the bakery across the street who called 9-1-1 waddled over and gave Duke a detailed accounting of the events.

"They must have been waiting in the alley. I was just putting challahs into the display case and I saw Velma and Harry get out of the car like they always do at three minutes to nine."

"Same time every day?" Duke held his pen in midair.

"Like clockwork." The baker wiped his brow with a rag from his apron pocket. "The big one had a shiny gun and he hit Velma behind the ear, then the one with the Yankees cap punched her."

"Who hit Mr. Klein?"

"The female."

Duke started to write, but stopped. "You saw a woman as part of this trio?"

"Yeah. She was the one shouting orders." The baker took a quick look around. "She had big tits."

The robbers didn't get much from the jewelry store. Mr. Klein had unlocked the door for them after his wife was shoved to the ground. They grabbed what few pieces were on permanent window display but ran with the sound of approaching sirens. Several witnesses gave identical descriptions of the assailants, but one of them, a woman in her eighties, swore they were speaking Japanese.

With the jewelry store locked up for the day and the two Kleins off to the Emergency Room, the team from the 84th Detective Squad got back in their cars. Paperwork beckoned, there were DD5s to write. Duke breathed a sigh of relief. It was police work as usual. He needed the status quo.

Both his partner and Detective Albertini had returned from the range. Loviccio scored three points higher than Albertini and was taping his target onto the wall next to her desk.

"You're up on Friday, Garvey. I saw your name on the schedule." Loviccio pointed at the target. "Beat that, and I'll buy you dinner."

"At the prospect of grazing with you, I'd intentionally shoot one point lower." Duke dropped his notepad onto his desk. "People are scared out there, Ronnie. I just watched a man and his wife argue over getting someone caught for a crime because they were a different human variety. They both saw the criminals, but the husband was doing his best to convince his wife that she'd seen nothing and should keep her mouth shut."

Loviccio shrugged. "That's old news, junior. You think it's bad now? Imagine what it was like when the Mafia was running wild in the streets. Remember the riots of the sixties? Race has always been the sandpaper in this city. All this bullshit about getting along? Nothing will ever change. Old folks will fear the kids. White kids will always feel superior to blacks. And the Hispanics will bounce from one side of the street to the other, trying to fit in."

"You have a very dim view of the people we're here to protect and serve."

"Hey, you were a street cop. Am I sayin' anything you haven't heard before? Am I sayin' anything untrue?"

Duke shook his head. "Ronnie, I'd love to say you're wrong, but I saw it in action again today. There's way too much fear on the streets and it's working against us."

"Fear's a great a motivator, partner."

With the full complement of two shifts entering reports, the 84th Detective Squad resembled a typing pool. Two laptops were set up on The Ghost's desk, with Sean Collins and his partner arguing over who got to use Nussbaum's chair. A report of a body on the baseball field at Red Hook Park sent Jackson and Albertini back to the street, and the clicking of keystrokes was reduced to near normal.

Duke finished the DD5 and sent the file off to the archives. He printed two copies: one for his files, the other he signed and put into the rack by the lieutenant's office. Protocol called for the boss to review the file, but Moscowitz had closed his blinds and was shouting at someone on the phone loud enough that he could be heard in the hallway.

It was almost four in the afternoon. Duke walked over to his partner's desk and read the screen. Loviccio was finishing the report on Barry Mulholland. The case was going to the District Attorney in the morning so the killer could be transferred from the Roslyn jail to Riker's Island in the city. Duke pointed out a misspelled word to the senior detective and was shoved out of the way for his efforts.

"You going home?"

"No. My mother's demolition company is working a job on 110th Street. There's a Caribbean restaurant on 112th Street that she's been touting and I told her that I'd meet her there for an early dinner."

"Touting? That like tooting?" Loviccio shrugged. "Junior, I'm gonna need a dictionary to speak the same language as you."

Mother Garvey was seated at the first table inside the door of Best In The East. The fragrances of island cooking made Duke smile. He knew his mother had already investigated the kitchen and probably dipped her finger into every pot. Three large glasses were on the table. One held only a straw and the remnants of a drink. The other two were filled to the top with what appeared to be chocolate milk.

Duke gave his mother a kiss on the cheek and sat down opposite her. "What's this?"

"Jamaican Browning." She slurped the straw. "Taste it, mon."

He lifted the glass and followed her lead. "Mmmm. It's a really rich chocolate shake." And then the rum kicked in. "Whoa. An adult chocolate shake. How much rum is in here?"

"Not enough." Mother Garvey turned and shouted at the bartender. "Mon, you mix dis for de baby? You forget de rum?"

The bartender poured two shots and carried them over to their table. He dumped the first one into her glass and slid the other one across the table to Duke.

"Mine's fine. Thanks." Duke picked up the shotglass and put it at the far end of the table.

Mother Garvey reached over and grabbed the shot, spilling it into her drink without a word. They ordered dinners and a couple of glasses of water with the bartender still standing there. He left to enter their meals into the terminal on the bar, and Duke gave him a moment to get out of earshot.

"I had a long talk with my girlfriend and my partner about this whole reincarnation thing."

"It not a ting, Duke, it real."

He nodded. "Yes, mother, that's the part we agree about. It's as real as you want it to be."

She opened her mouth to retort, but Duke held up his hand. "Hear me out."

"Speak, den."

"My entire life has been about the truth. You never lied to me. Every bad thing that's ever happened to you is out in the open. Your belief in the Rasta way is something I've always admired, even though I couldn't understand or agree with all of it." He took a quick sip of the drink and continued. "Whether or not I am the reincarnation of someone is no longer the issue. Everything that's happened comes back down to my job as a detective."

"You take de job over de Rasta way. Dat obvious."

He shrugged. "I wish it could be the other way around, but these are modern times and old-fashioned belief structures are crumbling."

"So, you don have de belief no more?"

"I don't know how much I had to start, mother." Duke reached over and took her hands in his. "You dragged me from your world and brought us into a new one when I was still young enough to accept the change."

"Me not lookin' for me son to change."

Duke sighed. "But I have, and so have you. Look at what you do now, mother. You blow up buildings for a living even though you don't need the money. How do you explain that?"

"Me give jobs to dem dat can't get none."

"A noble cause."

"Dem all Rasta."

Smiling, Duke released her hands and sat back in the chair. "Because you insist on it. How many of them are true believers, mother? How many of your workers would worship the Empire State Building if you told them to? You can't make someone believe just because you sign their paycheck."

"What dis got to do wit you, Duke?"

"This has to do with me putting religious beliefs in the backseat in favor of keeping my job and my sanity." Duke shook his head. "I can't go through life believing something horrible about myself that I have no way of proving. If I was a serial killer before, I'm not one now. I'm not responsible for anything that Alice Roman did, just like she had no future stake in my life."

"No one ever say you responsible." Mother Garvey wrapped both hands around her beverage and held it tight.

"And since I'm not responsible, there's no reason to ever discuss this with anyone again. Especially anyone who works for the NYPD."

His mother nodded twice. "Make sense."

"Good. Then we have no reason to talk about this anymore."

"If dat what you want."

Duke looked up as a server arrived with their meals and frowned. "I hope this is as good as you make at home, mother."

Mother Garvey shook her head and reached for the jerk sauce. "Nevah happen, mon."

Chapter Thirty-Two
From Beyond The Grave

Promotions came slowly in the NYPD. With the budget crisis and the City of New York once again on the verge of bankruptcy, even the most worthy cops spent years waiting for their just reward. Lieutenant Moscowitz had put Duke in for a promotion to Second Grade the day after the detective had signed the DD5 on the last of the twenty homicides. It was now three weeks later and nothing had come down from One Police Plaza.

With the summer heat reaching close to triple digits, the crime rate slowed. It was too hot for murder and robbery. Even the drug dealers had gone into the shade. Duke and his partner were on their way back from a car-jacking when the dispatcher re-routed them to the Captain's office.

"This is it, Duke." Loviccio punched his partner in the shoulder. "Second Grade in less than two months. Man, you are setting records that will never be beat."

"Maybe it's for you. Maybe you're getting your First Grade bump."

"For what? My good looks? My wardrobe choices?"

Duke pinched his nostrils. "Your choice of aftershave would be my guess."

Captain O'Malley ushered the two detectives into his office and closed the door. He told them to take seats, but remained standing behind his desk.

"This paperwork was given to me by your commanding officer more than three weeks ago." He dropped a sheaf of official-looking papers on the desk in front of them. "At first glance, I was ready to sign off on your promotion."

Duke looked at Loviccio. Concern was spread across his partner's face.

The captain continued. His tone was one of puzzlement. "Then the strangest thing happened." He lifted the top sheet off the stack. "This letter appeared on my desk in a plain white envelope. It had my name on the front, but no other markings. Normally, this would never have gotten as far as my office. Someone would have opened the envelope to make sure it wasn't filled with anthrax or an explosive. So when I found this in my daily mail, I was first concerned that security had been breached."

Duke was about to speak, but his partner put a hand on his knee.

"I had Sergeant Williams come in here and slit it open while I watched from across the room." The captain laughed. "When nothing but a single sheet of paper fell out of it, I made him swear not to tell anyone." He handed the document to Duke and slid into his chair. "Read it, detective, and tell me what I should do next."

The letter was handwritten and dated the same day that Nussbaum retired. Having seen hundreds of pages The Ghost had written in his DD5s, Duke recognized the penmanship instantly.

I have seen my father's killer in the eyes of David Garvey. He is young and does not remember, but death has a face no one ever forgets, even as they move from life to life. Look into his eyes and see who he was before. Look into his heart and know that a killer lurks there, waiting to be released. Twenty souls went to heaven at the hands of David Garvey. More will come before he's stopped. My father's death may have been the last in his previous form, but his new life is prepared to begin the slaughter anew.

It was signed Francis Herman Nussbaum, Detective NYPD Retired.

"I don't know what to say, captain." Duke put the letter back on the pile. "I'm a killer waiting to happen?" He laughed nervously. "You've seen all my psyche evaluations. Do I sound like a killer to you?"

"No one sounds like a killer until they pull the trigger the first time." Captain O'Malley sat down at his desk and folded his hands in his lap. "Why would Frank write this letter? Is he trying to warn me about something that he knew about you, Garvey?"

Duke looked at Loviccio and shrugged. "I only spoke to him once in the squad."

"Did you ever visit him at home?"

"Not him, but I went to do a follow-up interview with his sister." Duke pursed his lips. "He was there, but he was watching television the whole time. I don't recall him saying anything to me."

The captain leaned closer to Duke. "What's he mean about your eyes?"

Duke opened them as wide as possible and stared at O'Malley. "I don't know. Do you see anything unusual, sir?"

"I see a bit of bloodshot. You getting enough sleep, detective?" Sitting back in his chair, Captain O'Malley smiled. "Frank Nussbaum was a crazy old coot. I graduated from the academy with him and we both walked a beat in the South Bronx for a couple of years before his father was murdered."

"I didn't know that, sir." Loviccio raised his eyebrows. "I thought you were born with bars on your shoulders."

"If you didn't have less than a year to retirement, I'd bust your ass back into uniform, Loviccio. Don't push your luck." Getting up from his seat, the captain looked out the window, shaking his head slowly. "Frank went nuts after his father died. The captain that promoted him did it just to get Nussbaum off the streets. He was afraid that Frank was going to beat on suspects, hoping to force a confession...even if he killed someone."

Duke nodded. "Sounds like it was a wise choice."

"Maybe, but over time, it turned out to be a mistake that we couldn't fix." Turning, Captain O'Malley folded his arms across his chest. "I tried to transfer him, but Frank had made friends all over the department. He played golf with the Chief of Police and personally handled the protection details for three different Mayors. To say Frank Nussbaum was connected was like agreeing that the sun would come up in the morning."

Loviccio leaned over and looked out the window. Clouds had rolled in and the sky was completely overcast. "Not always a safe bet, captain."

Captain O'Malley ignored him. "The sheer number of friends and enemies Frank collected in his forty-year stint with the NYPD is more than impressive, it's almost frightening." He picked up Frank's letter. "And then we have this. Who knows how many of these letters he sent out? I've been waiting for a call from the Mayor's office ever since I opened this one."

"But with Frank dead, how could these letters have any validity?" Shaking his head, Duke looked back and forth between his partner and the highest ranking officer in the precinct. "You said Frank went crazy. This certainly reads like the musing of a madman."

"I'd agree with you if I knew for sure that he hadn't reached out from beyond the grave and made someone else in the department aware of his feelings." Captain O'Malley put his palms on his desk and leaned in close to the two detectives. "What if he sent a copy of this letter to Internal Affairs?"

"Well, then we're all in the deep shit, captain." Loviccio got up from his seat. "Garvey deserves the promotion and you know it.

If you're gonna hold back because of the fear of a ghost, then maybe IAB should shove a scope up your ass...captain."

A week passed and then another. Duke and Loviccio worked their cases, entered the DD5s, and did their best to push the stalled promotion off to the side. Rita Jankowsky stopped in to say that her sister was doing much better, and that she expected to return to work by the end of August. It was a month earlier than planned. Duke was pleased that she was coming back and hoped that she and Loviccio would partner once again.

Juliana had moved back in two days after the shooting. Their runs were now a full twenty miles and both of them had filled out entry forms for the New York Marathon coming up in the fall. And then to add a dollop of cream to the mix, she announced over Sunday dinner that she was taking the sergeant's exam just before Labor Day.

"You'll outrank me if you pass."

"Yeah, but no gold badge."

"Stripes are better." He winked. "And easier to get."

"Oh? I'd like to see you pass the test, smarty."

Duke shrugged. "Not if it means putting on the bag each morning."

"Yeah, I knew you couldn't walk away from that closet full of sport jackets and slacks."

They were sitting on the balcony with the second of three wine bottles opened and ready for drinking. Juliana had gotten up to look out at the fading sun when the two blue and whites, a Cadillac Escalade, and an unmarked Chrysler pulled up in front of their building.

"Something's going on here." She stood and pulled her semi-automatic from its ankle holster.

Duke ran over and looked down. Uniformed cops were racing from the two cars to open the doors of the Escalade. Lieutenant Moscowitz got out of the unmarked Chrysler and waved at him. Captain O'Malley stepped out of the other door and looked around the street as though he was entering a war zone.

"Did you invite my bosses for dinner?"

"Uh, uh." Juliana pointed at the gray-haired woman stepping down from the big Caddy. "Did you invite the Mayor?"

The ceremony was brief. Even with Duke's air conditioner set to freeze meat, six cops, three detectives, and the Mayor of the City of New York were far too many warm bodies for the little unit. Duke was promoted to Detective Second Grade wearing sweatpants and a t-shirt with a dancing man and the words "No Problem, Mon" in red, green, and yellow print.

Duke tried to get in touch with his mother using the live video conferencing app on his phone. He wanted her to see a reincarnation go up another level. But her phone went straight to voicemail. Juliana shot video so he could share it with her when she surfaced.

It wasn't until the visitors were filing out of the apartment that Duke finally got the chance to talk to Captain O'Malley in private.

"What changed your mind, captain?"

The senior officer waited until everyone had boarded the elevator before he spun around and looked at Duke with his hands on his hips. "It was your eyes, Garvey. Something in them told me you were speaking the truth. Something said that every word that came out of your mouth was the embodiment of honesty."

"Thank you, sir." Duke reached out his hand.

Captain O'Malley shook it and pulled him close enough to where the detective could smell the garlic on the commanding officer's breath. The senior officer looked up and down the hallway before whispering, "Plus, we've both been here before."

Epilogue

Cynthia Carson sat in the first pew at Saint Oda's. The check in her pocket would not only cover the cost of repairing the crack in Christ's leg, but a full renovation of all the statuary and cleaning of the stained glass windows. Nunzio Hernandez, the carpenter originally tasked with the repair, had died, but his son was a regular at the church and agreed to take on the job.

Her brother's funeral had been delayed for almost a month due to the autopsy and a letter that had been found in his nightstand stating that he didn't want the city to waste the money and effort. Cynthia tore up the letter after Loviccio read it and threatened to sue everyone from the Mayor down to the city hall janitor if her brother wasn't given the proper sendoff he deserved.

It was an affair that brought out the rich, powerful, and famous from every corner of the globe. The Vice-President flew in on Air Force Two, shutting down La Guardia Airport for the bulk of the day. The Governor was sick in bed, but sent his wife and two aides. Every detective in the 84th Squad put on the bag and stood shoulder to shoulder as they carried Detective Francis Nussbaum's coffin down the steps of Saint Patrick's Cathedral. Even the Pope sent a video message.

The sermon was shared between the head rabbi for Brooklyn and Father Mulcahey of the New York Archdiocese. A cop standing behind Duke cracked a joke about mixed marriages, but the snickers quickly faded. Most of the speeches and accolades were short and said nothing about the thirty years that Frank Nussbaum had wasted trying to find his father's killer. Those cops that got up to speak were the ones The Ghost had worked with while he was still in the patrol division.

Not one of the detectives from the 84th Squad took the microphone.

They buried The Ghost in his own backyard, next to his father and mother. Cynthia spent two days moving the lawn furniture, barbecue grill, and dragging three dozen tomato plants in pots to one side of the house to accommodate the crowd. The roar of news helicopters drowned out the rabbi and a late afternoon thundershower cut the event shorter than planned.

In the four weeks it took to repair the broken leg of the black Jesus Christ, Duke visited the church twice. First was to arrest Emilio Cortez for the robbery of ten thousand dollars and the golden crucifix. The cash box had been recovered by a fisherman hunting for fluke. The seals had held and the bills inside were in pristine condition. Father Xavier raised a stink when they came for Emilio, but he relented when Duke handed him the bounty.

His second visit to Saint Oda's came on the Sunday when the repaired idol was returned to its base. The sanctuary was filled to capacity and two large television screens had been set up on the church's steps so the overflow crowd could watch the dedication. Duke had arrived early enough to get a seat inside. Juliana was with him and remarked that it was the first time she'd seen Christ as a black man.

"Does the color really matter?"

She shook her head. "No, but it just looks weird."

Duke squeezed her hand. "Try to imagine seeing it through my eyes."